Her Australian
Cattle Baron

Her Australian Cattle Baron

Margaret Way

LYRICAL SHINE
Kensington Publishing Corp.
www.kensingtonbooks.com

LYRICAL SHINE BOOKS are published by

Kensington Publishing Corp.
119 West 40th Street
New York, NY 10018

All Kensington titles, imprints, and distributed lines are available at special quantity discounts for bulk purchases for sales promotion, premiums, fund-raising, educational, or institutional use.

Special book excerpts or customized printings can also be created to fit specific needs. For details, write or phone the office of the Kensington Sales Manager: Kensington Publishing Corp., 119 West 40th Street, New York, NY 10018. Attn. Sales Department. Phone: 1-800-221-2647.

Lyrical Shine and Lyrical Shine logo Reg. U.S. Pat. & TM Off.

First Electronic Edition: June 2017
eISBN-13: 978-1-5161-0159-7
eISBN-10: 1-5161-0159-6

First Print Edition: June 2017
ISBN-13: 978-1-5161-0160-3
ISBN-10: 1-5161-0160-X

Printed in the United States of America

Chapter 1

Royston Stirling left his favourite mare, Marika, a true coal black, in the capable hands of Eddie Emu, one of a group of aboriginal stable boys he relied on. He had bred Marika from two outstanding black horses, ex-racehorses, bought in by the station. Eddie had a gift with horses.

Weariness was lapping at all of his senses—it had been one hell of a day—nevertheless, he took a few moments to check if Eddie had any concerns.

"On top of everythin', Boss!" Eddie assured him, flashing his dazzling white smile. At sixteen, Eddie, in his navy singlet and cut-off trousers, considered himself to be one of the boss's right-hand men. In another year or two, Royston would move Eddie up to stock-man. He had grown fond of Eddie, born on the station to their best tracker and his part-aboriginal wife, although there had never been a kind word for Eddie and his hard-working parents during his father's time. Charles Royston Stirling's heart had been pure granite.

There had been no tears at his huge Outback funeral, only regret for what might have been. Mercifully, life went on.

Living at Kooralya now was far less traumatic than it had been under his father. He had made a point of that. His people were important to him. No resentments were allowed to grow. Every man, woman, and child on the station was treated well or he wanted to know why. Running a remote cattle station was no different to running a small democratic kingdom.

It had been another long backbreaking day of pulverising heat. An extra problem had been thrown into the mix. He'd had to call in the Royal Flying Doctor Service. One of the jackeroos had broken his leg. A fall from his horse. No unavoidable accident, just a silly piece of derring-do that caused temporary chaos. It could have been much worse. Working cattle stations were dangerous places. This station, in its 150 years' history, had suffered its fair share of disasters both to family and station staff.

With his long stride, he crossed the broad, cobbled courtyard to the home compound as the first of the stars were coming out. The walls were surrounded by high terra cotta walls draped in a beautiful native climber that broke out in a profusion of fragrant white flowers for most of the year. The scent enveloped him. The high walls had been built for a purpose. They protected the home gardens from high winds and the occasional dust storm. The women of his family had laboured down the years to establish a garden in the desert heartland. All of them had been determined to impose beauty and order on the wilderness. To their great credit, they had succeeded.

Kooralya's main gardener, Will Vernon, an English horticulturalist who had migrated to Australia for his health, had come to them some ten years previously. Living in the hot dry conditions of the Outback, he had thrived. Will was now in his eighties, though no one would ever know it. Being passionate about what one did in life was a great driving force.

"Take control of your life. Don't allow life to control you," was one of Royce's late father's many dictums. Of course, his powerful, feared father, one of the biggest landowners on the continent, hadn't been able to control his own wife. The credo wasn't foolproof. He had learned that early. Women had power of their own.

There were no long twilights in the bush. The sky was already a bewitching indigo-blue. Dusk was descending softly and rapidly. In less than ten minutes, the night sky would turn deepest, black velvet, a magnificent background for blazing stars. Big and small, they were packed so closely together there was scarcely a space between them. It was always like that in the pure, unpolluted air of the Outback. He had travelled the world in the year following university, where he had gained a double degree in law and business management. His grandfather, Sir Clive, had insisted he be given a gap year, but his father had protested vigorously he should stay home and start learning how to run the station. His grandfather had won that argument.

In his opinion, the starry skies of the interior, much like the stars of New Zealand, were unrivalled. Something to do with their isolated geographical position, he reasoned. Wide open spaces, a small population. As usual, he paused a moment to admire the colonial mansion where he had been born. It didn't surprise him when visitors from home and abroad called their first sighting of his home surreal. It had to be said, the setting *was* bizarre. One saw historic mansions similar in style in Sydney, Melbourne, and Adelaide, but in the middle of the Australian desert? He had often wondered what his ancestor, John Spencer Stirling, had thought when he rode around his vast Outback holding trying to settle on the best place to build a homestead. There had been no law against constructing a manor house in that empty, forbidding region few people had even seen. Because of John Spencer Stirling's love for his homeland, England, he had attempted to recreate in his own Outback castle what he had left behind. As a second son with little inheritance to speak of, he had made the decision to set sail for the New World, Australia. He had been determined to make his mark. Brilliant at everything he did, John had founded a great pioneering dynasty.

Lit up at night, the house reminded Royston of a liner at sea, only the house was anchored firmly to the most ancient soil on earth. On Kooralya's western and north-western borders lay the Simpson Desert, possibly the most feared of the ten deserts that covered some half-million square miles of the interior.

The Stirling desert stronghold lay in the legendary Channel Country, the home of the nation's cattle kings. Essentially, it was a desert that flooded. When a major cyclone came courtesy of the tropical monsoons, the landscape went underwater. At times, the flood waters spread eighty kilometres across, an extraordinary sight, though the homestead had never had water lapping at the door.

Instead, the flood waters rushed headlong to Lake Eyre, a vast area of shimmering, bone-dry white sand in the very centre of the continent. Lake Eyre had only filled three times in the past 160 years. His much-loved and respected grandfather, the late Sir Clive Stirling, knighted for his contribution to the industry, had always called the Channel Country "Kidman Country" as a mark of respect to the great Sir Sidney Kidman. Sir Sidney had created the largest pastoral empire on earth. The Kidmans—the beautiful Nicole was a relative—were still among the largest landowners on the planet. The biggest chunk of privately owned property on earth, roughly the size of England, was owned by the Kidmans. It was up for sale at the moment, with overwhelming interest. He had taken a look himself with a view to forming a syndicate, but with bids starting at well over $300 million, he had climbed back into the Beech Baron and flown off home.

A few moments later, he reached the rear door to the house, opening and shutting it quietly. He was always quiet in his movements, controlled and measured in his actions. It was part of who he was.

"Move like a panther, you do," Pippa Reed, their housekeeper, often commented whenever he gave her an unintentional start. Even in his high boots, he knew he hadn't made a sound, whereas his late father had as good as bashed his way through doors.

Indoors, it took a second or two for his eyes to adjust to the brightness of the house lights. The sooner he headed upstairs, the better. It wouldn't take long to wash off the effects of the day. He had started to stride down the long, polished hallway with its panelled walls before he detected another fragrance in the air. Not the flowers that always filled the house. It was a woman's perfume.

Memories, locked deep down, rose abruptly to the surface. He dreaded these moments when he wasn't fully in control. He glanced up sharply, almost expecting to see a ghost. As if ghosts existed! Though his aunt, Anthea, claimed they did, and Anthea was a very level-headed woman.

From a safe distance, he had his first glimpse of Jimmy's "golden enchantress." One glance was sufficient. She perfectly fitted that description. Not pretty little Marigold, the young woman who was to marry Jimmy in two days' time. This young woman was no apparition. She was flesh and blood, Marigold's older sister, the solitary bridesmaid. Jimmy had been *adamant* he didn't want a large wedding when it had been apparent Marigold had wanted, in Anthea's words, "the works."

Jimmy's fiancée, on the surface so artless, with the bubble of yellow curls, bright blue eyes, and a breathless style of speaking, had something disconcerting about her. Some defining personality trait she sought to keep under wraps for whatever reasons. It was a disturbing thought, but he couldn't shake it. Pretty little Marigold could well be a ticking time bomb once she joined the family. Marrying James had been her grand plan. Within hours of meeting her, Royston had learned that.

Now the sister. Amelia. He remembered now. This was the woman who actually held his brother in thrall. He was shocked. He couldn't understand how this wedding to Marigold had come about.

Swiftly he glanced down at himself, aware he must look like a wild man. Best to stay silent and hidden. His work clothes, blue denim shirt, jeans, and high boots were covered in a layer of red dust. His hair had grown too long. It was even curling up at his nape, but there was little time to worry about hair. He needed a shave. He had been counting on a long cold beer, and then a hot shower.

He fervently hoped Pippa wouldn't arrive on the scene and call out his name, alerting the young woman. He had no wish to meet Marigold's sister now, who in no way resembled the totally misleading picture Marigold had drawn for them. Why, for God's sake? Had it been Marigold's idea of a joke? If so, it was unacceptable.

Apprehension like a giant wave began to roll over him. He could even feel the rush of blood through his veins. He had seen a woman as beautiful as this before, although the colouring couldn't have been more different. This young woman was beautiful in much the same way his mother, Frances, had been beautiful. They had the same look of refinement, the same exquisite bone structure, the tenderness of expression. His mother very strangely had never married the man she had run off with, Henry Mansel. The Mansels were long-time friends of the Stirlings, so the shock had been enormous. "Uncle Harry," of all people! Even more confounding, the relationship hadn't lasted. His mother had never remarried, unlike his late father, who had wanted more sons to help run the station. Frances was still very beautiful, or so one or two of the family's inner circle had made it their business to tell him. They all hoped and prayed since his father's accidental death five years before that reconciliation could begin.

He had never been able to bring himself to start the process. His mother had not wanted him. She had never tried to contact him. He had turned thirty a few months back. A reconciliation was highly unlikely to occur twenty years later.

This young woman appeared infinitely more interesting than her younger sister. That in itself was a profound cause for concern. She had a glorious mane of golden-blond hair. It was caught back from her face with some kind of sparkling adornment. The length spilled over her shoulders to the small of her back. She had the true blonde's creamy-pale complexion. His mother's hair had been the same blue-black as his own. His mother, "the traitor," as his father had always referred to her. His "dark enchantress." Less than twenty feet away from him stood Jimmy's "golden enchantress." There were no words for his shock and feelings of outrage.

He had time to back away. Why didn't he? The reason was obvious. The sight of her held him prisoner, subjugating his will. Being held prisoner by a woman, no matter how beautiful, was far from normal for him. No woman—and there had been quite a few—had as yet swept him away. They had all tried. It went with the name. From Marigold's description, he had visualized the older sister as being another version of Marigold. Maybe not so pretty. Marigold at twenty-four had confided that Melly didn't even have a boyfriend, whereas Marigold could lay claim to a string of admirers before Jimmy. Personally, he had taken that with a huge pinch of salt. Marigold Boyd was no heartbreaker, at least in his opinion. Maybe he was too hard on the girl, though he relied on his instincts. They were rarely wrong.

Here now was Amelia. She appeared to be weaving all the light around her. The only reason she hadn't noticed him was because she was staring up intently at the portrait of his mother painted after her engagement to his father. The painting had her seated in a highbacked antique chair, her lovely, long-fingered hands crossed to show off her magnificent diamond solitaire engagement ring. Amelia's expression as she looked up was entranced yet somehow saddened by what she saw. Most people knew the story. His parents' divorce had been very public, very acrimonious. His father had been full of a raging fury that knew no bounds. Even so, he had refused to take the portrait down even after he remarried gentle little Sally, who had learned very early her husband had no need of her after she managed to produce a son, which she had done in agony when his father had insisted the baby be born on the station and not in the nearest rural hospital.

In those terrible early days after his mother's defection, everyone on the station steered well clear of the boss, who was going through hell and ready to lash out at anyone who dared approach him. His father had even called for him to come home from boarding school, although the mid-term hadn't been over. Charles Stirling, the iron man, needed his son, his heir and only child.

He had listened quietly and very sadly hour after hour to his father's rants that were as bruising as body blows. He had adored his mother. It had been excruciatingly painful listening to his father calling her ugly names. None of them could have been true. His mother, to him, to *everyone*, was a great lady. Her goodness had shone out.

"She betrayed both of us, me, her husband and you, her only child, her son. She and that traitorous bastard, Mansel. They were just waiting to crush me. Guilty as hell, the pair of them. Mansel always envied me from when we were boys. He *had* to have what was mine. He had to have Frances."

He remembered the tears that had stung his eyes, but never fallen. He had never cried in front of his father, though the agony had never left him. No one else had been privy to his father's ravings. At that dreadful time, his grandfather was staying with relatives in Scotland. So it was just him, a boy of ten who had lacked the words, let alone any experience of life, to handle the great burden that had been laid on him. His grandfather had hastened home the very day he heard the shocking news, appalled by the burden his son had inflicted on his grandson.

"You might just as well have plunged a knife into him, speaking so vilely of Frances. He adores his mother."

He had been swiftly sent back to boarding school. His grandfather, until his death, had made sure he stood solidly between him and his father. He had never said one bad word against his mother.

"Poor Frances! She must have had her reasons. Your father always did want too much of her."

He could still hear his own imploring young voice. "Why didn't she take *me?*"

"Your father would never have allowed it, Royston. He was the worst husband I know, but he wasn't going to lose you. Besides, my boy, Kooralya is your birthright."

What had always been difficult to understand was that over the years, he had caught his father countless times staring up fixedly at the glorious portrait. It was as though he couldn't bear *not* to see her. He had taken deeply to heart his father's expressions: agonized, intensely nostalgic, furiously angry. Nothing and no one had ever gotten away from Charles Stirling, master of Kooralya, the Stirling Outback kingdom. His mother, so kind, so beautiful, so much fun, with a formidable intelligence, had abandoned her son just as she had abandoned her husband.

The enchantresses of this world had always had a profound effect upon men, he thought grimly. They took hold of a man's imagination. Only strip away beauty, then what did you have? He could only hope this young woman, for all her beauty, lacked real magic and was as vapid as her rosy-lipped sister, who nevertheless had a few tricks up her sleeve.

Maybe the older sister fancied she did too, except he couldn't suppress the certainty that Amelia Boyd could have any man she wanted. Either way, he had no intention of being deliberately drawn into any woman's web, although he knew better than most that beautiful women had a powerful sexual field. He had been caught in hers from the moment he had laid eyes on her.

He must have made the faintest sound—an indrawn breath—because on the instant, she swung her blond head, staring down the long hallway. A series of expressions began to flit across her face. First, he thought he detected an instant of shock. It was chased away by an expression of trepidation. Surely not? He wasn't his father. Yet if her expression was anything to go on, she must have taken it into her head to fear him on the spot. A second later, her lovely features settled into calm.

"You must be Royce?" she asked, a charming lilt to her voice.

Even her voice was special. Something else to contend with.

"I'm Amelia." She began to move towards him, as light and ethereal as a ballet dancer. Such fluidity conveyed a definite sensuality, all the more dangerous because it was entirely natural. She was dressed in a simple white slip dress of some weightless fabric that floated around her ankles. For all the simplicity of her summery attire, she couldn't have looked more alluring.

As a consequence, he overreacted, responding curtly. "I'm sorry if I startled you." He was caught now. He had no other option but to join her. "I won't shake your hand." Close now, he was inhaling the subtle scent of her against his will. "As you can see, I'm covered in dust."

"Then I won't keep you."

His tone, he was quick to recognize, had taken him a step too far. Goddesses didn't countenance hostility. His downward slanting gaze, unknown to him, was extraordinarily intense. Not friendly. Not welcoming. Not indulgent. She had large, oval green eyes within the sweep of long lashes. Why wouldn't she? She was an enchantress. Her eyes weren't a light green, but the deep, lustrous green of Kooralya's permanent lake, Lake Serenity, which everyone on the station called Serendipity because it never ran dry.

She was much taller than her sister. Willow-slim. Five feet, seven inches, he guessed. With his superior height—he was six-three—he was able to look down at her, causing her to tilt back her head. She seemed so incredibly different to her sister, it was difficult for him to get his head around it. Even he and Jimmy shared their height and a certain familial look.

He found himself mentioning it, as though the differences demanded an answer. "You and Marigold don't share a resemblance." Still the crisp tone, but he didn't seem to be able to do a darn thing about it.

"Marigold is my adopted sister," she answered, looking slightly baffled. "Didn't she tell you?"

"I've only just heard it now from yourself." His voice and expression had turned sardonic.

She glanced away from him for a moment. "My parents adopted Marigold as a child," she said gravely. "Her parents had been their close friends. Tragically, they were killed in a car crash. Marigold has always looked on me as her big sister, the relationship has been so close. I expect her not telling you has a psychological element to it."

"Jimmy didn't tell me either." Jimmy was very good at not telling him everything he should.

"Of course Jimmy knows," she confirmed quickly. "Marigold would have told him right at the beginning."

"You know my half-brother well?" Even he recognised the peculiar inflection in his voice. Accusatory? She was part of something. A triangle?

It was as though a shadow had fallen across her. She was silent for a moment, but her answer came with perfect calm. "Of course. I've come to know Jimmy well. Marigold and Jimmy wanted me for their bridesmaid. That's why I'm here, Royce. I may call you Royce?"

"Please." His name was actually Royston. It was his mother who had shortened it to Royce.

The shadow was still there. Was he upsetting her in some way? If he were, he had to stop. She was a guest in his home.

"You're very welcome, Amelia." Deliberately he lightened his tone. "Now you must excuse me. I seriously need to make myself presentable. It's been a long day."

"I'm sure it has." She didn't mention she had already heard from Jimmy, his aunt Anthea, and the family's engaging housekeeper, Pippa, how extremely hard Royce worked. It was obvious to her they worshipped the ground he walked on, so he had to have his lighter moments, she reasoned. One thing was certain: Hard, exhausting work wasn't harming him in any way. He looked stunningly fit with a tall, wide-shouldered, lean body. Jimmy too was tall and lean with the same elegance of stance, but he lacked his half-brother's level of physical fitness and his powerful charisma.

Royce Stirling, master of the vast Outback station Kooralya, was a truly arresting man. Intimidating too. One of the big players in life. There was little trace of gentleness about him, rather a kind of inner turbulence he kept under control. Clearly, he hadn't taken a liking to her. In itself, that was unusual. Most people liked her.

She found herself passing the remark before she could call back the words. "You have a strong look of your mother."

She gazed back at the portrait, then at him. Indeed, he did. There was the same thick blue-black hair with a decided tendency to wave, the brilliant near-black eyes, the sculpted features. The feminine beauty of the mother transposed into the supreme alpha male. Royce Stirling was a totally different species to Jimmy. Small wonder Jimmy had grown up feeling like he was walking in another's man's shadow, though Jimmy had always maintained his half-brother had been "endlessly good" to him.

"Royce shielded me and my poor little mum from our dad. In all honesty, our dad was a black-hearted bastard. No one could blame Royce's mother for making her escape. Dad was impossible to live with. He just used my mother. He never loved her. He never respected her. The only woman he had ever wanted—I won't use the word *loved*—was the *femme fatale* Frances, even though she put herself in danger."

In danger? How, she wondered? A feeling of trepidation was understandable given the station's extreme isolation and the late Charles Stirling's allegedly harsh nature. This was no happy family. Highly dysfunctional, from all accounts. One had to marvel at the workings of the human heart and mind. It was a great mercy for Jimmy he'd had an older, stronger half-brother. She glanced back at Royce Stirling. Her remark about his resemblance to his mother had shocked him out of his composure, if only for a moment. Very few people, she guessed, made reference to the resemblance, although they would all have seen it.

She watched him nod in acknowledgement of an indisputable fact, but he obviously didn't trust himself to speak. Instead, he took deliberate steps away from her. "I'll see you at dinner," he clipped off, momentarily lifting a hand. "Until then."

With that, he turned about, taking the steps of the divided staircase with the same elegant rhythm of movement she had noted.

Thoughtfully, she remained at the foot of the magnificent mahogany staircase, staring after him. There was a knot of emotion in her throat that was new to her. She could imagine women being besotted by Royce Stirling, so blessed by the gods. As far as she was concerned, he was best left well alone. Essentially, they were not comfortable with each other. She was sure that would never change. First impressions remained the strongest. Their link in the future would only be Marigold, soon to be Mrs. James Stirling. Winning Jimmy had been a tremendous coup for Marigold. She had gone after him with single-minded ambition and perhaps very little real emotion. That had been a worrying thought that had never gone away. Marrying money had always been Marigold's aim. Now her small feet were firmly planted on her desired path.

The big concern was that Marigold wasn't fond of children, but she realized she would have to provide Jimmy with at least one child. Marigold lived within a cloud of resentments and unresolved problems that had continued from childhood into adulthood. No matter how hard she and her parents had shown Marigold unstinting love and support, nothing seemed to change. Sadly, there was no magic formula to create happiness. A child could be crippled in later life by unresolved feelings of abandonment. Only Marigold's parents had not abandoned their much-loved little girl. They had gone to their early deaths in a tragic accident. Fate had stepped in as Fate always did.

"It's an absolute mystery to me how you stick up for that girl," Lara Richards, good friend and fellow lawyer, often said. "She doesn't love you, Mel, but you keep falling into the trap. God knows you're clever, but you can't seem to cotton onto Marigold's true nature. Darkness has pierced Marigold's soul. Take it from me. I have *your* best interest at heart. Little Marigold is deliberately allowing her life to be shaped by her childhood tragedy. Can't you see that? She hugs it to her as if her parents who died so horribly had been trying to destroy her and her happiness in life. If I had an adopted sister like that, I tell you, I'd be scared to death."

Her answer? "You're saying I have a dilemma on my hands?"

Lara had shaken her head. "Yep, I do! She looks like such an innocent little thing with the big blue eyes and the breathless voice, but only from a *distance*. Not close up."

She preferred not to criticize Marigold in front of others, even Lara. She knew perfectly well that Marigold had the capacity to create disharmony. Lara had cottoned on to Marigold from the moment they met. Marigold had been going all-out to convey to her friend how much she loved her big sister, Melly. It hadn't worked on Lara.

It wasn't that Amelia was blind to Marigold's faults. What she chose to be was loyal. Marigold was family. She had always allowed for some jealousy. Sibling jealousy in families wasn't unusual. It had to be said in Marigold's defence, she had always applauded Amelia's successes.

"You're so clever, Melly, brilliant really. So much Daddy's daughter. His *real* daughter."

Her father, Jeremy Boyd, was an eminent barrister. She had followed her father into the law, specializing in family law, a fraught area, as she had swiftly found, but it had made her parents so proud. She had a framed photo of the family taken on the day of her graduation. Her beaming mother and father, a frowning Marigold in the foreground, her shoulders being held by Jeremy. Marigold had always been included in everything. Nevertheless, Amelia had spent endless time soothing Marigold's ruffled feelings over one thing or another. One had to make allowances, so she always took the considered approach. Though why they all spent so much time placating Marigold she didn't really know.

"Is it a fault in us, darling?" her mother had once asked her. "The more we try to please Marigold, the more it leaves her unsatisfied."

Her father had been blunter. "It would take a miracle to change Marigold. For some reason, she wants to make us all feel guilty. It's not fair to you, Mel, to always be the peacemaker."

The peacemaker. She was stuck with that role until Jimmy took Marigold off their hands.

She gave Royce Stirling time to reach the upper floor. His suite of rooms was in the west wing. She and Marigold had been given adjoining rooms in the east wing with the added luxury of *en suites*. She had never been inside such grand bedrooms in her life. The high ceilings were beautifully decorated with plaster scrolls and garlands. Crystal chandeliers hung from a central rose. Everything about Kooralya made her wonder about the kind of people who had put down roots in such extreme isolation but still lived like establishment families in city mansions.

The house was enormous, three stories high, built of sandstone and brick. The only concession to the symmetry of the Georgian-style façade was the broad wrap-around veranda on the first floor. She hadn't as yet been shown over the house, so incongruously grand, but Anthea had promised a tour of the house and surprisingly lush gardens the following day. It had been easy to tell the gardens were Anthea's pride and joy. There was an extensive vegetable garden, "entirely Pippa's domain." She had noted the affection in Anthea's voice. Pippa had obviously become one of the family.

Deep in thought, she made her way up the divided staircase, pausing for a moment to admire the stained-glass window above the landing. The sun shone brilliantly through it during the day, splashing jewel colours—turquoise, emerald, sapphire blue, ruby—over the landing and down the stairs.

At night, as now, the exterior lights were used to illuminate the tall, arched window. Huge as the house was with its labyrinth of rooms, she felt no sense of gloom. There were glorious Persian rugs on the warmly polished floors to add colour. Vases of flowers were everywhere. The valuable furniture wasn't overpowering. By day, the sun shone brightly through the front door and the many large windows, lightening the entire atmosphere. All the same, the household staff under Pippa's supervision couldn't afford to be slouches. She had become aware it was considered a great honour to be chosen to work up at the Big House.

She found herself pausing for a moment outside Marigold's door. Marigold's decision to stick largely to her room wasn't the best way to go. Since Amelia had arrived that afternoon via the freight plane, which she had boarded at the Outback domestic airport, there had never been the slightest suggestion Marigold wasn't well liked and most welcome to the family. So why did she have the unsettling feeling this marriage wasn't being looked upon as a marriage made in heaven? God forbid the family had picked up on Marigold's wayward streak. It had grown more pronounced over the past few years as Marigold moved into maturity.

She wasn't really looking forward to this. Briskly, she knocked on the bedroom door.

"Come in."

She had correctly read the signals. Marigold's answer was so full of angst it dismayed her. Every bride had her moments of anxiety, she reasoned. Marriage was a huge step. Maybe the grandeur of the Stirling homestead had swept her away. When she entered the room, she found Marigold in a very unattractive pose. She was lying on the four-poster bed, on top of the expensive brocade quilt, her smooth, rounded arms and legs splayed.

"Sorry, did I disturb you?" She didn't understand that well why Marigold had wanted her for a bridesmaid, though it had to be said, Marigold was short on girlfriends. That had to do with Marigold's pronounced lack of empathy.

Marigold didn't look at her. She continued to stare up at the plastered ceiling as though the answers she sought might be written in large letters up there.

"I hate this bloody house," she muttered, with such a great surge of feeling it lifted her torso.

"Really? I love it," Amelia said.

"*You* would."

It wasn't an implied compliment: more like an insult. "For pity's sake, Marigold, settle down," she said briskly. "You'd better learn to like this house a lot. This is Jimmy's family home. You will be expected to visit often."

Marigold spoke coldly. "They will never include me in anything. They think Jimmy should have picked another girl entirely." For emphasis, she slammed her head into the mound of pillows as though she lacked the strength to get up and start dressing for dinner.

"Try to calm yourself," Amelia urged. "Jimmy did pick you. Aren't you feeling well?"

"I feel awful," Marigold put up her two hands, dragging her fingers through her short curls. "You all seem to have forgotten I'm here. I'm the bride, for God's sake. Where the hell is Jimmy? He's made a point of disappearing since we arrived. Kowtowing to God Almighty, I suppose."

Amelia sank into one of the armchairs, searching without much hope of success for the right words. "I assume by God Almighty, you mean Royce?"

"Ah yes, the awesome Royston!" Marigold cried. "He has all the authority in this godforsaken place. He doesn't like me. I'd go further and say he doesn't trust me. I'm sure he's doing his level best to get Jimmy to back out of this marriage. Only he *can't!*"

Amelia felt her heart tremble. Marigold sounded furious. "You're overreacting. You've done this sort of thing many times before, Marigold, only I've had enough. You have to get yourself together. Jimmy's Aunt Anthea is a very sensible, kindly woman."

"Oh yes, except for her *eyes.*" Marigold gave a weird chortle. "She doesn't like me either. She will never like me. So don't bother patronizing me. His dear little mum won't like me either." Jimmy's mother, Sally, who continued to live on Kooralya, was due back from a short trip to Sydney where she had been staying with her sister and brother-in-law. They were to be special guests at the wedding.

"I know what I'm talking about." Marigold ground her teeth. "I'm not good enough. I'm second-rate. I got a bit drunk the other night. Vodka. I like vodka. They're so bloody starchy, aren't they? The aunt looking down her straight nose at me. Jimmy doesn't defend me. Even the bloody housekeeper, Pippa, doesn't like me, silly bitch. As for Royston! Just you wait until you meet him at dinner."

Amelia eased back in the chair, feeling the level of anxiety mounting. "I've already met him," she said. The worrying thing with Marigold was she had developed a tendency to binge drink.

"Trust *you.*" Marigold bounced up and down on the bed. "So what did you think?"

"He's a very impressive man." Amelia's answer held a touch of acerbity.

"Larger than life? Made you feel all glowy inside?" Marigold gave her a silly smirk. "He's a far cry from your dreary old Oliver."

"Dreary old Oliver is a brilliant mathematician and a lovely man," Amelia said. She had lost count of the number of times Oliver had asked her to marry him. Oliver had his charm. She knew a lot of people regarded them as a couple of sorts. She was praying one of these days Oliver would meet the right woman. It wouldn't be her.

"What the heck do the two of you talk about?" Marigold asked, truly puzzled. "He hasn't a bloody thing to say to me beyond, "Hello, Marigold, how are you?"

Amelia could have pointed out that Marigold had very limited interests beyond what pertained to herself, but she refrained from doing so. Instead she asked, "Are you sure you're okay?" She was wondering if Marigold should be on some sort of medication to calm her. She was certainly in one of her moods. To be fair, Royce Stirling had sparked her own anger. Why not Marigold's?

"No, I'm not okay. I'm *sick!*" Marigold began massaging her stomach with one hand.

"That's because you're upsetting yourself unnecessarily." Amelia softened her tone. "Perhaps you could make more of an effort. You can turn on the charm when you want. There's no doubt you charmed Jimmy. He had his pick of all the pretty girls. They all chased him."

"Except *you,"* Marigold retorted, with unmistakeable bitterness.

Amelia let out a patient sigh. "Please don't go on with this,' she begged. "I like Jimmy, but I'm not attracted to him in any romantic fashion. You know that perfectly well, so don't try to make something out of nothing. I will say this. Jimmy has been frittering away his life. It's time for him to settle down and pull his weight. For all his conquests, he chose you. The day after tomorrow, you'll be Mrs. James Stirling. Isn't that what you want?"

"It's what I'm going to *get!*"

The vehemence of the tone was so astonishing Amelia felt a quick chill. "You love him, don't you?"

Marigold clenched her small fists, her knuckles showing white. "He doesn't love me."

Amelia felt her anxieties mount. Jimmy wasn't acting like he was in love, either. "For pity's sake, Marigold, if there's a problem, tell me. If you want to back out, you can. There's time if you feel you're making a big mistake."

Marigold turned her head away, so sharply her fluffy curls bounced.

"I'm talking to you, Marigold," Amelia said sternly. She had to get Marigold's attention. "Please answer. Why are you so uptight?"

"Haven't I reason to be?" Marigold turned back to give Amelia a withering look. "You're the only family to attend me. Not a whole gaggle of Boyds. What do you suppose people will think? My adoptive parents not here for my wedding?"

"Your fault entirely, Marigold," Amelia pointed out crisply. "All you ever told Mum and Dad was you'd met James Stirling. Nothing more. No hint it could be serious. You've put a lot of distance between yourself and them of recent times. That hurts them. Don't you realize that?"

"Can't be helped," said Marigold. "Anyway, they're away on their travels. Italy again. They can't seem to keep away from the blasted place. They've even learned the lingo."

"As have I. Italy is *my* favourite holiday destination as well. You know that, Marigold. I invited you along at least twice, but you weren't interested. If Mum and Dad aren't here, it's because you elected to keep them in the dark. The last I heard from them, they were in Tuscany, where they'd caught up with the Westbrooks."

"Dear old Graham and Paula," Marigold crowed. "Two of the most boring people on earth."

Amelia didn't bother addressing that ridiculous charge. "What did you tell Jimmy?"

"I told him they had better things to do than attend our wedding. He would have told his family."

"Then I'll make sure they all know the truth." If it came down to a choice of defending her mother and father or Marigold, Marigold wasn't going to be allowed to get away with that blatant lie. She was sure Marigold hadn't wanted their parents here. Marigold had a proven track record of being able to go the distance with betrayal.

"And make a liar out of *me*?" Marigold looked shocked.

"You *are* a liar, Marigold," Amelia replied.

Marigold bounced up in the bed. "Made you feel good, did it, telling me that?"

"For what it's worth, I pray you will change. You'd do well to tell the truth from now on in."

"Ah, spare me the sermon," Marigold said, falling back against the pillows. "You can be such a fool, Melly, for all your much-lauded brain. The only reason Jimmy is marrying me is—are you listening, Melly? I'm fed up with keeping it to myself. I'm *pregnant with his child*."

The announcement was directed at Amelia like an arrow shot from a bow.

The impact was ferocious. Leaning forward, Amelia clutched her arms around her like a woman in pain. "Sweet Lord," she exclaimed.

There was a hard glint in Marigold's sky-blue eyes. "I'm not so sure there is one."

"Oh, there *is* one and you were raised to believe in Him," Amelia shot back. "I'm having trouble believing you."

"That's not important right now." Marigold reached for a glass of water on the bedside table, gulping it down. "I admit I do have a talent for lies."

"That's not a talent, Marigold. It's a character flaw." Amelia suddenly felt as weak as a kitten. "We both know you say anything at all to make life easier for yourself." She gathered herself as she rose to her feet. "Tell me the truth now or I'll leave you here on your own. I can't deal with lies. I want the truth."

"Save your breath, Melly. You'll *never* leave me. Strange but true. You're my big sister. You should be a guardian angel with your pure heart. Always so patient. A tower of strength to your difficult little sister—only I'm not your sister. Not your sister at all. Your parents are not my parents. *Never. Never. Never. Never. Never.*" With every denial, a thump of the pillows. "Adoption doesn't mean *blood.* I could be your enemy and you'd still treat me well. Why can't you be a bitch just for a change?"

Amelia felt sick to her stomach. "Being a bitch isn't me, Marigold. Nastiness isn't good for the soul. You're not my enemy. You're family. You would think you'd have learned that by now. If you'd really gotten yourself pregnant you would have told me, surely?"

Marigold gave a big, insulting yawn. "What a terrible shame I didn't. I don't tell you everything, Melly."

"Do you think I don't know that? I know about your deceptions, little secrets, and your downright lies. But I always remind myself that you're family. You're like a soldier constantly at war. You go through life as though you have to defend yourself against all comers."

Marigold gave a malevolent grin. "You'd have made a great psychiatrist, Melly. You've just hit it on the head. I do have to defend myself. I suffered a catastrophe. I have no parents. Yours weren't taken from you. I know how hard you've all tried to make me part of the family, though I think *your* parents are finally fed up. *You're* the one everyone loves. Everyone prefers you to me. Go on admit it."

"Maybe things would change, if you'd stop feeling so sorry for yourself," Amelia couldn't prevent herself from snapping. "Our world is full of catastrophes. Terrible suffering. Victims who survived the horrors of the Holocaust didn't throw in the towel. Anyone would think you'd been maltreated instead of loved. Mum and Dad couldn't have been kinder or more supportive. I've done my best."

"Actually, you've done quite well," Marigold admitted, suddenly seeing how Amelia had knit her arched brows together. "It's being pregnant that's making me like this," she said, coming up with an excuse.

"So it *is* true?" Amelia turned back to slump into the armchair. Her legs had suddenly given way. "And you've kept it all to yourself?"

"Except for Jimmy, of course." Marigold's full rosy lips were set in a tight line. "He doesn't care about *me*. He cares about our coming child. Jimmy loves kids."

"Thank God for that!" Amelia tried hard to compose herself. "You can't be playing games, Marigold?" She needed to ask one last time.

"Do I look like a kidder? No games, Mel. Not anymore."

"Jimmy hasn't breathed a word to me," Amelia said, wondering why he hadn't.

"It's a wonder!" Marigold flashed back. "If Jimmy were to love anyone, it would be you. Beautiful, kind, clever, Melly."

"I'd advise you not to pass any of your ridiculous comments on. There is not and never has been the faintest suggestion Jimmy is attracted to me. What we share is *you* and a friendship."

Marigold decided it was time to revert to her soft, breathy voice. It was vital she retain Amelia's support. "Have it your way, Melly. I don't want to talk about it, anyway. You're the closest person in the world to me. The *perfect* big sister."

"So what you always dreamed of has come to pass," Amelia said, no pleasure, let alone approval in her voice. "You're marrying into a great deal of money and power. Whatever you say, I would like you to *swear* to me you're pregnant."

"If I have to." Marigold placed her hand on her heart. "Anyone would think it was a bloody catastrophe."

Amelia stared across at the young woman on the bed. Marigold's bosom, naturally full, especially for her petite stature, was looking fuller, though she wasn't showing in any other way.

"How far along are you?"

"Two months without a period. That's not like me. I'm as regular as clockwork. I feel sick in the mornings too. Damn it, Melly!" She gave a sudden heartfelt sob. "I'm one hundred percent sure. I should be congratulated. It's not a horrible tragedy, you know. Why are you staring at me like that?" Marigold started to rub her flat stomach again.

"Doesn't it weigh on your conscience you deliberately trapped Jimmy?" Amelia felt sick at heart. "This isn't a child conceived in love. Then there would be no problem at all. This child was conceived out of avarice."

Marigold fired back, her expression one of outrage. "What's wrong with that? Women do it all the time."

"Men don't like being trapped, Marigold."

"So I'm sorry, sorry, sorry!" Marigold returned to beating the pillows. "I mean, bloody hell! It takes two to tango. Jimmy and I had a lot of sex. You know what he's like. That's all he wanted. When I found out I was pregnant, I couldn't believe it. I was so ashamed." Tears spurted into her blue eyes. "I didn't tell you. I wanted to. You're my only friend. You've always stuck by me. You're my bridesmaid, for God's sake!" Marigold's voice suddenly cracked. "I didn't want you to find out like this. Jimmy and I were going to pretend I fell pregnant on our honeymoon."

"He hasn't told a soul?"

"I didn't ask him *not* to," Marigold lied. "It was all his idea. He knew he had to step up to the mark. He worships his brother. They all do. Royce is the sun, moon, and stars around here."

"He's going to find out sometime," Amelia said grimly. "They all are."

"They won't know one hundred percent," Marigold answered with complete confidence. "The baby will be premature."

"Dear God!" Amelia closed her eyes, letting her shock show. "Is this marriage going to work?"

"Come on, Melly." Marigold turned a pretty pleading face. Her blue eyes were glistening with ready tears. "It isn't the worst thing in the world. I don't like kids, but I'll deal with it. Besides, everyone loves babies, even the bloody Stirlings."

Amelia came to a decision. "I think you and Jimmy should tell the family before the wedding, Marigold. Honesty really is the best policy. Jimmy's mother, his aunt, and uncle are arriving tomorrow, as are all of the guests. You and Jimmy can tell the family privately. No one else needs to know."

Marigold bounded off the bed like a gymnast. She looked frantic. "*No one* is going to know," she shouted. "Jimmy doesn't want to tell them any more than I do. It's for us to make the decision, not *you*. Jesus, can't you keep out of anything?"

"Sure, I can." Amelia rose from her chair. "I can go one better. I can go home."

"And desert me?" Marigold cried, throwing up her small hands. "Wonderfully kind and supportive Amelia taking the easy way out?"

"Don't try to dump your failings on me, Marigold," Amelia warned. "If you and Jimmy have made the decision not to tell the family, and that includes *our* family, that you're pregnant, you can be absolutely certain I'll keep my mouth shut. Do it your way."

Marigold sucked in a breath. "I knew you'd agree."

"I'm *not* agreeing with you," Amelia said. "I feel more like curling up in a corner to weep. This could have been handled so much better."

Marigold shook her head in denial. "Jimmy and I have talked it over. Our decision is made. You're such a comfort to me, Melly. It's early in my pregnancy. That's the beauty of it. I can pull it off."

Amelia remained silent as she rose and walked to the door. "This isn't the best way to go about things, Marigold. Your plans could all backfire. Did you bring that pretty blue and silver cocktail dress I bought you?" she asked, one hand on the brass doorknob.

Marigold shook her head. "No, I didn't. I like it, Melly. I *was* going to bring it with me, but I've already decided on a little red lace number. You know me. I like to make a splash."

Amelia's hand curled around the heavy knob. "Please lay off the alcohol tonight. We both know alcohol goes straight to your head. If I were you, I wouldn't drink at all during your pregnancy."

"But you're not me, are you, Melly?" Marigold waggled her fingers. "I promise I won't lash out on the vodka again. They've probably hidden it anyway, but I'll have a couple of glasses of vino."

"I think you might settle for one," Amelia said repressively. "You owe it to yourself and Jimmy to make a good impression."

Marigold moved to the walk-in wardrobe, waving a careless hand. "That's your provenance, sweetie. You're here to make a good impression for me. You know I really should be wearing a ball gown. They're so posh."

"Well, posh *you* aren't," Amelia retorted, making her escape.

Chapter 2

Marigold hadn't been that far out when she had joked about wearing a ball gown to dinner, Amelia thought. The formal dining room set a very high tone. The long, polished mahogany table was surrounded by beautiful antique chairs, cushioned in ruby velvet to match the predominant colour in the gorgeous Persian carpet. The high ceiling was coffered with a splendid rock crystal chandelier at its centre, its lights reflected in the two tall, gilt-framed mirrors that hung on either side of the room. She understood the formal dining room was only used for celebrations or when there were special guests to dinner. At other times, the family used the informal dining room that led off the kitchen.

Marigold, who wasn't a bit shy when there were men around, looked very eye-catching in her short scarlet cocktail dress, the low-cut bodice showing off too much bosom. Though many a man in a fever of male excitement couldn't have resisted long, admiring glances at the bosom on display, Jimmy wasn't looking at all charmed by his fiancée's frontal assault.

Big brother Royce's expression predictably revealed very little. That was something Amelia had expected. She wondered why he wasn't married or at least engaged, given he was one of the most eligible bachelors in the country. It wasn't as though she could ask, though. She couldn't. It wouldn't be polite. It was entirely possible, however, that some extremely attractive daughter of one of the landed families would turn up as a guest for the wedding.

The unsettling notion filled her head that Royce Stirling would be a fabulous lover. Up until now, she had thought she lacked the capacity to be bowled over by a man. *Well, there was always a first time for everything,* she thought. Very sensibly she shut down on her notion, focusing on the glorious flower arrangement instead. She feared where unsuitable thoughts of Royce Stirling might take her.

In the space of an hour or two, he had turned from a hardworking cattle man into a suave dinner party host. She thought it would be all right if she acknowledged how good he looked. But then he had looked good in dust-splattered work clothes, sporting a scruffy black stubble on his cheeks and chin. Tonight, he was clean-shaven. His white banded shirt looked very stylish beneath his lightweight charcoal jacket. The pristine white threw his bronze skin, raven hair, and dark eyes into high relief. It actually bothered her he was so handsome. Although handsome didn't say it. Jimmy was handsome too, but he lacked the special aura given to powerful men.

The five of them were seated at one end of the long table. Spread out, they would have had to resort to shouting at one another. On the surface, it looked like an enjoyable occasion, only there was a fragile balance in play. Royce presided at the top of the table. Where else? Marigold, the bride-to-be, was at his right. Jimmy was seated opposite his fiancée to his brother's left. Anthea Stirling, striking in dark blue silk, long-skirted like Amelia's, sat beside Marigold. Elegant white linen decorated the table. Fine porcelain, sterling silver cutlery, crystal glasses, four matching silver candlesticks, the tapering candles alight. As a centrepiece, a silver punch bowl with a lovely lustre had been filled with the most exquisite, slightly open red roses with a light sweet fragrance.

Amelia turned her head to smile at Anthea. "Yours?" Gently, she reached out a hand to stroke a petal.

"Mine," Anthea acknowledged, with a pleased smile.

"I'll take a punt. Black Velvet? I'm going on the velvet texture of the petals."

"That's remarkable, Amelia," Anthea said. "I haven't had a single visitor who could identify it. It was bred in the U.S., but oddly enough it does better in Australian climate conditions."

Marigold's light voice was mocking. "If you're looking for bucketloads of enthusiasm, Anthea, you can't go past Melly. She's mad about gardens. Takes after her mother."

"Surely *your* mother too, Marigold?" Royce intervened smoothly.

"Well, yes, of course." Marigold answered sweetly. "Melly's most recent trip to London was timed so she could take in the Chelsea Flower Show, would you believe?"

"This was?" Anthea's fine-boned face was alight with interest.

"Last May. I only had a fortnight, but I wanted to see the show. It was superb. The displays were astoundingly beautiful. I even managed to catch sight of the Queen, who looks remarkable for her age. She was chatting to David Austin, probably the world's most famous rose grower, as you would know, Anthea. They both looked engrossed. Kate and William were there as well."

Marigold cut in, bright-eyed. "Please! You can stop there, Melly. I find talk about gardens terribly boring."

"You don't know what you're missing out on, Marigold," Anthea said with a softening smile. "We can speak more about roses tomorrow, Amelia," she promised. "I want you to meet our dear friend and my mentor, Vernon. Vernon lives in a bungalow in the grounds. He's come to dinner countless times over the years, but he's over eighty now and likes an early night."

"I'd be delighted to meet him," Amelia said. "Our mother is very keen on her garden. She, too, has her helper. He's English. He once worked on an English estate. He's an expert on roses, though he did put in a garden of marigolds in honour of Marigold here."

"Marigolds are very common," Marigold said.

"They look wonderful in a mass display." Quick to read signals, Anthea had realized Marigold had conflicting feelings about her beautiful adopted sister. It was very unpleasant. Jealousy, of course. Probably the seeds had been sown in early childhood.

Jimmy, who had been unusually quiet, suddenly spoke up. The skin over his handsome face was drawn tight. "You totally lack Amelia's artistic eye, don't you, darling?" It was delivered with a smile, yet every word seemed heavy with something dangerously close to dislike.

Aaaah! The first crack in the façade, Amelia thought. She was now on tenterhooks. Should this marriage go ahead, pregnancy or not? Marigold seemed incapable of working out what it was to be gracious, but she did flush at Jimmy's comment. Mercifully, Royce chose that exact moment to raise his champagne glass. "To Marigold and James," he pronounced, his brilliant dark glance embracing them both. "Wisdom and happiness."

Amelia was glad he had put it in that order. Wisdom first. Happiness to follow. She felt distressed, but she knew she couldn't show it.

"We're so sorry your parents aren't able to attend the wedding," Anthea addressed the bride-to-be, locking onto the possibility Mr. and Mrs. Boyd may not have been asked.

"Italy beckoned." Marigold laughed, as though that explained everything. "I couldn't compete with that. They adore the place."

Without hesitation, Amelia rose in defence of her parents, who had been so kind and good to Marigold. "You left it far too late to tell them, didn't you, Marigold?"

"Marigold's idea," said Jimmy.

"Come on, Jimmy!" Marigold scoffed. "You said as long as the two of us were together. That was *all* you wanted."

Amelia badly wanted to explain their parents knew nothing about Marigold's wedding, but she couldn't predict what the outcome would be. Marigold was looking very flushed. She had always flushed up as a child when she was about to throw a tantrum.

"There will be other times," Royce Stirling said, smoothly. "Italy has to be one of the great travel destinations. I made the grand tour of Europe the year after I graduated. I'd say Italy came out tops. For a trip totally different, Antarctica was right up there. It's extremely worrying how the big glaciers of the world are melting. For the life of me, I can't understand how anyone could reject climate change."

The conversation continued for a little while in that vein.

Despite the swirling undercurrents, Amelia remained serene throughout an excellent dinner. There were three courses: sweet and sour prawns, spiced duck breast, and for dessert, a delicious lemon and coconut tart with melt-in-the-mouth pastry.

Beset by anxieties or not, she found she was hungry. Besides, it would have been nigh-on impossible not to enjoy such beautifully cooked and presented food from the Stirling home's treasure, Pippa. The Stirlings were as appreciative as she. The only one to push her food around the plate was Marigold. Her tummy could well have been rejecting a full meal, Amelia would have thought, except for the fact Marigold was drinking too much, even taking the sauvignon blanc bottle out of the ice bucket and refilling her glass without waiting for their host to do so.

"Sweetheart, I think you've had enough," Jimmy suggested, staring hard across the table.

"Anyway, it's time for coffee," Royce said. "We'll take it in the drawing room."

"Just when I was having a great time." Marigold drained the last drop.

Jimmy was very quick to come to her, pulling back her chair and taking her arm. Marigold lurched, so he was forced to grab her around the waist. For some reason, this made Marigold laugh explosively. "Giddy-up!"

Amelia didn't glance at anyone. *Giddy up?* An alternative to thank you? Marigold didn't even like horses. Anger and a sense of humiliation began to boil in Amelia. Royce moved to hold back his aunt's chair, then hers. She knew he was looking down at her, but she didn't raise her head. She was mortified by Marigold's behaviour, which was sadly on the vulgar side. Marigold had been raised to do better.

Yet Marigold was no fool, even if she were playing the fool. Was she punishing Jimmy for something? God knows. Marigold obviously felt no guilt over embarrassing Jimmy in front of his family, but then Marigold didn't understand guilt like other people. She had embarrassed Amelia countless times in the past and never once apologized. Maybe she had been far too accepting? In which case, she was largely at fault. She had pointed out many times to Marigold how she offended people with her careless comments, but Marigold had always shrugged off all admonitions. Marigold was predictable in some ways. She always had an agenda of her own. The primary agenda had been marrying James Stirling. She didn't love him, if indeed she understood love. In itself that was extraordinary. How did anyone enter into marriage with *no* love in the heart?

Royce Stirling led the conversation, both entertaining and stimulating over rich Italian coffee. Unfamiliar with some of the subjects, Marigold made little effort to conceal her boredom. Amelia knew the expression. Marigold felt trapped. It wasn't surprising then when she excused herself, claiming to feel tired. Jimmy took her arm as he escorted her out of the drawing room into the hallway. If Marigold were not careful, she could lose Jimmy forever, baby or no baby.

Amelia had no difficulty reading his pent-up emotions. She hoped to God an argument wouldn't break out on the stairs. The family surely had seen happier brides and grooms.

Afterwards, when Royce and his aunt were discussing some item of family business, Amelia wandered out onto the wide veranda, admiring the white pillars wreathed in a blossoming lilac vine. Everything seemed utterly unreal to her. The splendid colonial mansion in the wilds. The way the Stirlings lived like royalty in such extraordinary isolation. It was like some fairy tale.

She lifted her head to the dazzling star-struck night sky. She had never seen so many stars in her life, all so brilliantly clear. It was easy to pick out the Southern Cross, a constellation very familiar to Australians and represented on the national flag.

She knew the stars figured largely in aboriginal legend. Australian aborigines, after all, were recognised as the world's first astronomers. For tens of thousands of years, they used the stars to predict natural occurrences and to work out their calendar. Kooralya employed a good many aboriginal and part-aboriginal people in their workforce. Nomadic tribal people came and went freely on their travels across the station. It could not be forgotten Kooralya was once aboriginal land until the white man arrived.

She felt more than heard a presence behind her, a presence who had followed her out here. His shape was already forming in her mind. It wasn't Royce Stirling. Her highly tuned senses would have recognized his approach. Her whole body would have quickened its pace. She turned, fully prepared to see Jimmy. He looked like a young man in pain, his nerves all but charred.

"Jimmy, what it is?" For a moment, she felt like picking up her long skirt and hurrying away from a problematic situation. She was acutely aware Jimmy was strongly attracted to her. Whatever the reason, it never ceased to amaze her. She had never given Jimmy the slightest hint of encouragement.

He came to stand very close to her, as if for comfort, but essentially invading her space. "I've a dilemma on my hands, Amelia."

Thankfully, Jimmy had never called her either Mel or Melly. "Tell me." Get it over.

"I should have told you before." There was a silence, then it came in a rush, "Marigold is pregnant." He let out a strangled breath. "Honest to God, I don't know what to do anymore."

"*Do*, Jimmy?" Amelia had to lower her voice hurriedly. "When Marigold told you she was pregnant, you immediately offered to marry her."

"Of course I did," he agreed, as though he were two different people. "I was the one who got her pregnant, after all."

"Then you're something of an idealist, Jimmy. I know you love children, but what is the point of your marrying Marigold if neither of you is happy? Other arrangements, surely, could have been made? Can still be made."

"What? On the eve of our wedding?" His face took on a tortured expression. "I really can't change anything, Amelia. I can't bring shame to my family."

"There *is* no shame, Jimmy," Amelia insisted, grasping his arm to give it a brisk shake.

Jimmy seized the moment, covering her hand with his. "You're so beautiful," he said in a voice that betrayed his intense, physical yearning.

Amelia had no course but to ignore the emotion so apparent in his voice. As gently as she could, she withdrew her hand. "Jimmy, your family aren't rigid moralists. One mistake is rarely enough to alienate a loving family and they do love you. But if *you* don't love Marigold and she doesn't love you, it would be utterly wrong to go ahead with this wedding even if you have to call it off at the last minute."

There was the glitter of tears in Jimmy's eyes. "What, and watch Marigold play the innocent victim? The betrayed woman. She's *determined* on this marriage, Amelia. She wants to be Mrs. James Stirling. Not my *wife*. Not even my child's mother, I suspect. She told you she was pregnant? I know she tells you everything."

"Indeed she doesn't," said Amelia bleakly. "I only found out this evening. If Marigold didn't tell me, *you* should have, Jimmy. Seeing you so unhappy is hard to bear."

"That tender heart of yours!" Jimmy said, struggling to keep his composure. "I have been feeling pretty grim."

"It shows, I'm afraid."

"Well, I don't have Royce's iron control. I know he's worried about me."

"With good reason." It was good to know Royce Stirling did care deeply about his half-brother.

"I don't suppose *you* could ever love me?" Jimmy asked, with no real hope.

"I do love you. As my *friend*." Amelia faced him with anxious eyes.

"And that's the nub of it. All the difference in the world." Jimmy gave a twisted smile. "You're miles too good for me. You're the sort of woman a man only meets once in a lifetime. I could *never* have you. I'm a bloody coward anyway."

Amelia searched for the right words to say. "You're no such thing! I won't accept that. If you decide to tell the family, I'll stand by you. You acted in a way you thought honourable, but you've now realized that decision could have appalling consequences if there's no love between you and Marigold."

"I never did love her." Jimmy spoke with a kind of despair. "I never told her I loved her. What I did was fuck her." He broke off abruptly. "Sorry, Amelia," he apologized. "I shouldn't be so crude. Forgive me. I've met plenty of girls, but none like Marigold with her issues. She's madly jealous of you, did you know? If you want to know *why*, I'll tell you. You're everything she's not. My one criticism of you is you're far too generous towards her. You should call her out as a conniving manipulator. I don't relish the thought of marrying her, but marry her I will."

The night wind picked up, blowing Amelia's long hair around her face. She pushed it back with a shaky hand. "Jimmy, you simply *can't,* not feeling as you do. There's no depth of connection. You're not even *friends*. A genuine friendship between lovers I would think absolutely essential. You're allowing Marigold to blackmail you."

"And isn't she good at it," Jimmy retorted, with blackest humour. "It's okay, Amelia. The wedding date is set. Guests will be arriving tomorrow including my mother, my aunt, and uncle. Really nice people. Everyone is expecting a wedding. I should never have acted as I did in the first place. I've continued too long as the playboy. I've left everything to Royce, not that he needed my help, but I know he wanted me to be here by his side. I'm desperate for his approval, for the family's approval. Everyone has been waiting for me to settle down."

"*Happily*, Jimmy," Amelia stressed, not believing the drama that had unfolded within a few short hours. "I urge you to speak up and get it over with. You will have to speak to Marigold first. This isn't high treason. There's nothing fixed in stone."

Jimmy clasped her bare shoulders with his two hands, turning her towards him. "I'm not only in love with you as a beautiful woman, Amelia. I'm in love with your soul. Every man needs a good woman to take him in hand. Even Royce, who has everything. I've made my decision and it's *final*. The wedding will take place just as a divorce will in due course. I can't have Marigold moving away with my child. I have to protect my precious unborn baby. You know Marigold. You've seen her in action for years and years. I'd say she was wicked, only I don't think she *knows* what she does. It's as though something vital has been left out of her. The ability to make the right moral judgements."

"Ah, Jimmy!" Tears sparkled in Amelia's green eyes. Marigold always acted on what she considered her own best interests.

"The wonder of it is, I've come to know what love is," Jimmy was saying gently. "I love *you*, Amelia. I know I shouldn't, but once you fall in love, you can't change course. The decision isn't in your hands. Love can lift a man to the heavens or destroy him. May I kiss you? Just once," he begged. "I'm going to miss you terribly."

She couldn't possibly agree to it. "Jimmy, this isn't a good idea!" Her eyes flashed a warning.

"I know that," he said, but still he lowered his head. "I want to take you into my heart, into my mind. I'm afraid I'm not going to have a happy life, Amelia." His mouth was barely an inch from hers.

Amelia knew a sensation of precariousness. She should deny Jimmy the comfort he wanted, only she was transfixed by his very real anguish. For that moment in time, Jimmy's emotions had kicked into over-drive.

"Jimmy, you *can't!*" she whispered "You mustn't do this. It's crazy and totally inappropriate."

"I know," said Jimmy, like a man in agony.

Royce Stirling was forced into acting as witness. A man sees a woman. He wants her. There was no question Jimmy wanted his golden enchantress. Royce stood immobile, just inside the French doors leading onto the veranda that had been his destination. His shoulders momentarily slumped as though beneath a heavy burden.

How we keep our souls secret.

What he was watching was tremendously upsetting, yet it was also a blatant display of disloyalty. Infidelity on Jimmy's part and on *hers*. He knew the image of the two of them locked together would forever haunt him. Jimmy and his blond enchantress. Her head was thrown back so far it had to be painful for her long graceful neck. She looked incredibly beautiful. Incredibly desirable. Fragile beside his brother's tall frame. Jimmy had his arms locked around her as though he would never let her go. They could have been posing for a passionate love scene.

What the hell was Jimmy playing at?, he thought with a great spurt of helpless anger. Jimmy had deliberately chosen one woman when he was crazy for another. This wedding was no more than a mockery. It should be called off. Loving one woman and marrying another was a recipe for disaster.

And what was behind Amelia Boyd's lovely face with its open expression? What was in her soul? He felt strongly he should call a halt to this illicit love scene. He didn't see himself as someone lurking in the background, a stalker. He was horrified. He wrenched back the long filmy curtain that was floating in the breeze, only to see her break away, her beauty in full bloom from that passionate kiss. She was running down the veranda to the short flight of steps that led into the garden.

His brother didn't go after her. Instead James began to walk, head down, back into the house.

He stepped out to confront him. "What the hell was that all about?" he asked angrily, turning his brother back onto the veranda and forcing him down to the shadowed end.

James gave a discordant laugh, but he didn't pull away. Royce was taller and far stronger than he was in all departments. "I've been desperate to kiss Amelia ever since I met her," he confided, striving for his usual flippant tone, but only succeeding in sounding wretched. "That was my only opportunity before I become a married man."

"Are you *crazy?*" For a second, Royce's voice boomed. "I *saw* you. You're madly in love with her."

"Infatuated, certainly," James confessed. "Yes, indeed. I'll get over it. Amelia doesn't share my feelings. I'm about to marry her sister. My sweet little Marigold."

"God knows why," Royce shot back, lowering his tone. It was just as effective near-soft. "You definitely don't love her."

"I do too," James maintained. "Well, in my fashion. Marigold suits me. I don't want a superior woman like Amelia who would always be challenging me. Marigold enjoys the same things I do. Like me, she's not encumbered with a full set of brains."

"Why do you always sell yourself so short?" Royce was sick of this sort of thing. James had been studying architecture. He had shown a considerable aptitude for it before abandoning his course.

"Maybe because our father christened me useless," James suggested, with a bitter laugh. "I'm not a complete person like you, Royce. You're the most complete person I have ever known. You experienced Dad at his worst, but you pulled through. You had *stature* even as a boy. I love you. Damn it, I revere you."

"Jimmy, please stop," Royce begged, with great patience and infinite sadness. He was painfully aware of his half-brother's lonely soul. Damn it, *he* was lonely in his own fashion. Their father's harsh nature had affected them both.

"With a bit of effort, you can take your life in your hands," Royce told his brother. "I'm here to help."

"That's not how it's going to be," James Stirling said, as though he knew something his brother didn't. "I can see clearly who I am, Royce. As I've always said, life would have been a whole lot worse for me and Mum without you. You shielded us from that wretched man. I bet Beelzebub himself escorted him straight to hell."

Royce cast his half-brother a compassionate sidelong glance. "We've done better, Jimmy. We're better men. But this is all wrong!" Royce clasped his brother tightly on the shoulder. "Does Marigold have something over you? She's not pregnant, is she? She strikes me as the kind of woman who would consider getting you that way."

James had a moment of pure indecision. He knew this was the time for him to come clean; to tell Royce everything, but he had learned more of Marigold and her excesses than just about anyone, including Amelia. He genuinely dreaded what Marigold might do if her plans were ruined. Marigold was a very odd young woman with a capacity for cruelty if driven. He felt sure of it. His heart was pumping wildly. He was desperate for his brother's comfort, desperate to escape his brother's piercing regard. He had made his decision. He had made his bed. Now he had to lie in it.

"Marigold *isn't* pregnant, Royce," he said, in a voice that even fooled him. "I *want* to marry her. I'm going to marry her."

"Hell, you said that like you were saying goodbye," Royce protested, his strongly defined features drawn tight. "I can't figure this out at all. There's no way you can fool me. You're madly in love with Amelia, not Marigold. You were kissing her like you never wanted to let her go."

"So?" James gave a crooked smile. "I bet you'd like to kiss her too."

The words came as a direct hit. "Your golden enchantress, Jimmy," he said, in a sombre voice.

"Dad used to call your mother 'his dark enchantress,' remember?" James responded.

Royce nodded. "Dad made a prison for himself. He locked himself in."

"Him and his memories," James said. "He hurt my poor little mother terribly. I guess he hurt your mother terribly too?"

It was issued not as a challenge, but a question that might need to be addressed. Royce looked away across the garden, wondering where Amelia had sought refuge. "My mother was the one who ran off, Jimmy. She didn't take me with her. She didn't even contact me afterwards."

James snorted. "As if she could! We both know Dad was a violent man. He would have killed her. And you. Can't you see it? Insanely jealous men kill. It happens every day all over the world. It would have made him feel good for a minute. If you can't figure out me, I can't figure out you, Royce. Why don't you contact your mother? You're the man who can slay dragons."

Royce didn't have to search for an answer. "I survived without her. In her way, she was as implacable as Dad."

James took his courage in hand. "Quite sure about that, are you? I think it's time for you to go looking for answers, Royce. Your mother might have had help getting out of here, but she never did marry that guy. For a beautiful woman, she has never remarried."

"Maybe she learned about marriage the hard way." Royce shrugged. "Anyway, we're not talking about me. We're talking about *you*. I don't know what *you're* doing. I don't believe for one moment Marigold is the woman for you, but if you're determined to marry her, there's always divorce."

"Thank God for that!" said James, as though he had thought the whole thing out.

When his brother walked back inside the house, Royce decided on the spur of the moment to follow James' golden seductress. He walked with his big cat's tread down the veranda into the dark purple night like a man compelled. This was a woman who had done and was *still* doing a whole lot of harm. He now had all the evidence he needed to back up his initial strong suspicions.

The warm air was awash with the scent of gardenias, oleanders, frangipani, all sweet and heady. His love for his runaway mother, all mixed up with anger at her betrayal, came and went in cycles. Now suddenly Amelia Boyd's entry into his life made his locked-down memories flare into life. He bitterly resented the fact men were astonishingly susceptible to beautiful women, astonishingly immune to learning from experience. He found himself wondering whether Amelia Boyd was one of those women far more interested in gaining power over men than giving them power over her. He tried to shake off Jimmy's comment that he, too, would like to kiss Amelia. If he did, it would be far from love. It would be unequivocal desire. It had penetrated his skin like so many arrows.

He must have walked for a good six or seven minutes. The beauty all around him revealed by the exterior lighting didn't calm him as it usually did. She couldn't have found her way back into the house. He would have seen her.

Fruit bats stuffed with mangoes and pawpaws streaked across the night sky and into the small woodland of trees a short distance away from the intensely cultivated main gardens. A lot of attention had been given to the section of the garden he was now skirting. A large pond had been created some four years back with his approval. It was fed by a subterranean spring with its source the Great Artesian Basin, the largest, deepest artesian basin in the world, underlying nearly a quarter of the continent. It was also the only reliable source of fresh water for much of the Outback. The pond's glittering surface was densely ringed by all manner of ferns and thick clumps of iris and arum lilies growing with their feet in the water.

These were Anthea's gardens. Anthea's territory. The gardens kept his aunt happy after she had suffered a doomed love affair in her youth. Anthea's fiancé had been killed defending a woman, the wife of a native worker, gone berserk on the family's New Guinea coffee plantation. The loss had been shocking. Anthea had never been the same again. There had been a lot of heartbreak in his family, he thought. Out-of-the-ordinary stuff. Now Jimmy!

He finally sighted Amelia sitting in seclusion at the far end of a tunnelled walkway dripping with morning glories. At the back of his mind, there had been the thought they would seek each other out. There was a tautness, a special awareness between them that had taken root within moments of laying eyes on each other. He was a man who enjoyed women's company. He'd had his share of affairs, but he had never met the woman to turn his mind to marriage. He knew a lot of people expected him to eventually settle down with Charlene Warrender. He and Charlene had enjoyed an on-and-off-again relationship for some years. Charlene was immensely suitable. Outback born and bred, the daughter of Charlie Warrender, owner of Jambawa station, their closest neighbour to the southeast. He had considerable affection for Charlene—he had known her since they were children—but affection wasn't the totally irresistible wild burn of passion. He knew in his heart he wanted a great flume of emotion, not affection. He had begun to think he wanted far too much.

Not you!

Amelia stood up to confront Royce, a violent lurch to her heart.

In the vine-dappled lighting she caught sight of him: tall, incredibly fit, stalking towards her. She felt incredibly tense and nervous. She knew she was in a shameful position. Yet it seemed too much, just too much, for one evening. He must have seen Jimmy kissing her. Now he had come to demand an explanation. Was she supposed to drop to her knees begging his forgiveness? Royce Stirling, self-appointed judge and jury. He had been making on-the-spot judgements his whole adult life.

She felt totally inadequate to deal with him and the devastating situation they were all in. It must have looked bad to him, seeing Jimmy kissing her so passionately. There was Marigold's adoptive sister and her bridesmaid within the tight half-circle of Jimmy's arms, betraying everyone's trust. Guilt, even when she wasn't truly guilty of any wrong-doing, hit her with excruciating force.

"Well, well, so this is where you've hidden yourself away?" he called, moving so quickly he cut off any chance she might take flight. "Don't run away, Amelia. You and I are going to have a little chat."

She stood her ground, tossing back her head on its long graceful neck. "You're not out here to be sociable," she said. "And I'm not running away."

"Then you must be completely shameless." Coming on her like this in the perfumed darkness, he had the insane idea time had stopped altogether. They were *alone* in the world. Light rays crossed her, giving her hair a rich, golden sheen. They outlined her slender figure, so incongruously dressed in innocent white. So beautiful, yet so morally blemished.

His aura put Amelia on her mettle. She was far from an accommodating ninny. Not with Royce Stirling, master of all he surveyed. "Shame doesn't come into it," she said sharply, though to her consternation, her knees felt like they might buckle.

"Really?" There was a cutting edge to his voice. "So James is madly in love with you and all the rest is a façade. Is that it? You're going to continue your affair even after he marries Marigold?"

She knew she should remain calm for her own sake, but she couldn't. Not with *him*. "Don't be ridiculous!" she flared. "There *is* no affair."

Even in the half-light, his striking face showed his disbelief. "So how did you achieve your hold over him? Witchcraft, is that what you used? Jimmy used to talk about his "golden enchantress." We all thought he meant Marigold, but when we got to meet her a few months back, she didn't fit that image. A pretty girl, certainly, but someone quite different from an enchantress."

Amelia looked away. She was deeply reluctant to speak about Marigold, much less Marigold's problems. "Jimmy's feelings are a mystery to me," she said. "What you saw is not as it seemed."

He clicked his fingers in contempt.

"Jimmy has never before kissed me," she said, desperate to convince him, even though she knew she had to see it through his eyes. "Can't you understand? I don't lie."

"You *do*," he contradicted her flatly. "My instincts were correct right from the start."

She needed understanding. She wasn't going to get it. As far as he was concerned, she was a woman with her mind set on conquest. "Then you're a man who jumps too fast to conclusions. What you saw was in the nature of a goodbye kiss."

He gave a deep sigh of admiration as if for a magnificent lie. "I hardly think you could call it that. A goodbye kiss is rarely a revelation."

He spoke with such cool contempt she hardly knew how to respond. She couldn't run back to the house and call a cab. She might as well have been his prisoner. "I should have stopped him, I know, but I wasn't really given a chance." Even to her own ears, her excuse sounded poor.

Royce groaned. "Oh, stop it, Amelia. Stop it, please! I'd say you're a woman who knows how to lay down the law, so if that's your explanation, I'm not buying it. You know *exactly* what you are to Jimmy. His golden enchantress. I'd say you revel in your power over him. Are you going to tell me now you love him?"

She threw up her hands. "No. No. *No!* Of course, I don't. Maybe you're the one who doesn't know about love?" She knew the sensible course was to stop right there, but to her peril, she was too far gone.

Royce could feel his temper rising to the insistent drum of his heart. "You don't know a damned thing about me."

"And you don't know a thing about me, either," she retaliated. "What I do know is you have never given your mother a chance." It was delivered like a strong accusation. He towered over her—a man's height and strength could be so intimidating—but she continued to stare up at him, her emotions on the boil. "Did you judge her like you're judging me?" she challenged.

For an instant, he felt she had gained the whip hand. Clever, so clever! "That is none of your business. I remind you you're a guest here," he said in his most formidable voice.

"Then don't you have a duty to be courteous to your guests? I'm not so dense I failed to miss the fact you didn't want me here."

He wanted to be away from her, but the way he was feeling prevented him from turning on his heel. "Perhaps you can clarify what we heard at dinner? Your parents chose to go on holiday to Italy over attending my brother's and Marigold's wedding, or Marigold decided there was no place for your parents in it."

A feeling of utter defeat came over her. "Something like that."

"Well, well!" he said. "Doesn't Marigold worry you?"

"She exaggerates."

"I must meet your parents," he said.

"They're wonderful people. They'll be stunned when they hear about the wedding."

"Surely *you* should have told them?"

"Can we stop now?" she said. "After Marigold's parents were tragically killed, my parents, close friends, adopted Marigold. You know that much?"

"Of course. It sounds like Marigold didn't deserve her adopted parents."

Amelia shook her head. "No point in talking about it. What's happened, happened. Marigold needs time to mature."

"So what's your excuse? You're taking your revenge?"

"I have no idea what you're talking about. Revenge? I'm no vengeful person. Maybe *you* are?"

"News to me."

Amelia felt like she was being plunged into a nightmare. She had to cling fast to her self-control, only she couldn't, he so rattled her. "Just about the whole country knows your story," she said, even knowing it was ill-advised. "You *are* Outback royalty. There's a whole mystique attached to our cattle barons. I'm certain you've never considered asking your *mother* her reasons for leaving?"

Damn you, he thought. He had considered it a million times but he could never bring himself to do it. His mother hadn't even sent him so much as a note. She could have sent letters to him through his school, even university. "Might I remind you we're not talking about me," he said, very coldly indeed, his emotions on a knife's edge. "I know exactly what you're doing. You're trying to turn the tables."

Amelia's breath caught in her throat. "I'm sorry." She dropped her head in apology. "I shouldn't have spoken to you about your mother, but you're making me so *angry*. I have no romantic interest whatsoever in Jimmy. I promise you. Our only relationship has been friendship."

He too was making efforts to calm himself. She couldn't have been angrier than he was. He saw that. Only no one, absolutely *no one,* caused him to lose his composure. This woman was having no difficulty at all. "I can't believe you." There was a hard nuance in his voice. "There had to be a good reason for James to have acted the way he did. That wasn't some parting kiss with all necessary restraint. Jimmy is marrying Marigold, yet he was holding *you,* the bridesmaid, like he never wanted to let you go. I'm *amazed* you're trying to suggest something different. You must know you're playing a dangerous game."

Her head drooped like a flower on its long stalk. She was so weary of it all. Weary of Marigold. Weary of Jimmy. "The challenge for you is to find out the truth. It seems there is nothing *I* can do to convince you. I've always known Jimmy is attracted to me. There, I've said it. But I've never taken any real stock of it. I have never given him the slightest encouragement."

"So why didn't you rebuff him?" he asked, aware his emotions were fast arriving at the point of consuming him.

"Okay, I breached the rules. I'm not at all happy about it. But sometimes . . . sometimes . . . *kindness* prevents one from—"

"Amelia, stop," he ordered. This unwelcome desire for her was eating away at the self-control he took such pride in. He could smell her subtle fragrance, feel the heat off her graceful body in her gauzy dress. A breeze had sprung up, lifting the long diaphanous skirt, sending long locks of her hair cascading over her shoulders. He realized she was as angry as he was. Angry at being caught out, as illicit lovers were so often caught out.

Despite his long-entrenched sense of caution, she appeared to him as the most thrilling representation of her sex. It should have hardened him against her, yet it was having the opposite effect. To combat it, he spoke too harshly. "This has to come to an end," he warned. "James is hell-bent on marrying Marigold for his own peculiar reasons. Your adopted *sister,* I might point out. Where's the loyalty, Amelia? You mightn't want any binding relation with my brother, but you'd better forget all about keeping up the association. If you disregard what I'm saying, I can and will make things very difficult for you."

A shadow crossed her face as she moved closer to him. She hadn't intended to do so. Or perhaps she did? "Am I supposed to be afraid of you? Am I supposed to break out in a cold sweat?'

He felt the blood rush to his head. Hot. Swift. Fierce. "I'd advise you to listen," he repeated. "You have to be very careful. Many eyes will be upon you. Upon you, James and Marigold. You would have to see very clearly Marigold can't hold a candle to you in the looks department. I hope you're not going to upstage her."

"God, you're a hateful man," Amelia exploded.

"I wish I knew how you can look and sound so innocent and be so damned guilty," he returned by way of challenge.

The very air around them seemed to have caught fire. She gave him the only answer she knew. One that would offend and shock him as he was offending and shocking her. "And you had better be careful you don't turn into your father." After the words were out of her mouth, she took fright. She had taken a step to the very verge.

The pulse of his heart was loud in his ears. Myriad scents were streaming towards them. Gardenias. Tropical roses. Jasmine. Innumerable heat-loving plants. Soothing, but they had no calming effect. She had pushed him too far. This was the way she worked her spells. "I know what you are." His low-pitched voice was almost a panther's growl. "And you're very, very good. I'm nothing like my father. You won't find anyone to tell you differently. What I *am* is head of the family. You won't achieve anything setting yourself against me. I'll make sure you fail."

"Am I supposed to crack under the strain?"

High above them, a falling star shot swiftly towards earth.

She stared up into his arrogant face. She wanted to lash out at him, but she was fighting to form the right words. Instead, her hand flashed up without conscious volition. How dare he threaten her? How dare he presume he had control over her? She, who was totally against violence in all its forms, now felt the same helpless anger as her abused women clients.

Men!

The world was run by arrogant men! It was wrong. All *wrong*. She had seen the effects of men's domination over and over again. The least she could do was stand up for herself. For *women*.

Her fierce slap was destined to never reach its target. Royce caught her narrow wrist mid-air. "Here's your chance, Amelia. Test me out. You know you want to. Teach me what a kiss is," he taunted.

The truth struck her. She was frighteningly attracted to this man. An attraction that had propelled her into free-fall. "I feel sick at the thought," she said.

"Really? You'd have fooled me." He gave her a scornful look.

"I don't even *like* you."

"Who said anything about liking?" he countered. "It's simply an experiment. Don't imagine for one moment you have any power over *me.* "

She was barely breathing. "Sometimes things just happen."

"I bet they do around you. Is it possible you're panicking?"

"Go on then," she challenged. "Surprise me. As if you could."

She was to pay for that.

Royce pulled her into his arms as though taking action was his only possible course. This was a woman beyond imagining.

Beyond imaging too was the way their bodies came together as if fused. They fitted perfectly, one to the other, man and woman, feeding off the other's compulsive physical needs. If nothing else, their *bodies* weren't going to lie for them. The need transcended anger, condemnation, rage, even sorrow. He hadn't overpowered her. He hadn't trapped her. If she had cried out, he would have instantly let her go.

Tension held and gripped. She was *melting* into him, hungry for what he could offer. It was all part of a glorious, blatant seduction. It was her great gift, enslaving a man. His only protection was his certain knowledge he was a man who would never worship at her feet. What he was doing was taking advantage of this streamlined attempt at seduction. He told himself it would never work.

Their kiss was so deep, so searing it couldn't be explained away. It was fiercely compulsive, as though neither of them had a say. All that existed was an overpowering physical hunger, a primal appetite, a fascination, the devastating loss of self that kept them locked in a sensual trance. Whatever the huge barriers between them and the deep distrust, he knew she wanted him as much as he wanted her.

She stayed within his arms even when he began tracing the long slender lines of her body. She could not have been closer to him, her breasts crushed against his chest. Their hips clamped their lower bodies together as if they were desperate to be one flesh. He had never felt like this in his life. He wanted to tug the dress from her. He wanted to lay her down on the thick green grass. His self-control was hanging by a thread. He needed to shatter her power, when all he was doing was kissing her over and over as if that was what it took to make him complete.

The kisses grew wilder. More demanding. Nothing gentle or lover-like about them. Nothing sanctifying. The hell of it, he knew, was a mad desire. Spasms coursing through his aroused body were so strong he was in pain. They had to move forward to the point of no return. Or *stop.*

He wrenched his head back, still holding her firmly. Even so, she quivered in the aftermath of disorienting emotion. He kept one hand on her shoulder. One thin strap of her gown had fallen down, almost entirely revealing a small perfect breast. The whole episode was unbelievable. The one thought in his mind was he would never forget it. The impossible had happened. He had been dethroned, defeated, by a woman. It was a scenario he knew well from the painful past.

Amelia felt she could never go back to the way she was. Her throat was so tight she could barely speak. Her voice, when it came back, was splintered in her throat. It didn't even sound like her own anymore. "I'm leaving after the wedding," she told him, trying to sound vehement and succeeding only in sounding vulnerable. "I hope I never have to see you again." Hand trembling, she slipped the white strap back on her shoulder. "I just dreamed you up, Royce Stirling. You're a dangerous man."

He stood as still as a statue, determined not to kiss her again. His customary feeling of being the man in control had as good as crumpled. All that brought about by a woman? "Famous last words, Amelia. You *will* come back," he predicted in an ironic voice. Well used to making love to women, he was severely shaken.

"I'll be an old lady before then," she promised him. "Try to get a handle on this thing you think I have going with Jimmy."

"What you have going with my brother fills me with the greatest unease," he swiftly informed her. "Time you got yourself a man of your own."

That comment pierced her like the tip of a blade. "Look who's talking!" she cried. "You're thirty, aren't you? You've reached the decade in your life when you'll have to think about finding *yourself* a bride."

"I've already got someone in mind," he said, very crisply indeed.

"God help her!" Amelia lifted her long skirt, preparing to run back down the tunnelway. "Who would ever want a man with such a monstrous ego?"

"Search me," he responded, "but plenty are determined."

Amelia could well imagine. "Maybe they're convinced they can tame you? Who knows? Women can be very blind."

"You sound like a man-hater."

"Once in a while, I am," Amelia freely admitted. "I've seen too much suffering of women at the hands of men."

"So you feel bound to make men suffer in return? Is that it?" It was a theory.

"You should be giving me absolution, not condemnation, but you've lost your heart somewhere along the line. Good night, Mr. Stirling. I won't say it's been a pleasure to know you."

"Ditto!" He bowed low, one arm held elegantly in front of his body.

He watched her until she had almost reached the end of the flower-wreathed bower. Her long diaphanous skirt was floating like a cloud around her. She had moved with a swiftness that didn't seem to him like that of an ordinary woman, but a goddess. He gave a brief discordant laugh. She had paused once, looking back. He gave her a satirical wave. She would hate that. A moment more and the purple darkness swallowed her up.

How had he arrived at this point? he was forced to ask himself. He had never behaved so wildly, so out of character in his entire life. It shocked him. It also tormented him far into the night.

On a perfect cobalt and gold Saturday afternoon, James Stirling and Marigold Boyd were married in the presence of the extended Stirling family and their closest friends. Amelia was intensely aware of the surprise of family and friends, especially Jimmy's mother, his aunt, and her architect husband, a fine-looking man. The wedding was so low-key. They had expected when James married, it would be to much fanfare. Even more surprising was the tension between bride and groom.

Only she and Royce knew the reason. Amelia was furious he could think her the sort of woman who would deliberately destroy another woman's happiness, let alone that of her adopted sister.

The guests were dressed to the nines. Hopefully they would put the tension between bride and groom down to the fact James had been too long a playboy.

Now he was facing up to a far more responsible life. In other words, marriage was a culture shock for Jimmy. The bride was a pretty little thing. That was the universal opinion. Not exactly what they had all expected knowing James's taste in women. But she *was* his choice. That was all they needed to know.

A Stirling cousin declared himself delighted to walk the bride down the aisle of the picturesque stone church adjacent to the main house. It had been built in the mid-1880s for the master, staff, and servants of Kooralya to worship.

To Amelia's eyes, Marigold looked like a storybook bride in a feminine, short, white wedding dress with a strapless bodice adorned with rhinestones and dazzling beading and frothy layers of tulle for a skirt. She had opted for a fingertip white tulle veil held in place by a lovely jewelled bandeau, a family heirloom that Anthea had lent her.

Amelia had known even before Marigold had shown her the bridesmaid gown she had picked out for her that she was meant to look like the *mother* of the bride. The colour was a shade of pink that many would call insipid, but at least the fabric was lightweight chiffon. She had discarded the short taffeta jacket that was meant to go with it. It was a cover-up quite unnecessary in the heat. Later, after turning this way and that, she had taken her scissors to the bulky corsage of taffeta flowers sewn to the side of the fitted waist.

She had intended to wear her hair up. She had brought with her two very pretty jewelled combs, but Anthea had presented her with the prettiest headpiece she had ever seen: a coronet of exquisite pink and cream rosebuds interwoven with a tracery of baby green ferns. It was meant to encircle her head and forehead, so they both decided on leaving her hair long.

"Have a happy day, Amelia, dear," Anthea said, a glitter of tears in her eyes.

"You too, Anthea." Amelia leaned forward to kiss Anthea's cheek. She was touched by their rapport.

"I know I shouldn't speak ill of the bride," Anthea said with a wry little grimace, "but I think our Marigold was rather frantic to make sure you didn't steal the limelight. That pink could easily have been a disaster on someone else."

"I think your beautiful head piece clinched it for me," Amelia smiled. She was well aware of Marigold's intentions. She knew Marigold too well. On the other hand, she wouldn't have minded all that much if she had looked a bit on the dreary side. This was Marigold's day, after all. She prayed things would settle down between Marigold and Jimmy. A baby was on the way. Nothing mattered now but they should find happiness and raise their coming child in peace and love.

The reception was held in what the family called the Great Hall. It had been purposely built for all manner of large functions. Even for a small wedding, the hall had been splendidly done out. The high ceiling was draped in miles of the same filmy pink material, the same shade as the floor-length cloths that covered the eight-seater tables. A low-set arrangement of pink roses acted as centrepieces. It was all Anthea's idea. The bridegroom's mother, Sally, had left Anthea to it. Anthea, in turn, had flown in a team of wedding planners to help her.

As the chief—one and only—bridesmaid, Amelia sat at the lavishly bedecked bridal table. Jimmy's mother, Sally, the prettiness of her youth faded by time and more than her fair share of unhappiness, Amelia assumed, was feeling some concerns. She was Jimmy's mother, after all, and Jimmy wasn't looking the way he should.

Marigold, on the other hand, looked positively radiant, even ecstatic. She now had everything she had ever wanted. A rich husband to indulge her at every turn. They all watched on as the best man, looking stunningly handsome in his wedding finery, rose to give a short speech. Touchingly, it was filled with love, humour, and congratulations for the presumed-to-be happy pair. Amelia found herself raising her crystal flute along with everyone else.

She could see the smiling faces of the guests, all ages, glasses raised for the toast. She couldn't help noticing how a very attractive, beautifully dressed young woman never took her eyes off Royce. She was wearing an enchanting, wide-brimmed cream hat that dipped to one side. Her glossy dark hair was caught in an updated chignon at the back. It was a style Amelia often adopted herself. The young woman's dress was perfect. Form-fitting without being tight, cream silk scattered with tiny sprigs of rosy apricot-coloured wildflowers.

It had to be the neighbour, Charlene Warrender. Anthea had filled her in on the guest list. The Warrenders were close neighbours, if a couple of hundred miles apart could be deemed close, but apparently was in the Outback. Anthea had made no further comment, but Amelia realized this could very well be the woman Royce Stirling had in mind for marriage. So suitable! No question at all, Charlene Warrender was under his spell. She could see it. She could *feel* it. Charlene's blue, near-agonized glances fell into adoring mode.

A group of musicians had been hired to play at the ceremony and reception. They were very good. Not only did they excel at classical music, but they knew exactly how to get a party going. Jimmy and Marigold led off the bridal waltz. After a few moments, the younger guests moved onto the floor. Amelia saw Royce take Charlene into his arms. She saw the vulnerable softness in Charlene's expression, the faint quiver to her lovely smile. Poor girl, she was madly in love with the man. Really, someone should warn her, only all the other guests seemed to be delighted to see them together.

She found herself in great demand on the dance floor. This was a wedding after all. She was determined to enjoy the day. Only her heart skipped a painful beat when Jimmy tapped her partner on his shoulder. "Hi, Dave, do you mind?" he smiled. "It's my delightful duty to dance with our bridesmaid."

David, a charming young man still at university, where he was training to become a doctor, assured Amelia, "I'll be back!"

"Lucky devil!" Jimmy breathed close to Amelia's ear. "You look beautiful. I should have told you before."

"Thank you, Jimmy," she said, keeping her tone light and affectionate. "You're a married man at last."

"That was the whole idea, wasn't it?" Jimmy said.

"God, Jimmy, you can't go on like this," Amelia was endeavouring to keep a carefree smile on her face. People would be watching as they always did. "You have to make an effort; otherwise, you'll never be happy. Marigold looks lovely. Everyone thinks so."

"You mean everyone is wondering how we came to get married," Jimmy answered as if he wanted to yell the place down, get drunk, or both. "Marigold is not my type at all."

"You should have thought of that before you got her into bed," Amelia moved in closer so she could murmur her disapproval in his ear.

Jimmy laughed. It wasn't a pleasant sound. "Amelia, darling, I was known for my dalliances, but not a one of them set out to trap me."

"Then you were lucky. You know I care about you and your happiness. I'm always your *friend*. If you try hard, you can have a life."

"How can that happen when I'm in love with you?" he said, his dismal mood unhappily on show.

"Jimmy, you're destroying yourself," Amelia said, almost feeling his heart break.

Across the floor, Royce, who had been keeping an eagle eye on the pair, made a swift excuse to the female cousin who was hastening towards him. Without drawing too much attention to himself, he made it over to his brother, the bridegroom who had Amelia, the bridesmaid, locked in his arms.

"May I?" he asked, a totally misleading smile on his face. "Dance with your bride, Jimmy," he ordered in an undertone. "Go on. *Move.*"

Jimmy moved.

If they had been anywhere else, Amelia would have rushed away as well. Instead, she allowed herself to be taken into Royce's arms as if they didn't have a care in the world.

"Poor Jimmy, desperate for your sweetness and understanding?"

"Don't take it out on me," she said.

"Smile."

"Smile yourself," Amelia answered, tartly. "God knows you were positively beaming down at . . . Charlene, is that her name? She's lovely, by the way. I'm assuming she's the one."

His dark eyes blazed out of his dynamic face. "Quite a few people are starting to think something is amiss." His arm was curled hard around her, carrying hints of a fatal attraction.

"Does anyone believe in perfect love?" She raised her blond head, giving him a brilliant smile to complete their happy picture.

"If you have any regard for Marigold, you'll leave Jimmy alone," he said. "Let them get away. They'll be in the States a good two months."

"It's their honeymoon. They shouldn't waste it."

"No." He pulled her even closer as if he didn't know how to do otherwise. They were moving in perfect unison. Not easy to do. No other partner had. Not even Charlene, the young woman he had danced with a million times. But with *her*. He brought his head down so they were cheek to cheek. "Act enthralled," he said.

"You're kidding me." There had been compulsion in his voice. "The man who has to be obeyed?"

"If you don't, you won't be able to predict what I'll do next," he said.

"With Charlene watching?" she scoffed. "Not that you wouldn't have had your ups and downs, I dare say, you being what you are."

He could feel the slow burn. "Do it for my family's sake," he said.

She couldn't resist that appeal. "I'm sorry." She was conscious of the full rush of excitement with his arms around her. She had come to Kooralya never dreaming in a million years this could happen. "I feel the same as you do, Royce. I'm terribly worried about Marigold and Jimmy."

"As well you might be," he said, curtly.

"Why are you so cruel?" she implored. "This is a party. A wedding reception."

"And you look like spring. As exquisite as the roses on your brow. They're starting to open up. Such a delicate, delicious perfume! Tell me, do all witches have emerald green eyes?"

"What colour are Charlene's?" she asked.

"A heavenly blue."

"You haven't done too badly then, have you? I hope you've considered the possibility Charlene might think you're flirting with me."

"Never mind the flirting," he said. "I'm deadly serious."

"No need to be, I'm leaving in the morning."

"Might be time to give *me* a goodbye kiss," he suggested, his smile sardonic.

Amelia moved in consternation. Heat was flowing from him to her. It flowed down her arms, her highly responsive body, her legs. It even tingled in her toes.

"What are you up to?" she said on a breath. "Obviously, there's a method in your madness."

"Perhaps we can persuade James, who is watching us compulsively, that he's lost you."

"He never *had* me." She gazed up at him, near-hypnotized.

"You're so much the seductress, your sights have been set on me as well," he suggested. "Another conquest. Another enslaved male."

"Damn you," she said sweetly, lifting her hand to let it lie gently along his darkly tanned cheek. His polished skin was warm to her touch. "Goodbye, Royce, *dear.*"

"Play it for James," he murmured, low voiced. "Don't hold back."

"Men!" she said with some contempt. "You're cruel, all of you. What will Charlene think?"

"She'll be less sure of me," he said, bending his raven head.

Across the Great Hall, Marigold moved closer to her husband, taking his arm. At long last, she was the woman in possession. It was a heady experience. Mrs. James Stirling. She'd had a plan and gone after it. The plan worked. "Better move on, Jimmy darling," she said with mock gentleness. "It appears our precious Melly is after your big brother. She does this sort of thing all the time."

She didn't get the response she wanted or expected. "If Royce and Amelia fell in love with one another, it would be the best thing that ever happened," he said, in a quiet, sincere voice. "I love both of them. They both have character. We don't."

Chapter 3

It had been a long and upsetting day in the battleground that was the family court. Couples who had once sworn undying love for each other within a few years and a child or two were at one another's throats. It had almost grown into a family custom. Just for a change, Amelia found herself on the husband's side. Many men, she had come to realize, did get a rough deal. Sympathy most often lay with the wife and mother. It was on record, however, that the police had never been called to the marital home. Family, even his wife's family, had made statements to the effect the husband had never shown physical violence towards his wife and small children.

He *had* broken the conditions that had been imposed on him after the split-up, to see his children once a month. So deprived, he had soon taken to turning up at all hours and unestablished weekends not entirely sober. On those occasions, his wife had refused him entry, claiming later to social workers and the police he was not only harassing her, he was threatening her, a charge that was vigorously disputed.

Marriage breakdowns were a sad and sorry business. Many times, Amelia had heard judges, solicitors, and barristers harangued by couples out of control and not of sound mind. She had been threatened herself and called a few ugly names. Very few patted her on the shoulder. Her work had made her wary of men.

The last thing she was prepared for when she finally arrived home was to find Marigold waiting outside her apartment door.

Surprise, surprise. Not a good one. More like a warning bell. What was Marigold doing here? Ordinarily, visitors had to be buzzed into the complex, but Marigold would have been recognised as family to most of the tenants. Some obliging soul not bothered by the rules had let her through the security door. This could only be trouble. Trouble all the day long! Amelia found herself gulping air in an effort to maintain her composure.

"Marigold," she called, as she strode out of the lift. "What are you doing here?" If she lived to be a hundred, and Marigold still walked the earth, Marigold would always be able to shock her. She started rummaging in her handbag for the keys. Was there any sort of handbag that gave up keys willingly?

"Where's Jimmy? Aren't you supposed to be away for another fortnight or so?" Neither Marigold nor Jimmy had made contact. Understandable if they were madly in love, but neither appeared to have given a toss for the other when she'd last seen them. The most alarming thing was Marigold's stomach. Instead of starting to show her pregnancy, it was as flat as an ironing board. That confounded Amelia, though she did have a friend who had worked for seven months without showing at all. The ballooning had come later. Even in silhouette, Marigold was flat.

"Getting drunk, I suppose," Marigold answered her question as to Jimmy's whereabouts in an offhand voice.

"Surely not?" Jimmy couldn't have been in such bad shape. "Come inside." Amelia's heart was beating hard. Had Marigold lost the baby? She was so tired and depressed, she found herself fighting the urge to burst into tears. Marigold was a rarer than rare species. She was looking very chic in what had to be a designer label dress. She wore her trademark very high heels. No flatties. Surely if she had miscarried, she would be looking ineffably sad? Losing one's baby had to be the worst possible outcome for an expectant mother.

Inside the apartment, Marigold moved from the hallway into the nearby living room with its welcoming elegance.

Melly was just so clever about everything, Marigold thought. So *cultured.* A lovely word. There were paintings, not prints, on the walls, flowers, always flowers, top-quality furnishings, *objects d'art* in every strategic place. Marigold had never bought an *object d'art* in her life and didn't plan to. Disgruntled, she moved to sit on one of the two plush caramel-coloured sofas that were separated by a gleaming mahogany, circular cocktail table. It looked like a big wooden bowl to Marigold's unappreciative eyes.

"Can I get you anything?" Amelia asked, depositing her handbag on the nearest chair. "Tea? Coffee? Have you eaten?"

Marigold ignored Amelia's offer of refreshments. She was on a diet anyway. "What I really want is a divorce," she said in a gust of anger, knowing full well how much that would shock Melly.

Amelia had already braced herself for shocks. "You're not serious, of course, Marigold. Couples don't sue for divorce while on their honeymoon. They stretch it out a bit. Everything is still all right with you and the baby?" she asked, with an anxious frown. "You're not showing at all."

Marigold drew her hands down over her shapely breasts. "I hope I don't break your heart, but there's a reason for that. There *isn't* any baby."

The force of that piece of news hit Amelia like a blow. "You mean you miscarried? Sympathy went to the very core of her being. "God, how awful, Marigold. I am so, so, sorry. You must be heartbroken, and poor Jimmy!"

"Bugger Jimmy!" said Marigold, a fevered glint in her eyes.

Amelia felt her knees sag. There was a total lack of sensitivity in Marigold's expression. "You sound as if you don't care."

"I don't." Marigold clashed her small white teeth.

"I'm sorry. I'm just so shocked. This is devastating news." Amelia slumped onto the sofa opposite. "Jimmy must be broken-hearted. He was so looking forward to your coming child. So was I. A little niece, a little nephew to love."

"Hey there, ease up!" Marigold threw up her two hands. "I'm not in mourning. In fact, I've got news for you. I don't give a fuck." It was delivered with a mix of crudity and callousness.

"I see." No one could beat Marigold at throwing out shocks. She hadn't been reared to fling crude language about.

For a moment, Marigold felt panic. Amelia looked sad—worse, *disgusted*. She had always been able to run to Amelia for help. She instantly softened her tone. "I didn't have a miscarriage, Melly, if that's what you're thinking. Baby was a myth. Turns out I wasn't pregnant at all. I *thought* I was." She rose to join Amelia on the sofa, but Amelia waved her away.

Marigold sat down again. "Look, Melly, I'm not the first woman to think herself pregnant when she wasn't. I definitely blame my youth and ignorance. I had missed two periods, just like I told you."

Amelia's mind was reeling. "Jimmy married you because he believed you were pregnant with his child."

Marigold shrugged the charge off. "Stop looking at me as if I'm wicked. I made a mistake, right? Can't you get your head around that?"

"No, I can't," Amelia said. "You missed two periods. That's it? Two periods. You didn't consult anyone, a doctor. Take one of those pregnancy tests?"

"I didn't feel I needed to, Melly." Marigold was back to her little girl breathy voice. "You know I hate doctors. I did have morning sickness . . . or so I thought."

Amelia took another deep breath. She was feeling quite light-headed. Marigold might have been saying she thought she had irritable bowel syndrome, but as it turned out, that wasn't the case. "You'd better go," she said, putting a hand to her aching head. "Go on, clear off, Marigold. You're twenty-four years of age. You're not a child. You have money. Just look at that dress and those shoes! There's something wrong with you."

"Maybe there is." Marigold gave a careless shrug. "There's something wrong with everybody, even perfect old you. I'm not the kind of person you are, up and coming pillar of the establishment like your dad. Actually, I wouldn't want to be. You're not a bit of fun."

"You think *you* are?" Amelia gave a brittle laugh.

"Come on, Melly," Marigold urged. "I desperately need your help."

"Not any more, you don't." Amelia was thinking of the countless times she had been there for Marigold. It was high time to pull back. Marigold had only been using her. Using people was Marigold's game plan. "I can let you have the name of a very good woman psychiatrist," she said with the utmost seriousness. "You need that sort of help. I can't help you. I've tried and tried, but it was all wasted effort. Poor Jimmy!"

Marigold glared. "Poor Jimmy! He's a sorry piece of work and that's the truth."

"How did he respond when you told him you'd lost the baby?" Amelia asked, catching Marigold's darting eyes.

Marigold stood up, smoothing her short skirt that had ridden high. "You know what, Melly dear? He *cried*. A man crying, I ask you!"

"For what it's worth, Marigold, I think you're fast turning into a despicable human being."

Marigold's lips curled. "That's no way to describe me, Melly. I'm a realist." She gave Amelia a brazen stare. "Are you involved with Royce?" She spoke as if she had scored quite a point.

"How can you ask me that?" Amelia gave an exhausted sigh.

"Come off it, Melly!" Marigold snorted. "I was witness to the two of you sharing a humdinger kiss at my wedding."

"It was nothing. It wasn't real," Amelia said quietly.

"Was it to let my pathetic lovelorn husband know you weren't interested in him?" Marigold asked shrewdly.

"Forget Royce Stirling." Amelia roused herself to issue the warning. "I can see tragedy here, Marigold. Tragedy of your making. You told Jimmy how and when this bogus miscarriage happened, did you? He couldn't have been around. You may have convinced him *and* me you were pregnant, but you can't talk yourself out of this mess. He won't believe you. You would have called out for help. You would have needed it. Where were you anyway?"

"He took off for two whole days. Abandoned me."

"You were in mortal danger in your luxury hotel?" Amelia asked.

Marigold chose to ignore the implied sarcasm. "When he finally came back, I told him the baby went down the toilet."

"God Almighty!" Amelia visibly recoiled.

"I'm sorry, but I had to say something. What would he know anyway?" Marigold flashed back. "Let him believe he brought it all on himself. He's been so nasty to me. He believed I was pregnant, yet he gave me a tough time. He was out most of the time. He didn't want to be near me."

"Jimmy married you because of a baby that never was." Amelia spoke not to Marigold but to herself.

"He was awful to me," Marigold maintained. 'I genuinely thought he would settle down and we could make a go of it. Only what did he do? He banged on and on about you all the time, like I meant absolutely nothing, mother of his child or not. He pushed me once."

Amelia's golden head shot up. "He did *not!*" She spoke emphatically. "I won't accept that. I know Jimmy. I know you. You're a pathological liar, Marigold. Both of us need to face it. You lie and lie about everything you don't want people to know."

"Like you were there?" Marigold challenged, her cheeks flushed. "Are you against me too?"

Amelia gave her a drained stare. "You freak me out, Marigold."

"Please . . . please . . . don't say that."

"Stop the playacting, Marigold," Amelia said, her tone dropping in disgust.

"Melly, please don't be mad at me," Marigold implored.

"I haven't *started* yet," said Amelia. "I want you to go, Marigold. Truth to tell, I can't bear to look at you one moment more. I should question whether you believed yourself pregnant at all. You were determined on marrying Jimmy. You could have lied about it."

In the blink of an eye, Marigold turned into the picture of despair. "I respect you too much to lie to you, Melly," she said, dipping her head in shame. "I beg of you, please don't tell Jimmy. He's bound to come to you for sympathy. He believes I had a miscarriage. He'll get over it. You putting him straight won't help. It's best this way. We won't have to say a thing to the family. They don't need to know."

"Jimmy may decide to tell them," Amelia said. She walked to the door, opened it, and held it back. "You said you wanted a divorce. I'd advise you to hold off to a more appropriate time. Learn patience, Marigold. Couples don't normally talk divorce on their honeymoon."

"Yeah . . . well, I'm not the first and not the last to consider it." Marigold forced herself to walk to the door. She had confidently expected Melly would ask her to stay. "Jimmy is the one wanting the divorce. He's damn near an alcoholic, you know."

"I bet you can match him drink for drink. Stoli on the rocks?" Amelia gave Marigold a hard look that nevertheless held a measure of pity.

Marigold reached out, laying her hand on Amelia's arm. "I need you to back me, Melly. I know I might sound as if I don't care, but I'm someone who was badly scarred as a child. I'm sure that's the way a psychiatrist would explain it away. I'll get that woman's name in a day or two. I mean it, Melly. I'll heed your advice. For now, I'll say goodnight. You look so pale. I'm sorry I shocked you, but you're the only one who truly cares about me. I love you, Melly. *You're* my rock." With the saddest smile, she inched up to kiss Amelia's cheek. "You're a good woman."

"Don't I wish *you* were," said Amelia crisply.

On her own, Amelia sat down on the sofa, head in hands. She didn't know what to think anymore. All thought of a little niece or nephew was gone. She had really been looking forward to a brand-new member of the family, although strictly speaking, there was no blood line. But that didn't matter. There was a strong link between her and Marigold.

But did anyone truly know Marigold? There had been no real proof of Marigold's pregnancy before the wedding. Jimmy, apparently, hadn't even asked for proof. He had accepted Marigold's news as the truth. Jimmy had revealed himself as desperately worried that Marigold, if thwarted in her ambitions. would seek an abortion.

Amelia clasped her hands together tightly. Marigold had trapped Jimmy, but Jimmy had to answer for his irresponsible lifestyle. Tonight, poor Jimmy would be in the abyss. It wasn't as though he and Marigold could grieve together, a loving couple facing this unexpected tragedy in their lives. Would Jimmy talk to his brother? He worshipped Royce. She really didn't know what Jimmy would do. Marigold had begged her not to say anything either to Jimmy or his family.

Think, Amelia. Think!

This was all going to be extremely harrowing. She was caught in the middle. What would Royce Stirling think of her? His opinion of her now was bad enough. Jimmy, under enormous stress, might not stick to the plan and tell his brother Marigold had lost the baby. He would say he and Marigold were devastated. Only she feared Royce Stirling's natural capacity to read people. He might be wrong about her, but he wasn't wrong about Marigold. Marigold, with her devious tongue, would probably have painted her in a less than admirable light. It had become a habit with Marigold over the many years. Despite all the little betrayals, Marigold always came to her for protection. Maybe it was high time she started to consider whether she was the one who actually needed protection.

Anthea waited until dinner was over and they were having coffee before she took a print-off of James's email out of the pocket of her skirt and passed it to Royce, who had had a full day with a pre-Christmas muster. Beside her on the sofa sat Sally, who had read her son's email many times, all the while shaking her head sadly. It was obvious Sally was acutely conscious of the anger and disappointment that was gathering around them.

Anthea watched Royce read through the email carefully. Even when he had finished absorbing the contents, he continued to stare down at the print-off in a grim silence, his strong features drawn taut.

"So that's why he married her," he said, directing a glance at his aunt.

"I'd say so," Anthea agreed quietly.

"What?" Sally was aghast. "But he loves her!" Sally was not the most observant of women.

"He loved the idea of becoming a father more," Anthea said.

"But why didn't he tell *me*?" Sally looked from one to the other for the answer. "I *am* his mother. Didn't I have the right to be told? Didn't we all have the right to be told? That beautiful girl, the sister. Why didn't she tell us? She must have known."

"Of course she knew," Royce balled the piece of paper, no emotion on his handsome chiselled features.

"Even if Amelia did know, Marigold must have insisted she say nothing." Anthea sprang to Amelia's defence. She had developed a strong liking for Marigold's sister. Alas, not for Marigold. "Amelia aside, James was the one who should have told us Marigold was pregnant."

"Then what on earth prevented him?" Royce asked, suddenly looking angry. "What did he think we were going to say? Condemn him? How ridiculous. So Marigold got herself pregnant. I don't think the pregnancy was an accident in this day and age. We all saw how thrilled, one could say triumphant she was to become James's bride. I knew something was eating away at Jimmy. God, what a fool he is to think we would turn on him. He should have been honest and open. A baby! Okay, the baby would be arriving much sooner than anyone expected, but the initial shock would have passed off quickly."

"Now she's l-l-lost the baby," Sally wailed. She picked up her coffee cup and slurped the cold contents. "My poor boy! He can't seem to do a thing right. Like me."

Royce scarcely heard. Sally had been so traumatized by her marriage to his father putting herself down had become a lifetime habit. "He speaks as if the shock was brutal. He doesn't even say the *both* of us, like any normal loving couple. He's treating the heartbreak as if it's his alone."

"We know how much Jimmy loves children," Anthea said soothingly. "Maybe they didn't want to tell us until they were absolutely sure all was well with the pregnancy."

Royce gave a flick of his elegantly formed hand. "We were all *absolutely sure* nothing was well with the marriage. Jimmy wanted Amelia. He couldn't have her, so he took Marigold instead."

"Amelia, the bridesmaid?" Sally's expression was that of a woman who believed she couldn't possibly have heard right. "My son was in love with the bridesmaid, not the bride?" she gasped. "I don't believe that for a second. Jimmy wouldn't marry the wrong woman. He *wouldn't*," she cried over the hard lump in her throat.

Royce locked eyes with his aunt. Anthea didn't miss a thing. She would have guessed.

"Perhaps Jimmy fell in love with Amelia because he knew he couldn't have her?" Anthea offered by way of explanation. "She's beautiful, charming, a highly intelligent young woman, holding down an onerous job. Jimmy's usual approach would never have worked with Amelia."

"Jimmy's 'golden enchantress,' " Royce said, a blunt edge to his voice.

"That was obvious once we met her. I'd say Amelia is very fond of Jimmy, but I'm convinced she isn't in any way in love with him."

"In love with him!" Sally, a small woman, appeared to have shrunk. "I don't understand what the both of you are saying. You sound so sure Jimmy *did* this. He married the wrong girl?" she asked, looking frantic. "That's madness."

Gently Anthea patted the other woman's shoulder. "Please calm down, dear. We'll work this out together."

"We need to consider Marigold told Jimmy she was pregnant with his child," Royce said. "It must have come as a great shock to him, given his admittedly careless lifestyle. He made the decision to do the honourable thing, or what he considered to be the honourable thing. I have to say I wouldn't want *my* child to get away. I would want my child to bear my name. Be family. Jimmy obviously felt the same. God knows what's going to happen next. This email isn't all that far from despair. I need to get to him."

"I think you do," Anthea confirmed.

"Why didn't he phone when he was away?" Sally asked, suddenly belligerent. "Not a single postcard. Now this highly upsetting email. He's always been a problem boy. He really needs a hammering."

Anthea winced. Sally could and did come out with the most alarming things.

Royce answered for both of them. "I'm amazed you've even suggested it, Sally, knowing the hammerings Jimmy did get. Hammering doesn't work. I have to check on my brother. See he's all right. The bravado he goes on with is only a façade. James, when he feels,

feels very deeply. I'll fly out tomorrow around midday. I have a few things I'll need to delegate. Do you wish to come with me?" He knew Anthea would want to remain on the station.

Sally's slight body began to jerk. "I'll stay here with Anthea. It's you Jimmy needs, Royce. Not me." She couldn't have looked more desolate, at the same time not willing to go to her son.

"So that's settled," said Royce, having fully anticipated Sally's answer. Sally had never had the strength to be a hands-on loving mother. "I need to get on top of the whole situation," he said. "I think I'll ask them both to come back with me."

"Good idea," Anthea nodded her approval. "Will you see Amelia, too?" she asked, meeting her nephew's brilliant dark eyes. "Find out what really has been going on?"

"I'll certainly want to hear *Amelia's* side of the story, Anthea," said Royce. There was a hard intonation in his voice.

Amelia felt herself back in charge. She had read through any number of files, given orders, made decisions, consulted with one of the senior partners in the firm. Another hour and she could go home. Her phone rang. She picked it up. It was Megan, the pretty, very popular and efficient receptionist for the prestige Melbourne firm of Bannerman, Boyd, & Powers.

No businesslike tone from Megan for once. "The most *gorgeous* guy I've ever seen is asking to see you, Amelia," Megan murmured, her tone silky. "A Mr. Stirling. He doesn't have an appointment," she added almost breathlessly.

Jimmy *was* a very handsome man. She had been expecting this. "Send him through, Megan, and then get back to work, my girl. The man's taken."

Megan chortled.

Amelia rose to answer the door herself, a sympathetic smile on her face. The man she confronted, however, wasn't Jimmy, but Royce. She couldn't have been caught more off-guard. Her whole body rocked. Her smile faltered, and then faded away.

"Royce, how very unexpected," she said. "Come in. Have you business in town?" She marvelled at the composure in her voice when his sudden appearance threw her badly.

"Let's not playact, Amelia." Royce, too, was visibly rattled by the sight of her. "I'm here to see my brother. He sent us an email telling us Marigold had lost the baby. It sounded so stricken, I had to come." "Of course. Of course!" The bond between the brothers. "I know how much Jimmy means to you. Please sit down, Royce." She sought refuge behind her desk. "How can I help?"

He remained standing, a tall man exuding energy. *Royce Stirling was built for height and space around him*, Amelia thought. He wasn't a man to be confined. He looked strikingly handsome in a beautifully tailored city suit. Small wonder Megan had been so impressed.

"You've seen him, needless to say?" Royce gave her the brilliant piercing look Amelia had come to know so well.

"Sit down, Royce," she repeated, falling back on the knowledge this was her home ground. "I'll send for coffee, shall I?"

Royce took a chair opposite her. Her desk was impressive. It would certainly appear that way to her clients. Not modern. A walnut pedestal desk with a dark green leather writing surface. Though the desk top was packed with files, it was orderly. She would have been able to put her hand on exactly which file she required. "Thank you, no," he declined. "It's explanations I want before I see Jimmy."

"Explanations of what, precisely?" she asked, coolly.

He studied her across the desk. She was wearing what he knew was generally called a professional woman's power outfit. A superbly tailored black suit: a fitted jacket that showed off her lovely feminine shoulders and narrow pants that made much of her long legs. A crisp buttoned-to-the-neck white shirt was beneath. Her long, beautiful hair was drawn back into an elegant knot. She was wearing gold earrings and what looked like an Arts and Crafts gold brooch set with cabochon stones and gold beads pinned to one lapel. She looked what she was: a highly intelligent, successful young lawyer not about to be intimidated by any member of the public. That included him.

"You knew about the pregnancy, yet you said nothing?" he pressed on, regardless. He was a man who when he demanded answers, he got them.

She hoped she hadn't flushed. "It wasn't my place to tell you and Anthea, Royce. Jimmy and Marigold didn't want you to know. I couldn't go against their wishes."

"You're a lawyer," he challenged. "You could have pointed out to them the best way to go. Jimmy hangs on your every word. I'm very surprised he hasn't landed on your doorstep. Obviously, this wasn't a marriage made in heaven."

"So, both of them have made a serious mistake," she said, marvelling that his eyes, dark as night, yet could blaze.

"Your *sister* made no mistake. She set out to get Jimmy and she succeeded like scores of unscrupulous women before her."

She let him see her extreme annoyance. "It's the woman's fault, of course."

"*This* time it is. We wouldn't be talking like this if Jimmy loved her. I don't even believe he likes her. Not anymore. There's no point in denying it, Amelia. Misplaced loyalty in some way, I suppose. Marigold would have known how to protect herself from any unwanted pregnancy. The thing is, she wanted this one. Now on their honeymoon, she's miscarried. Is it out of order to say I suspect she mightn't have been pregnant at all?"

Her heart lurched, yet she managed to hide her sense of shock. "None of this is my business, Royce. You have to speak to Jimmy."

"I bet you've already spoken to Marigold?"

Amelia held her hands together tightly.

"So you have?"

She nodded. "Marigold always comes to me when she's in trouble."

"I'm pretty sure that happens all the time," Royce commented bluntly. "She had to know Jimmy is in love with you."

Amelia sighed ruefully. "She also knew I had no romantic interest in Jimmy. I do have a close male friend, an academic. Marigold knows him. Jimmy wasn't an issue between us."

"The close friend? Is it possible to get a name?"

"None of your business, Royce." Her green eyes sparkled, green as the cabochons in her antique brooch.

"You showed considerable interest in *my* business," he countered.

"I'm not saying any more, Royce." She picked up a file, put it down again. Taylor versus Taylor. Another marriage not made in heaven. "I was devastated when Marigold told me she'd lost the baby. I was so looking forward to the new little member in our family."

"And Marigold? Was she devastated too?" His tone was highly sceptical.

Amelia threw back her head. "Why wouldn't she be?"

"I have a great nose for odd behaviour, Amelia. So does Anthea, who sends not her regards, but her love. My aunt took a great liking to you even knowing Jimmy was in love with you, not his bride."

"Sadly, Jimmy was out of his depth," Amelia said with quiet conviction. "I'm very fond of him, but as I have told you repeatedly, there was no romance."

"Except you allowed him to kiss you passionately the night before his own wedding?"

This time, she felt heat flare into her cheeks. "As I recall, *you* kissed me in a way that would have startled and shocked the guests."

"Be that as it may, I suspect Jimmy will come to you, Amelia. Where does Marigold live?"

"She has an apartment of her own." She didn't say her father had paid for it.

"Address, please?"

She was intent on not giving it to him. "Marigold is in no fit state to talk to someone like you. She knows you don't approve of her."

"Neither do *you* approve of her," he said, starkly.

"I beg your pardon?"

There was disgust in his voice. "Anyone who gets to know your little sister wouldn't see her as an angel. You're the angel, aren't you, Amelia? Jimmy's angel."

The infuriating man was testing her. "Shouldn't you be out looking for him?" she challenged.

"If you think he's with Marigold, you have to tell me."

Amelia knew she had a responsibility to do just that. "Jimmy isn't with Marigold. She told me he was out getting drunk most of the time. I can tell you, they are definitely estranged."

"Good," Royce clipped off. "You are *most* kind to share that with me, Amelia," he said sardonically. "Now, what pubs does he frequent?"

An answer came to mind. "He likes the Docks on the bay. Any taxi driver will take you. Where are *you* staying, by the way?"

He named arguably the best hotel in the beautiful city of Melbourne, repeatedly rated as one of the most liveable cities in the world. "I need your promise you'll ring me when you see Jimmy," he said as he rose. "And you *will*. Here's the number." He withdrew a card from his inside breast pocket.

Amelia rounded the desk to take it.

"That's a promise?"

"*Yes, Royce*." She gave a deep sigh.

"Yes. Royce," he mocked her, abruptly taking her chin. "I do so have to watch myself around you."

How swiftly her emotions spiralled. "That's because you have a devil in you."

"The devil prompts me to kiss you."

Amelia stared into his mesmeric, dark eyes. Beautiful eyes. His mother's eyes. "Don't listen to him," she warned.

His laugh was brief, ironic. "How profoundly weak is human nature, Amelia. I listen to him a lot when I'm with you." He bent his dark head, unerringly found her mouth. Amelia tried hard to act as if it were beneath her dignity to resist, only his kisses did such *strange* things to her. A lifetime of such kisses would scarcely be enough.

"Listen to me, please," she said shakily when he released her. "You have to stop kissing me."

"Calm down, Amelia. It won't get you disbarred."

"Why do you keep doing it? Have you asked yourself that?" she questioned as she followed him to the door.

"Have you asked yourself why you let me?" he countered, turning back to her, a magnificent man.

"I might be attracted to you. Which is a very bad thing."

"But easy to understand," he said smoothly. "I'm quite willingly to admit I'm attracted to you too, Amelia. Don't worry. It's a chemical reaction."

"Of course it is, but it can't be allowed to grow into a problem."

He laughed gently. "Count on me. By the way, I know where you live, Amelia. Jimmy let that piece of information slide."

"Do I take that as *beware*?"

"That depends. Does your suitor, nameless for the moment, realize you don't love him? Or is he content to worship at your feet?" His eyes continued to run over her, shamelessly drinking her in. So much for the power suit! She couldn't have looked more feminine. Or sexier.

"Does that go for Charlene too?" she asked with false sweetness. "Goodbye, Royce. I hope you find Jimmy very quickly. He needs your support and guidance. It's a sad fact Jimmy doesn't have a high opinion of himself. I suspect he mightn't in your family."

At the implied criticism, Royce swung back. "I bear no guilt for that, Amelia. The time is going to come when *you* have to run to me for help."

"You really want me to believe that?"

"Believe it," Royce said.

Chapter 4

It was around 10 p.m. She was barely out of the shower, dressed in her nightgown and robe, when the intercom echoed through the quiet apartment. She felt her mouth go dry, knowing what this visit might mean. In the kitchen, she pressed the button on the wall unit to identify her late-night caller, even though she was certain it was Jimmy.

It all had to be a bad dream. She would soon wake up. Jimmy was here to tell her about his terrible loss. Tender-hearted, perhaps to a fault, she would want to hug him, but she knew she couldn't.

"Please let me in, Amelia." Jimmy stood there, imploring. He had taken a step forward so she could readily see his face. "I need to talk to you. I'm sorry it's so late. I had to pluck up courage. *Please.*"

She heard the frantic note in his voice. It occurred to her to ring Royce immediately, but she was already allowing Jimmy in. When she opened the door, it was a different-looking Jimmy to the one she was used to. Not the super-stud, the handsome playboy. His skin was drawn tightly over features that were nearly puckered. There were dark circles under his eyes. He looked as if he hadn't slept for days. "Come in," she said quietly. She allowed him past her, catching the strong whiff of whiskey. "Royce is in Melbourne. Did you know? He went looking for you. I sent him to the Docks."

"I was there, but not for long," Jimmy managed to turn about, albeit with a wobble. His dull, red-rimmed eyes suddenly brightened. "Royce is in the city? He flew all this way?"

"He cares about you, Jimmy," Amelia pointed out. "You haven't been fair to your family, excluding them from the truth." She stopped herself. This wasn't the time to chastise Jimmy. "I can't tell you how sorry I am you and Marigold lost the baby. It's a great blow."

"To *me!*" His answer was pure anguish. "It might sound awful to your ears, but Marigold doesn't care. She's so twisted inside, I'm surprised she got pregnant at all. We're finished, Amelia. Marigold is a singular woman in her ambitions, and woe betide anyone who gets in her way. I can no longer bear the sight of her. She can't bear the sight of me. She got what she wanted: my name. Even if we split up, which we will, she can trade off that. She's already run up huge bills."

Not on maternity clothes, Amelia thought grimly, feeling Jimmy's pain. "Sit down, Jimmy," she urged. "I have to ring Royce. I promised I'd let him know if you contacted me."

"Royce, being Royce, knew I would," Jimmy gave an off-key laugh. "You can't fool Royce. He's the man with the all-seeing eyes. Ring in a minute or two, Amelia. Please, can we talk first? When Royce arrives, he'll take over. That's his role in life. Royce is the man everyone admires, understandably."

"You're jealous?" Amelia asked quietly.

"I daresay, a bit. What younger brother wouldn't be? But I love Royce far more than I envy him."

"Would you like coffee, Jimmy?" Amelia asked. It was easy to detect Jimmy had been knocking back far too many Scotch whiskies. It was on his breath, in his side-to-side stagger.

"Yes, please," Jimmy accepted the offer. "I married Marigold because she was pregnant."

"We all know that, Jimmy." Amelia went quickly behind the kitchen counter, intensely conscious of her lack of dress. She needed to change out of her nightwear into something more appropriate. Her nightclothes were too revealing. She located the container of ground coffee, and then began to spoon it into the glass plunger. "Black, white, cream?" She had an idea Jimmy took his coffee black.

"Black. Thank you, Amelia. I am sorry to barge in on you like this, but I'm at the end of my rope. I'm heartbroken. What I feel seems even to me to be far out of the ordinary. There are lots of reasons for that, I expect. I have problems. Relics of my childhood I can't seem to shake. I actually think I'm manic-depressive. I yearn for Royce's respect."

Amelia held up a hand. Jimmy looked crushed with grief. "You have his love and loyalty, Jimmy. Count your blessings."

Jimmy gave her a sad, penitent look. "I won't be taking divorce

action against Marigold for some time. We have to wait a year anyway. I don't want to make perfect fools out of either of us."

"You won't be able to live together. You know that. It's total separation."

"I want to go home." Jimmy spoke so poignantly tears sprang into
Amelia's eyes. In another minute, they would start pouring down her
cheeks. She was so sad and tired. She feared for Jimmy. Underneath
the rich playboy, he was a vulnerable young man.

". . . back to the place where I was born," Jimmy was saying.
"Back to Kooralya. Marigold can tell everyone she hates the Outback. She does, anyway."

"That's your *real* world, Jimmy," Amelia said. "It was never
knocking around nightclubs with one pretty girl after the other."

"Any one of them would have been better than Marigold," Jimmy
said helplessly. "Why didn't you warn me about her? You're so
clever and beautiful, yet in a weird way she seems to dominate you."

Amelia didn't know why she was so shocked. "You're right, of
course," she said after a moment's searing reflection. "My family,
my mother and father, me, have fallen over backwards to try to make
Marigold happy. We did it every day. I believe it robbed us all of
tremendous energy. None of us could change Marigold, or even
make a difference. As it was, I've always tried to defend her. But
that's all over, Jimmy. From now on, my life is independent of
Marigold."

"God, I hope you mean that," Jimmy said.

Amelia set the coffee cups and saucers down on the black granite
counter. "You know I have to give Royce a full report?"

"Royce wouldn't accept less."

"Don't I know it!" The coffee had perked. Amelia poured Jimmy
a steaming cup of strong black coffee. She added two teaspoons of
sugar whether he took sugar or not. She would have to excuse herself
for a moment to change. She pulled a small tray from a cupboard, but
before she could make the next move, they were both startled by a
firm rap on the door.

"You're not getting broken into, Amelia, are you?" Jimmy tried
to pull himself upright. Dismally failed.

"I think we both know who it is." Swiftly she gathered her satin
robe around her, cursing the fact, given another few minutes she
would have had time to change.

"The Boss," Jimmy confirmed.

Amelia made her way to the door. She felt deeply disturbed. "Who is it?" she called senselessly, thinking this night would bring her yet another load of blame.

"Who do you think?" A dark, commanding voice answered. "Open up, Amelia."

Jimmy, on the sofa, managed to drag himself to his feet like a soldier about to be caught out napping on duty. "It's Royce, of course," she flung unnecessarily over her shoulder. She had no alternative but to give him entry. She was utterly fed up with always being caught in what looked like compromising situations.

"I've spent hours doing a futile pub crawl of all the so-called trendy bars," Royce announced, as he blazed into the hallway with its carved Italian mirror above a mahogany and brass console. "All of them seemed to know James, but claimed they hadn't seen him tonight. The last bar did." As he spoke, his dark eyes were sweeping over her, taking in her state of undress.

Amelia fought to hide her embarrassment. Who was she to blame? A malign fate? Her robe had a silk cord. She seldom bothered with it, allowing the robe to flow free. She was blushingly aware her nightgown did little to hide the shape of her body or her breasts. Her hair uncoiled, fell in thick ribbons over her shoulders and down her back.

Jimmy called out to them in a hoarse voice. "I'm here, Royce. Amelia was kind enough to let me in."

Amelia flinched at the expression that swept over Royce's face. The sheer awfulness of life!

"What can I say? Join the queue?" Royce stared down into her eyes.

Amelia couldn't bear the heat of her own body. She curled a protective hand over her heart, feeling its warmth. "Jimmy has barely been here ten minutes. I was going to ring you."

"What, tomorrow morning?"

Amelia didn't reply. She had never received such searing scrutiny in her entire life. "There's coffee if you want it," she managed to say, sharply. "I'll get changed."

"When I've never seen a nightgown and robe look more sumptuous."

"Why, what does Charlene wear to bed?" Amelia flashed back at him, hating the steely expression on his high-boned face.

"I can't be sure."

Amelia found herself on tiptoe. She leaned right into him. "Bastard!" she whispered very quietly in his ear.

Then she fled.

When she returned a full ten minutes later, dressed in jeans and a sleeveless top, she found Royce and his half-brother sitting side by side on her sofa. Seen together like that, it was easy to spot the family resemblance: height, build, a certain cast to their features. Jimmy's colouring was far more subdued. Bright blue Stirling eyes, tawny brown hair the sun had touched with golden tints. They appeared to be at peace with each other. Thank God! Amelia felt a great, coursing relief.

"Has Jimmy told you all you wanted to hear?" She addressed Royce with no show of hostility.

"Ah, there you are!" he said with mock welcome. "Jimmy has. He has also sung your praises."

"Why shouldn't he? Jimmy has a friend in me."

"He has indeed," Royce returned suavely, rising to his commanding height. "I'll take him back with me to the hotel. They can find him a room."

"He needs sleep," Amelia spoke gently, eyeing Jimmy, who was still slumped on her sofa, apparently on the brink of collapse.

"Royce is taking me home," he told Amelia, his voice a mere semblance of itself. "I'm so tired of it all."

"We'll find a way to make you feel better," Royce promised, catching Amelia's eyes. "Would you mind calling a cab?"

"No problem."

"I'd die for you, Amelia," Jimmy muttered, as Royce draped a strong arm around him, lending the very necessary support.

They stood at her door. Two brothers. One as impressive as they come. The other so vulnerable. "Thank you for being so kind to me," Jimmy said.

"It was easy, Jimmy," she said softly. "I'll go catch the lift for you."

"You'll tell Marigold I'm going home?" he begged.

Such a stricken face! "Yes, dear," she said, momentarily touching his cheek.

"I feel I'm to blame."

"No, Jimmy, you're *not!*" Amelia said in a voice that held strong conviction.

She moved off down the hallway to summon the lift to her floor. There was no one around. No witnesses to James Stirling's near-total breakdown.

"I'll come downstairs with you," she said. The lift had arrived and the two men had moved into it. "I can signal the cab driver."

"What would we do without you?" Royce murmured, his brother a deadweight on his arm and shoulder. "I intend to see Marigold before we leave."

"Whatever for?" Amelia suddenly felt icily cold.

"She *is* Jimmy's wife, part of the family."

He sounded far from happy with the knowledge.

On the ground floor, Amelia went on ahead. A cab was standing outside the complex. She ran towards it, calling, "Stirling?"

"Right, ma'am," the cab driver confirmed, bending his head towards her. "One of your friends had too many?" he laughed.

"Actually, he's had some sad news," Amelia said, opening the back door.

"I'm sorry to hear that." The cab driver sounded genuine. He got out of the cab, moving to help the big guy get his drunk pal into the car. "There you go, mate!"

"Thank you." Royce acknowledged the help, settling his brother more comfortably. He then shut the back door, watching the driver resume his seat in the cab.

"Take care, Royce," Amelia said, on a long, trembling breath.

Her hair and face glowed in the lights that illuminated the area. She looked heartbreakingly beautiful. No flutters of conscience about Jimmy? No mention of her state of undress when he arrived at the door, the half-naked sensuality that would wipe out any man's resistance. His arm shot out automatically, locking her to his side. "Good night, Amelia. Thank you for looking after Jimmy so beautifully. He won't be bothering you again. I can't say the same for myself."

She knew what was coming. She could see the glint in his eyes.

Her mouth half-parted in futile protest. "Go back inside now," he said, giving her one hard, memorable kiss. "I'll wait until you're in."

Colour stained her high cheekbones. Her green eyes sparkled like gemstones. "Jimmy's demons grew up with him," she said, with such a mix of sadness and resentment at the way he made her feel. She still felt the touch of his mouth. She would feel his kiss for hours. Only she was no instrument he could play at will.

"I know that, Amelia. Go on. Go inside. I wish I could say pleasant dreams."

"Yours won't be pleasant either." Yet she was fighting the helpless urge to turn to him, confide in him. She knew she couldn't. God knows what might happen if she revealed the shocking truth.

"There is, of course, more to it," he said, as though picking up on her wavelength. "I intend to find out."

Amelia shivered in the balmy night air. She knew though Jimmy had broken under the strain, Marigold wouldn't. Marigold's lack of empathy had always been a great mystery. In a curious way, her lack of empathy was also a strength. She remembered how as a child Marigold didn't weep. She had frequently called up glistening tears. Requisite tears for a given occasion.

Marigold had a shopping trip planned. She needed to get out. She intended to call on the best jeweller in town. Melly always wore beautiful jewellery. She'd had her ears pierced, so she could wear drop earrings like Melly's, though most of Melly's jewellery had been handed down to her. Nothing for Marigold. She wasn't *true* family. Just a charity case. They had always dressed her well. She had gone to the best schools, even if she had flunked the university entrance exam. Jeremy had bought her the apartment for a twenty-first birthday present. She was supposed to feel deeply grateful. She didn't. Life owed her. Besides, Jeremy was a very successful man with a successful man's income. No skin off his nose.

Marigold suspected Melly's beloved Mum and Dad were secretly glad to be rid of *her*. She wasn't thick. She knew for a fact Amelia's mother was on to her, even though the saintly Amelia wasn't. That's why she hadn't invited them to the wedding. She had almost convinced herself Melly was so loyal she would follow her into hell. Melly would never give her away.

On the other hand, she felt no qualms about messing with Melly's life. Jimmy's adoration of her was pitiful. She knew Jimmy's all-powerful brother, Royce, felt so too. Royce could become her ally. She knew sooner or later, Jimmy would file for divorce. It would be far better if she beat him to it. After all, there was beautiful Amelia, always on the scene, always coming between them. Three people in the marriage. Hadn't Princess Di said something like that? Of course, Melly was as white as the driven snow, but it was too easy to muddy the waters. Mud stuck, whether it was the truth or not. Marigold had long ago determined it gave her an advantage to be able to lie and lie and get away with it.

It would have been nice to go on to lunch with a girlfriend, but she was quite aware she wasn't liked. Well, not by Melly's many friends. Now that she had money, and plenty of it, she could find some friends of her own.

The intercom buzzer brought her out of her reverie. Who could that be? She considered not answering, and then decided she would take a peek.

Royce Stirling!

Shock-horror.

Then.

This was an opportunity to get back at Amelia and Jimmy. A feeling of power surged through her system. She *was* Mrs. James Stirling. They couldn't change that. Royce Stirling wouldn't question her about the baby that never was. Melly wouldn't give her up under torture. She knew exactly how to play it . . .

The day had started badly. Jimmy, after his drinking binge, had been violently ill. They couldn't fly home today. He had left Jimmy sleeping it off in bed. Marigold's apartment complex mightn't have been as exclusive as Amelia's, but it was nevertheless a desirable up-market inner city apartment block.

Marigold allowed him in, a near-smile sounding in her soft breathy voice. To his mind, Marigold had the air of a street kid more than a gently bred young woman. He hadn't needed a degree in psychology to gain that view. This was a newly married woman who had miscarried her child on her honeymoon. Sounding *close* to cheerful was a major feat in his opinion.

Marigold, looking the picture of health, greeted him warmly. She stood on tiptoe to kiss his cheek. "Come in, Royce. Come in. You've no idea how pleased I am to see you."

He followed her into the apartment, noting how stylishly she was dressed, obviously for going out. The same style didn't extend to her home decorating. The furnishings could best be described as ordinary. No paintings. No flowers. No personal touches. It could have been a rental.

"I'm so glad you caught me. Ten minutes more and I would have left."

"For where, Marigold?" he asked.

She gave a little shrug. "I have to distract my mind, Royce. You can understand that. I've cried so much I simply can't cry anymore." She injected credibility into her voice. "Please sit down. Have you come to help me?"

Royce took the single armchair. "I came to help my brother, Marigold. He's extremely distressed. I am at your disposal too, of course."

"Thank God!" Marigold sank onto the beige sofa close by, with only the scatter cushions adding colour. "I've never felt so *alone.*"

"You have Amelia."

Marigold gave a deep sigh. "If only I did. I love Melly, I really do, but she has caused a great deal of harm to my marriage."

Royce kept his tone neutral. "How so?"

Marigold raised her head, with its crown of soft yellow curls. "You're a smart man, Royce. A man of the world. You know perfectly well my husband is madly in love with Melly."

There seemed to be a coldness, a hardness in her despite the unhappiness in her voice. "So why did you marry him?" Royce asked, keeping his tone non-judgemental.

Marigold threw up a bejewelled left hand. "I loved him. I still love him," she cried, sounding infinitely hurt. "Melly doesn't. This is what she does. She has taken any boyfriend I've ever had away from me. I don't say she plans it. It's more like she can't help herself. That's why I forgive her."

"You love her, but you have no hesitation blaming her for the failure of your marriage?" Royce queried.

Marigold bit her lip, tears spurting into her blue eyes. "And for the loss of our baby," she said on a broken sob. "It was supposed to be our honeymoon. The first time we could be together *without* Melly, but what did we do? We fought and fought. Jimmy turned incredibly nasty. He didn't talk to me. He barked at me. He was always so angry. I was no match for him. He *missed* Melly, would you believe?

He missed Melly when we were on our honeymoon. I never had a chance. All I wanted was for us to be happy."

"And the baby? Why didn't you tell us you were expecting? It would have been no big deal, Marigold. We deserved to know. No one outside the family needed to have been told the news."

Marigold lifted her head. She spoke in a raw and tortured voice. "Melly has always been my closest advisor," she confided, as though excusing herself. "She convinced Jimmy and me there was no need to cause upset before the wedding. It would be easy enough to reveal a pregnancy in the months ahead, she said."

"And you went along with this?" Royce searched Marigold's small face. There was a light sweat on her dewy skin. Either she was one of the world's greatest unsung actresses, or she was telling the truth. Only he couldn't shake the feeling Marigold was a knowing woman, a crafty woman. She wanted to turn him against her beautiful, clever sister.

"Jimmy will back my story," she added, as though she had spotted his scepticism. "Jimmy didn't want you to know."

That much was true. "Was Amelia with you when you miscarried? You would have rung her if you were in any trouble?"

"I did ring her." Marigold sounded wrung out. "Then it was all happening."

"Where, exactly?"

Marigold put her two hands over her eyes. "I can't talk about it, Royce. It's far too distressing. I had to cope on my own. Jimmy had abandoned me. Melly had a court case. She's always got a court case."

"I find it hard to believe Amelia wouldn't rush to your aid, or send an ambulance if she couldn't make it on time."

"I was here quite alone." Marigold spoke with deep sadness. "I miscarried very quickly. You won't want to hear the details."

"I have heard them from my brother."

"Oh?" She turned on him tormented, tear-filled blue eyes. "It was ghastly. Even if Jimmy had been with me, I would have warned him away. It was women's business. Melly didn't come." Now there was anger and indignation written all over her. "I can never forgive that. Melly is responsible for so much." She was crying in earnest now. Sputtering, ruining her expertly applied make-up. "She needs bringing down."

Royce whipped out a clean, white handkerchief, passed it to her. Marigold used it, went to pass the handkerchief back.

Royce waved it away. "I have no wish to upset you, Marigold. We all react in different ways. Jimmy is heartbroken."

"As he should be!" Marigold spoke with considerable wrath. "He has to pay for the way he treated me."

"He *is* paying, Marigold," Royce assured her. "Maybe he married you because of the pregnancy?"

"He didn't have to," Marigold rallied. "I didn't twist his arm. It was Melly who did that. She made him believe it was his duty to marry me now that I was pregnant with his baby. He enjoyed having sex with me. Then he had to pay for it. Not that I could have stood a chance against Melly. She captivates every man she meets. Jimmy was a push-over."

"You're saying my brother was intimate with Amelia?"

Marigold gave one of her unattractive snorts. "That's exactly what I'm saying. A man doesn't get that way without sex. It may have been just the once, but poor old Jimmy very naturally craved more. Melly is a very sexy lady."

"Why then did you make out she was short on admirers? You did that, before we met her." Royce stared directly into Marigold's blue eyes.

"A joke, Royce," She gave a thin smile. "A joke. You would have seen at once Melly is a woman who breaks hearts. She's a professional in that regard. The guy she's with, Oliver, is as crazy about her as Jimmy is. She'll never marry him. She'll move on. I hope that's been helpful."

Royce stood up, thinking how dangerous Marigold could be. "I'm taking James back to Kooralya with me," he said.

"Good." Marigold nodded her approval. "He needs to get himself together. I intend to divorce him, Royce. I'm sure you understand? It's impossible now to save our marriage."

"No miraculous reconciliation," Royce said with some irony. "The marriage didn't work from day one, Marigold."

Marigold shot him an intense look, as though pleading for understanding. "It might have worked had Melly left us alone," she said.

Royce didn't believe anything would have come of his brother's brief affair with Marigold if she hadn't gotten pregnant. He walked to the door, where he paused. "As James' wife, you have a claim. You're talking divorce?"

"Indeed." The breathy voice turned strident.

"You will naturally be expected to provide proof of your pregnancy," Royce said, waiting on her reaction. That appeared to be far more than Marigold had ever imagined. She looked aghast.

"What on earth are you talking about, Royce?" She stood, frozen.

"I'm only letting you know proof would be required, that's all. You would be doing *yourself* a service, Marigold," he added, smoothly. "You lost your baby. You fully intend to claim Jimmy was having an affair with your adoptive sister. You were so distressed and unhappy about the situation, as any woman would be, you lost your baby. A tragedy for an expectant mother. There's only your word for the pregnancy, however. I'm preparing you for what you'll be asked by lawyers, Marigold. Your solicitor, when you get one, will advise you. Jeremy Boyd, the father figure who adopted you, is a highly respected lawyer. He would be there for you, surely?"

Marigold's expression contorted. "As if I'd ask him! Never in a million years would he bring scandal down on his beloved daughter. He'd kill me before he allowed that."

"Such an accusation! I wouldn't repeat it, Marigold. Your privilege as an adopted daughter wouldn't extend so far. Find the best lawyer you can," he suggested, his hand on the door.

That was the moment Marigold let her guard down utterly. "It's going to cost you," she shot back with a look of pure spite.

"You think I don't know that, Marigold?" Royce said, unimpressed. "Good day to you. I won't keep you from your shopping. I see you've already run up excessively high bills." His voice was so quiet and calm, it took a second or two for the comment to sink in, and then she laughed.

"So what? Jimmy's rich!"

"Only you're not dealing with my brother now, Marigold. You'll be dealing with me."

"That's wonderful!" said Marigold. "You're the only one in the family I can trust."

Chapter 5

Amelia drove to Melbourne's Tullamarine Airport to pick up her parents and bring them home. She had stocked the fridge so they wouldn't have to go out for a day or two. Seasoned travellers though they were, they would be tired after the long one-stop flight from Leonardo da Vinci International Airport in Rome. She hoped it had been a good flight, though as a family, they had all experienced far more jet lag on flights from Europe than flying there.

It was a long wait until Amelia finally saw her parents emerge from Customs, her tall, distinguished-looking father with his thick shock of prematurely white hair, pushing a laden trolley. Their faces lit up the instant they caught sight of her. Amelia loved her parents with her whole heart. She was so proud of them and their accomplishments. A handsome couple, they were in their late fifties. Not young anymore. She couldn't go near the thought of one day having to lose them.

They were home in their leafy affluent suburb in just more than 25 minutes. Both her parents had asked after Marigold, as expected, but she had made the decision not to worry them until they were properly rested. All she said in answer to her mother's enquiry about Marigold was, "She's well, Mum."

"She's grown away from us, hasn't she?" her mother said.

"I don't think Marigold ever wanted to be one of us." Her father spoke as though he too was beset by the knowledge. "I can't for the life of me think who Marigold takes after! It's certainly not Grace and Ian."

In the kitchen, Amelia opened the fridge door to reveal the contents. Ham. Chicken. A dozen eggs. Milk. Butter. Cream. A selection of cheeses. Salad ingredients in the crisper. In the pantry, marmalade and Vegemite. Freshly ground coffee. Fresh bread. An assortment of pastas.

"Thank you, darling." Ava Boyd wrapped her arms around her daughter. Ava was a beautiful woman who still turned heads. She had passed her blond beauty onto her daughter along with her high intelligence, her sense of humour, and her loving nature.

"What about if I take you both out for dinner tomorrow night?" Amelia suggested.

"That would be lovely," her father said, stifling a yawn.

"I'll pick you up around seven. Leo's, okay?"

"Couldn't be better. We can discuss Marigold then."

Her parents walked her to her car. "Drive safely, darling," Ava said, kissing her daughter on the cheek. "Let's have a good night's sleep before we hear about Marigold's antics." She spoke lightly, never guessing what Amelia had to tell them.

Amelia's expression was sombre as she drove away. This was one story she didn't want to tell, but she would have to bite the bullet. She couldn't lie to her parents. They were too astute, for one thing, and they knew the changeling who was Marigold.

It was a weeknight, yet the restaurant, one of three Leo owned, was full, but not packed. Leo, short for Leonardo, was present that night. He greeted them, showing them to their window table and asking after the trip. Leo, Milan-born, was a globetrotter. He always credited his mother for instilling in him a passion for food. At sixteen, he had been apprenticed at one of the finest restaurants in Europe. When he met and fell in love with an Australian girl ten years later, he shifted to Melbourne, where he had opened a small restaurant. It was a risk that had paid off. Leonardo was a world-recognised chef and an award-winning author. They were anticipating a delicious, imaginative meal.

Her parents were looking rested, all smiles. They had greatly enjoyed their holiday, but, as ever, they were glad to be home. What a pity it was she had to tell them about the mess Marigold had made of her life.

"Okay, you can unburden yourself now," her father said after they had finished their main course and the dishes had been removed. They had decided to wait a while before they settled on any one of the delicious sweet treats on the trolley that was being wheeled about.

"Am I that transparent?" she asked, with a wry smile.

"No, not at all. But we do know Marigold," Jeremy said.

"I just hope it's not bad." Ava's nerves were suddenly on edge.

Both her parents settled in to hear what Amelia had to divulge about their adopted daughter.

"This is as bad as it could be," Jeremy Boyd said, when Amelia stopped talking. He was wondering where they could possibly have gone wrong raising Marigold.

"This poor young man, Jimmy, has to know there *was* no baby. It will make him very angry, but it might ease his suffering," Ava said.

Amelia sighed. "The last time I saw Jimmy, I'd say he was on the verge of a total breakdown."

"That's very troubling," Jeremy said, with a frown. "You say his brother, half-brother, is a strong, compassionate man? I've heard of the Outback Stirlings, of course. Cattle kings in their legendary heartland, the Channel Country. The father, from all accounts, was a very unpleasant man. Apparently, no one dared go against him. The word was, Frances Stirling left the station fighting for her survival. It was a terrible tale. She lives in Adelaide, I believe. She never did marry the chap she was alleged to have run off with. Odd!"

"Jimmy's mother, Sally, the second wife, still lives on Kooralya. It's easy to see she was another one of her late husband's victims, totally dominated, too scared to be protective of her son all the while he was growing up. I don't think Jimmy would have survived without Royce. Royce is made of stern stuff. Jimmy idolizes him."

"So, one brother living in the shadow of the other," Ava said. "We'll have to speak to Marigold." Her incredible emerald eyes, passed on to her daughter, darkened at the thought. It was enormously upsetting to find out Marigold had kept them completely in the dark about her relationship with James Stirling, let alone that she'd gotten married and hadn't even invited them. She and Jeremy would never have made their annual trip to Italy had they known. Jeremy should have been the one to give Marigold away. Jeremy was the closest thing to a father Marigold had known since the death of Grace and Ian.

"She's after a divorce," Amelia repeated quietly.

"She'd be a fool if she thought the Stirlings—Royce Stirling—

will prove a push-over." Jeremy's calm voice overrode his mounting concerns. "So it was money Marigold was after?"

"Becoming Mrs. James Stirling, with unlimited money, was her great ambition in life."

"Anyone would think she had been raised in a desperately poor family," Ava said.

Jeremy lifted his eyebrows, but didn't say more.

Amelia punched the gate code to let them in. They had arrived back at the Boyd's large, Mediterranean-style house set off by a freshly mown lawn and flowering garden beds. She had supervised the upkeep while her parents were away.

The exterior security lights lit up the front of the house and picked up Marigold's petite figure. She was standing outside, obviously waiting for their return.

"Here's trouble," Ava said, her hand straying to the string of Tahitian pearls around her neck. The gesture calmed her. Marigold was no longer an adolescent, dependent on family support. Marigold was a twenty-four-year-old young woman who clearly didn't have any regard for her adoptive family.

Marigold didn't go to them. She waited for the family to come to her.

Short of stature though she was, the set of her body raised alarm signals. Marigold was there to make trouble.

"Welcome home, Mr. and Mrs. Boyd," she called.

"Hard to understand her," Ava said with a sigh. "You're not concealing a weapon, are you, Marigold?" She walked right up to the daughter on whom they all had lavished their love, time, and attention.

"Heavens, no, Mummy!" Marigold laughed aloud.

"So many disturbed young people arming themselves these days." Jeremy came alongside, taking Marigold's arm by the elbow. "We'll go inside, shall we?" The invitation fairly crackled.

"Fine by me, *Dad.*"

They took their places in the cool gracious living room. Jeremy and Ava sat together on one sofa. Marigold took the other, while Amelia sank into the arm chair nearest her parents, preparing herself for Marigold's bluster. They all waited for her to tell them why she was here so late at night. The walnut grandfather clock in the hallway had chimed eleven bells moments after they had walked in.

"Melly has told you all about it, hasn't she?" Marigold looked flushed, excited. She could even have been drinking. She was wearing a cling-to-every-curve silk dress in the same shade of blue as her eyes. Metallic, gold, high-heeled sandals were on her feet. She was also wearing some very expensive-looking gold jewellery none of them was familiar with. She had never looked so chic. Nor in such good health.

There had been no sign of her car on the street, although they hadn't given the street much attention. No car parked in the driveway. She must have taken a cab.

"You can go one better. *You* can tell us, Marigold," Jeremy said.

"I bet she didn't tell you my husband is madly in love with her." Marigold pointed an accusing finger at Amelia.

Ava cut in swiftly. "We're talking about *you*, Marigold. Not Amelia." This was standard Marigold. Changing the discussion away from her. "Your husband may well be in love with Amelia, but Amelia isn't in love with him or anyone else, for that matter. I would know. She would tell me."

"You can't find it in you to criticize Melly in any way? You're both so proud of her." Marigold managed to make it sound like Jeremy and Ava were totally witless.

"With very good reason, Marigold," Jeremy said. "I have a question for *you*. Why did you allow your husband of just over a month to believe you had miscarried your child?"

Marigold gave a bizarre crack of laughter. "Because I *did.*"

"No, you didn't," Ava broke in. "You must put an end to all these lies, Marigold."

Marigold's smile resembled a cat's. "Do you know how much the Stirlings are worth?" she asked with glittering blue eyes.

"So you're admitting it was all about money?" Jeremy's expression was grave.

"Millions," Marigold said, as if she hadn't heard him. "Millions and millions. The cattle station is little more than their home base. What it brings in is nothing compared to a huge portfolio of investments. They're *filthy* rich! I'll be demanding my fair share."

"So you went after James Stirling determined to get him, whatever it took?" Ava asked quietly, recognizing the ring of emotional blackmail.

"It's been done before, *Mummy dear.*" Brazenly, Marigold looked Ava right in the eye.

"Your mother, my dear friend, Grace, would have been ashamed of you, Marigold," Ava said.

"She's not around, is she? She hasn't been around for yonks. I had to come up the hard way."

"Stop a moment there." Jeremy cracked out the order. "You're talking nonsense. Most people would say you had a privileged upbringing."

"I'd have given anything to have had my own parents." Marigold blinked at the severity of Jeremy's tone. "I didn't need it drilled into me how *good* you all are. I'm divorcing Jimmy." She looked from one to the other as though they intended to stop her. Physically, if need be. "Melly would have told you. My story is I lost the baby. Jimmy believes it. He's not worth your sympathy. He was horrible to me."

"Not true," Amelia broke in. "Jimmy wouldn't know how to be horrible, whereas you're horrible for fun."

"You need to lighten up, Melly," Marigold scoffed. "Royce called on me before he took his pathetic brother off home. Did you know that? Royce is definitely on my side."

"Then you've misread him, Marigold," Amelia cringed at the thought of what a vindictive Marigold might have said about her to Royce. "Royce loves his brother. I'd say he knew what game *you* were playing from the moment you met."

"I told him all about you and Jimmy," Marigold continued, apparently for the sheer pleasure of it. "It's not as though anyone missed the way Jimmy kissed you at our wedding reception. I have never felt so humiliated. What kind of a man kisses the bridesmaid passionately in front of his bride and all their guests? You always did try to drive a wedge between me and every boyfriend I ever had. You mesmerized poor, old Jimmy. He didn't stand a chance. Royce knows all about you, Melly. You were Jimmy's, what was it again?' She tapped her forehead. "I've got it! Jimmy's *golden enchantress.* I reckon he got it from some poem."

Jeremy Boyd was ignoring her rant. "You will have to prove you were pregnant, Marigold," he said. "Can you prove it?"

"How would anyone know?" Marigold countered with wide-open eyes. "One in five women miscarry in the first trimester, I've been told."

"Not you, by any doctor," Amelia said. "The first thing a woman who suspects she's pregnant would do is consult her doctor to be assured all was well. For once, you told me the truth, Marigold. You were *never* pregnant. You used that as an excuse to get Jimmy to marry you. Another man might have laughed in your face. Denied you were pregnant by him. They wouldn't have fallen so easily into the trap."

"Okay. Okay!" Marigold threw up her hands. The huge solitaire diamond in the engagement ring she had chosen flashed its brilliance. "I want a promise from you, my family, that we stick to my story. I miscarried when Jimmy was away. He accepted it. Royce may have appeared not so accepting, but with you, Melly, to back me, the problem will go away. It was Jimmy who screwed up. Pardon the pun. It would serve no good purpose to tell him there was no baby after all. Many women have phantom pregnancies. Perfectly respectable women. *I* truly believed I was pregnant."

"We don't accept that, Marigold," Ava said. "You're too conniving for your own good, my dear. Perhaps it would make Jimmy feel better about things?" she considered. "He'd be angry, of course. He would have every right to be, but if he knew you hadn't miscarried, his child hadn't been lost at all, he might start to feel stronger. Pick up his life again."

"What *womanizing?*" Marigold glared back at her adoptive mother as though she hated her. "Serves him right."

"Jimmy should know the truth," Amelia said. "He's on the brink of a total breakdown. He has to be saved. You should tell him, Marigold. You can claim you truly believed you were pregnant. I'll go so far as to back you, but he must be told."

"*No!*" For one brief moment, Marigold looked terrified. "I'm going to divorce Jimmy. I'm going to take him for all I can get. Just find it in your hearts to protect me." She looked rather wildly from Amelia to Jeremy to Ava. "I'm *family*. It would rebound on us all. The press will stick their noses into all our lives. They would find out everything. I'll destroy Melly if you fail me. Royce knows poor, old Jimmy would give his life for her. It would pay you all to back my story. You're a legal man, a realist, Dad. I appeal to you."

"I don't want any part of this," Jeremy Boyd said. "The Stirling family won't either. We all keep quiet. How many people did you tell you were pregnant, Marigold?" he asked. "Truth now."

"No one except Melly," Marigold said. "She was the *only* one outside Jimmy. He didn't tell anyone either. We both agreed on that."

"Well then. We can keep it within the families. I know the Stirlings will agree. It's the way things are done in certain families too much in the public eye. We need not fear them. But your husband must be told, Marigold. Things will settle down in time. Then you can get your divorce in a year's time."

Marigold was looking back at Jeremy with an expression of astonishment. Even hurt. "You won't protect me?"

"It's perfectly clear you've been behaving badly, Marigold," he said. "There is nothing for it but to put things straight. You and James Stirling will get your divorce as civilly and quietly as possible. It's a great pity the two of you ever met."

"I mightn't get as much as I've been counting on." The words came out sounding worried.

"It might push you into making a real life for yourself," Ava said.

When Marigold looked up, there were tears in her eyes. "Can I stay the night, Mum? I don't want to go back to the apartment. I hate being on my own. I'm not like Melly. Beautiful or not, she's a born old maid."

"I wouldn't hold out much hope for that, dear," Ava said. "Of course you may stay the night. Your room is always made up. We've always been here for you, Marigold. Sadly for you, you've never seen it."

After consulting with her father, Amelia decided to take early annual leave. She was to accompany Marigold to Kooralya, where Marigold was to make peace with her husband. When the right moment presented itself, she would tell him she hadn't lost their baby. She was to say she hated herself for it, but she had been too ashamed to tell him she hadn't been pregnant. She had experienced a number of true pregnancy symptoms, which wasn't unusual in phantom pregnancy cases. Her breasts had enlarged. Menstruation had stopped. She'd had to cope with morning sickness. There were strong emotional and psychological factors underpinning the fairly rare condition. It could never be forgotten she had lost her parents in a horrifying car crash at the tender age of five.

Marigold had a gift. She was a natural-born actress. Consequently, she was word-perfect with the lines she was being virtually forced to deliver. She had even perfected wringing her hands. She knew the image she had to project was that of a defenceless young woman who had made a huge mistake.

Royce made it his business to prepare James for the visit. He wasn't at all sure James was feeling as good as he made out. James really needed help. More help than Royce could give him. What his brother actually needed was counselling.

They sat on their horses in the shade of the red gums that overhung the mossy flower-strewn bank leading down to the creek. It was washed sparklingly clean by all the rainfall the Channel Country had recently had. It still seemed to him incredible after the tough time Kooralya and the neighbouring stations had experienced after three long years of drought. Rain had made confidence soar. There was a big demand for the high-quality beef the area was famous for, on the home front and their regular overseas markets.

"Marigold is coming here?" James responded with a quick frown and a note of alarm. "What for exactly?"

"As I understand it, she is desperate to make peace with you." Royce controlled the cynicism he felt. Surely he could give Marigold the benefit of the doubt.

"On no account do I believe it," James jeered.

"Amelia is coming with her," Royce tacked on, closely watching his brother's face.

"Amelia?" James sounded both startled and thrilled. "Why would she come?" His hands on the reins tightened and then released. Tightened and released.

Royce shifted his black Akubra further back on his head. "To support Marigold, of course," he said as neutrally as he could.

"That's what I don't get at all." James shook his head. "Marigold is so bloody jealous of Amelia, a blind woman would see it. Yet Amelia doesn't. I see that as ominous for Amelia. Marigold is fast growing into a woman to be avoided. Yet Amelia continues to support her." He spoke with dismay.

"Not all that easy for family to disentangle," Royce said. "We have to remember, they grew up together from little girls. They lived in the same house. They were treated like sisters. Amelia is only two years older than Marigold. She has a protective nature. In any case, Marigold would have begged her to do it. You don't have to see Marigold if you don't want to, though I have to say her email went a long way to softening my hard, old heart."

"It would! Amelia wrote it. Marigold couldn't write a shopping list. Add to which she doesn't have a genuine bone in her body. She wants to come here to discuss a divorce."

"It's what *you* want too, isn't it, Jimmy?" Royce held his brother's eyes. It worried him that James appeared to have used up all his reserves of strength.

"Of course. Think of it, Amelia coming back here!" he exclaimed almost in wonderment.

"You have to accept Amelia doesn't return your feelings." Royce thought it necessary to issue a clear warning. "She's your friend, Jimmy. That's all."

"It's enough," James answered. "Marigold can come. It's showdown time for her. She's going to demand a fortune before she takes herself off."

"You did marry her," Royce pointed out. "You gave her *our* name. We'll sort this out quietly. Amelia and her family will agree. They won't want notoriety any more than we do. Jeremy Boyd is a high-profile lawyer, a senior partner in his own firm." Royce thought he would never forget the furore that had accompanied his parents' very public divorce. It continued for years after. His grandfather, a very private man, had abhorred all the publicity the family had been caught up in. The press had even got hold of Anthea's sad story. How her fiancé had been speared by a plantation worker in New Guinea. They had dug up an engagement photo of Anthea and her fiancé to post in the papers. Nothing the press liked more than ferreting out family secrets and sensitive family matters. Nothing personal. It sold papers and gave reporters a job.

The first time Amelia had flown over the remote southwest corner of the giant state of Queensland, images of the red planet had come instantly to mind. She had seen all the amazing pictures of Mars released by NASA. The vast landscape was the same uniform fiery red. The same eroded dunes, rocks, and shallow craters. Planet

Mars, the Outback counterpart, was at least studded with the ubiquitous spinifex that dried to a dark gold. Kooralya, with its homestead
and numerous outbuildings, had appeared to her fascinated eyes as
some remote settlement in outer space.

Now they had returned.

In the few weeks that had passed, unbelievably, a miracle had occurred. She had listened daily to the weather forecasts for the nation.
Outback Queensland was rejoicing. Late-spring rains had bucketed
down over a huge area, bringing joy to the drought-stricken state.
Drought had turned to boom times. Rain was everything the Outback
prayed for. Word was, remote satellite towns were celebrating as
well.

She was amazed by the happiness she, a city dweller, felt. Her trip
to Kooralya had stirred her imagination. What she saw now to her
delighted eyes was a formerly parched land turned not a light green,
nor a medium green, but a *brilliant* green. It had been reported to the
nation that *Uluru,* the great rock formation at the very centre of the
continent, sacred to the aborigines, towered above as luxuriant a
landscape as ever a desert could be.

Marigold, on the other hand, showed not a glimmer of interest.
She was looking increasingly fearful they might crash at any moment. The pilot of their light aircraft, whom Royce had hired, com-
menced the descent onto Stirling land. Amelia was able to look down
awestruck on an ancient landscape that slipped away into infinity. No
wonder the ancients had worshipped the rain gods. The vast territory
was covered in a thick mantle of wild grasses and beautiful wildflowers: millions of white yellow-centred paper daisies she could
readily identify and innumerable varieties she didn't know the names
of. The floral splendour blazed on forever.

"Marigold, do look! It doesn't seem possible such beauty could
rise from the sun-scorched earth." All it had taken was enough rain
for the wildflowers to come out in their billions from miraculous dor-
mant seeds.

She was utterly bewitched, even if Marigold didn't share her fascination. She had brought her faithful Pentax with her. It would be a
wonderful opportunity to explore the Wild Heart that could turn
overnight into paradise. The water courses and billabongs that criss-
crossed Kooralya and gave the Channel Country its name were filled
to the brim with life-giving water. The surfaces glinted a blinding sil-

ver. She could see station stockmen driving herds of cattle towards the numerous billabongs. She even spotted near the eroded red hills a herd of brumbies, the Outback's wild horses, galloping like the wind across the furnace-red sands. There were no half-measures with this incredible land.

Drought or flood.

Royce and Jimmy were there to meet them, both men lounging beside a station Jeep. They looked very glamorous to city eyes, dressed in cowboy gear that suited their tall, lean bodies and long legs to perfection. Not a skerrick of extra weight on either of them, though Royce would weigh in heavier.

Once out of the light aircraft and safely on the ground, Marigold's confidence was restored. She rushed ahead of Amelia, and then took her time to embrace not Jimmy, but Royce. She reached up to kiss his cheek. "Hey, big man!" she cried as if they were the greatest of friends.

Amelia winced. This was one of Marigold's tricks. She was determined to have Royce, head of the family, as her ally.

How little she knew him!

She continued to watch as Marigold turned to her husband, offering Jimmy her hand. "How ya doing?" she asked, looking into a face that had recovered much of its good looks.

Jimmy gave a twisted grin. "How *you* goin', Marigold? I've been counting the minutes until you arrived."

Marigold gave a whoop of laughter. "More like Amelia," she said, as though determined not to let the subject drop.

Time for me to approach, Amelia thought. She smiled at both men. Little tremors were running down her back. Thoughts of Royce had consumed her. He took her outstretched hand. Jimmy had no hesitation giving her a brotherly kiss on the cheek.

The astonishing immediacy of skin on skin! It was as though their entwined hands simply and directly registered what was and had been from the start an inevitable attraction. The kind of twisted passion Heathcliff had felt for Catherine Earnshaw? She had read *Wuthering Heights* many times. She had never thought she could be so caught up in such complex emotions herself. Now she wasn't so sure. Alone in bed at night, she had *felt* Royce's presence, his mouth on hers. She heard his deep, vital voice, caught the sparks that flew from his body to hers. It was all terribly melodramatic like Emily

Brontë's novel, but she couldn't wave away her real reactions. It would be a total disaster to fall in love with the wrong man.

And then there was Charlene.

She made an effort to appear totally normal. "I can't believe the transformation rain has brought," she said, her eyes a sparkling green in her smiling face. "It's a revelation. Kooralya turned into paradise! I'm going to have to explore it."

"We're not here for long, Melly." Marigold's breathy tones sounded sharp.

"I might not go back with you," Amelia tossed off, as if totally independent of Marigold and her wishes. "If the family will have me, I'll stay on a few more days."

"That's hardly what we agreed." Marigold was starting to show her natural pugnacity.

Royce cut in smoothly. "You're welcome to stay as long as you like, Amelia. I understand you're on vacation?"

"It couldn't have come at a better time. I've never seen such floral splendour in my life. I'll have to ask Anthea all about it."

"She's the expert," Royce answered, with obvious pride in their aunt. "Anthea has always said one day she'll write a book about Kooralya's wildflowers."

Amelia nodded. "She should. I expect she's taken loads of pictures of the desert in bloom?"

"Look," Marigold very sweetly interrupted. "Can we get out of the sun?"

They were actually standing in the shade of the hangar where the Beech Baron and a yellow helicopter were housed. Another yellow helicopter was parked alongside the hangar.

"Of course, Marigold. I'll drive you back to the house," Royce bent his head to look at her. Like Amelia, Marigold was wearing close-fitting cotton jeans with a sleeveless, oval-necked cotton top in a daffodil yellow that suited her colouring. Amelia's top was white. Amelia had cinched a wide leather and brass belt around her narrow waist. It was hard to miss Amelia. She had just the right body tight jeans loved.

"It *is* hot, Marigold," he said. "Jimmy and I won't be able to join you for lunch, unfortunately. Too much to do. We'll be back at dusk." A station hand was hovering. Royce beckoned to him to take their visitors' luggage up to the house.

*   *   *

The men having driven away, Amelia and Marigold walked toward the house. The front door was open. Marigold tugged at Amelia's arm. "You were only joking about staying on?"

"I'm in no rush, Marigold," Amelia said. Anthea Stirling appeared in the open doorway, waving. Amelia waved back as Anthea proceeded to skip down the short flight of stone steps.

"It's great to have you back again!" Anthea put her arms firmly around Amelia, who responded with a hug, before turning to Marigold. "How are you, my dear?" she asked, solicitously.

"I'll be all right, eventually," Marigold answered, her mouth turning down. "I need to take my next step in life." She spoke as if meeting Jimmy was the worst thing that had ever happened to her.

"We were devastated to hear you lost the baby." There was considerable sympathy in Anthea's cultured voice. "I've been saying prayers for you and Jimmy. Lots of them."

"We're going to need them," Marigold said, tartly, purposely standing aloof. Unlike Melly, she could never find common ground with Jimmy's aunt.

"Come into the house," Anthea invited. She had to keep reminding herself Marigold bore the family name. "Your luggage will be brought to your rooms. The same as before. Lunch is scheduled for noon."

"I can't wait to see the wildflowers," Amelia said with enthusiasm. She took Anthea's arm. It was a gesture so perfectly natural she might have known Anthea forever. "I've never seen a spectacle so glorious from the air. Now I have to see it close-up. Royce said you intend writing a book about Kooralya's wildflowers one day?"

Anthea laughed. "I've been saying that for years."

"It's something you've *got* to do," Amelia said. "You have to share all the glory around you. Push yourself. I'd love to help."

"What is it with you guys and flowers?" Marigold asked in an irritated voice. She looked and sounded like a woman under pressure. "Where would a book about wildflowers get you?"

"What a question, Marigold!" Anthea decided to laugh off Marigold's comment. "I would be giving and getting great pleasure. It is, as Amelia has just pointed out, a responsibility."

*   *   *

Pippa had prepared a light lunch of seared scallops flown in that morning from the tropical north. A capsicum salad served as a bed for the seafood. It was followed by a tangy-tart panna cotta with a silky lightness dressed with fresh strawberry and rhubarb compote. Anthea had invited Pippa to sit down with them, making four at the table, and then Sally joined them.

After lunch, Amelia and Anthea waited until the worst of the heat had worn off before taking one of the station's Jeeps to the spectacular desert gardens some half a mile from the home compound. Marigold, predictably, had declined to come.

"I'm sure you'll have a lovely time without me." It was far too hot for her to exert herself.

Sally could see Anthea and Amelia might well have a lovely time without her. It was odd to see two young women who had grown up together as sisters display markedly different characteristics. "Marigold and I can have a nice long chat," she said. with a touch of mischief.

Amelia could have laughed out loud. It was the very last thing Marigold wanted. Indeed, Marigold was frantic to get away from her mother-in-law. "That would be lovely, but I need to rest," she said. She hadn't taken to the frowsy little woman who was Jimmy's mother.

"I feel spent after the plane trip," Marigold explained, responding to an unspoken prompt from Amelia. "I hate flying and, of course, I'm physically drained. I may appear overly stoic, Mrs. Stirling, but that's just my way. All the sympathy has centred around Jimmy. I've had to learn to be strong. It grew out of my childhood."

It was quite a speech.

And it was so wrong.

Marigold always spoke as if she were a survivor of a bloody war.

Never had the world seemed so brilliantly clear! Amelia parked the Jeep in the shade of a huge coolabah, its leaves turned edge on to the sun as a protective measure. She knew all about the historic coolabah at Station Creek. It was linked to two relief expeditions to find the ill-fated explorers Burke and Wills. Both men had little or no knowledge of the huge, empty continent that was Australia. No knowledge of the interior. Wills would have made a far better leader. Unfortunately, the impetuous Irishman, Burke, listened to no one and disregarded all advice. It always paid to listen, Amelia had found.

She had left her camera at home. That had been Anthea's advice.

"This is your first sighting. You're here to *enjoy.*"

She was already experiencing enormous pleasure and exhilaration, but a degree of disappointment had crept in. Marigold should have come. But for some strange reason, Marigold was unmoved by the beauty of flowers and the love of literature. It seemed sad Marigold was missing out on so much joy. What did give her great pleasure was jewellery, clothes, shoes, and make-up. Marigold's aim right from adolescence was to look like a movie star. She would now have the financial resources to cut quite a swath.

Propelled by adrenaline, Amelia had to restrain herself from running headlong into a waving sea of feathery plumes, coloured lilac into purple.

"Lamb's tails," Anthea called to her, laughing at Amelia's enthusiasm. She waved an arm towards her right where large green plumes in great profusion waved in the wind. "Pussy tails. You'll know the paper daisies. The yellow flowers are the native poppies. That great swath of pink over there is the Parakeelya. I'm sure you'll recognize Sturt's Red Desert Pea."

Amelia looked towards the great ranks of the beautiful creeping vine named after the gentleman English explorer Captain Charles Napier Sturt. It was Sturt who had set out, full of high hopes, to find the continent's fabled inland sea. In 1845, he did find the extinct inland sea of prehistory, the Simpson desert, one of the most daunting deserts in the world. Sturt's Desert Pea was the state floral emblem of South Australia. It was a protected species found only in Australia. The petals in the brilliant sunshine radiated a deep, bright red with glossy black central swellings.

"There are lilies too," Amelia called to Anthea in surprise. Cool, pure, white lilies in the desert? She began to walk further into the desert gardens, minding where she put her booted feet. The hot sun was drawing out a great multitude of fragrances. Enough to make the head swim. Overhead, came a cacophony of bird calls. The Outback was famous for its bird life.

"Spider lilies." Anthea waded in, giving the white lilies the local name. She pulled her large straw hat further down over her eyes. "Those beautiful pink flowers are—"

"Don't tell me. Native hibiscus. And those lovely purple flowers?" she pointed to an ocean of blooms, thousands upon thousands.

"Morgan flowers," Anthea was taking great pleasure in Amelia's excitement. Amelia was a born naturalist. She felt inspired by Amelia's enthusiasm to make a start on her book. She had a great knowledge of desert wildflowers, native grasses, and plants living where she did. To Anthea, her desert home was the heart of the world. Too soon, these glorious desert gardens would fade and die, victims of sun and wind, but for now it was indeed paradise. She was delighted to pass some of her knowledge on to Amelia. Had her beloved fiancé not died and left her so terribly alone, she would have wanted a daughter just like Amelia.

Instinct told her she might not lose Amelia, yet at the same time, she was convinced something peculiar was happening. Marigold had clamped onto Amelia like a parasite. She relied on Amelia to protect her. Amelia in turn had probably spent her entire life doing just that as some sort of compensation for Marigold's losing her parents so young.

Was Marigold being entirely truthful about her baby? Who could tell what was true anymore? Anthea had to wonder what the following days might bring. She hadn't missed the deadly opposition on Marigold's face when Amelia had mentioned at lunch she mightn't go back with her, but stay on. There was something Marigold was desperate to keep quiet. Something she feared Amelia might feel compelled to reveal.

James was by no means strong, though his mental health had improved since he had returned home. He was trying his best to appear normal, to give Royce all the support he could, but James was no cattleman. He lacked the qualities it took to run a great station. As a boy, Jimmy had experienced considerable difficulty learning to ride a horse. Her brother's way of throwing his sons onto a horse as soon as they could walk hadn't worked with Jimmy. However, Royce, as expected, had made the expected grand job of it. No one was sorry when Charles had drawn his last breath. The overriding emotion had been relief. Charles had been a tyrant. Tyrants left damaged people in their wake.

Once, she had suggested to Royce they could invite Frances to stay. His father had been dead some time. It seemed to her the coast was now clear. She had never blamed her beautiful sister-in-law for fleeing her brother. She *had* blamed her for many years for abandoning the ten-year-old son who adored her. Frances could not be forgiven for that.

Royce wouldn't hear of her tentative suggestion.

"My mother walked out on us, Anthea. End of story."

Amelia was finishing dressing for dinner when Marigold burst into the bedroom without resorting to a token tap on the door.

"I'm a bit worried about you," she proclaimed, fixing Amelia with cold, blue eyes.

It had become increasingly apparent to Amelia that since her marriage, Marigold had grown far more aggressive. "You're frightened I might spill the beans, is that it?" she asked.

"You can't bust me," Marigold asserted, using her new gangster language. "We're family."

"We're family when it suits you, Marigold." Amelia reminded her, wondering how their relationship had lasted all these years. Marigold had rarely given an outward sign of affection to any of them. She had behaved toward Amelia as if Amelia was a glorified servant. It had to stop.

As usual, Marigold ignored what she didn't want to hear. "You and stuffy old Anthea have grown surprisingly close," she challenged, as if she found such closeness a real danger to her. "Who knows what you might confide?"

Amelia finished coiling her hair into an elegant, low-slung knot. "I hate lying, Marigold, but I made a promise. If the truth is to come out, you're the one with the responsibility to tell it. I don't believe Jimmy is as accepting of the situation as he appears. I need to warn you as you don't appear to see it. Jimmy, underneath the swagger, is a very sensitive young man, lacking confidence in himself. He was tremendously disturbed when I last saw him. I find it hard to believe all that torment has gone away. These are early days, Marigold. He needs time. If I were you, I'd take it very easy with Jimmy. Don't push him. I won't stand by if he starts to show visible upset."

"Boo-bloody-hoo for poor old Jimmy. So you'll betray me, is that it?" Marigold ran an agitated hand over her fluffy, yellow hair.

"I can't think many people would blame me. Your ... *romance* with Jimmy had only one purpose. You were after a rich husband. It scarcely mattered if you loved him or not. Jimmy was getting away, so that put increasing urgency on you to rein him in. I'm certain pregnancy had already entered your head."

"Pregnancies that have led to marriage are countless," Marigold said as if it were a course open to all women. "Don't think I'm going to ask your forgiveness."

"That's good because I can't give it."

"I won't lose any sleep about it. My ambition has been fulfilled. I'm Mrs. James Stirling."

"For your sins," Amelia said dryly, turning to face her adoptive sister. Marigold was wearing a low-cut dress that was new. It emphasized a certain ripeness that had overtaken Marigold's petite body at an early age. It was a beautiful dress that must have cost well over a thousand dollars, but Marigold's overall appearance was out of kilter with the role she had to play.

"I see you like the dress." Marigold ran her hands down over her hips.

"You look stunning," Amelia said, with perfect truth. "But is it a good idea? You look more like you're going to a celebratory dinner than a quiet meal with the in-laws."

"What about you?" Marigold flashed back. Her eyes whipped over Amelia as though she were far more elaborately dressed. Amelia was not. She was wearing a fluid ankle-length dress in her favourite shade of violet: sleeveless, high-necked, but her appearance obviously irritated Marigold.

God had certainly been on Amelia's side when she was born, Marigold thought with familiar bitterness. It was so much easier for clothes to hang well if one had height. Her signature high heels were an answer to Melly's willowy height. Melly was such a clotheshorse!

"I'm hardly overdressed, Marigold," Amelia pointed out mildly. The family knew Marigold had always longed to be taller. Marigold had always believed they had grown up in competition. How had all these obsessions started?

"Sorry. No hard feelings." Marigold dipped her head. "Our temperaments simply don't match." It was becoming increasingly difficult for Marigold to hide her true feelings. And why not? No matter what the outcome, Jimmy had married her. She was Mrs. James Stirling, even if she found it difficult to remember at times. She knew she had to remain quiet and careful before she could live out her dream, but it was *hard*. For all her assets, she realized she might be a tad lacking in patience. The great thing was she was no longer the one in the background.

No longer in Melly's shadow. She was starting to get people to sit up and take notice. She was a Someone, the subject of society gossip. That would work for her with the divorce. She was ready to sweep her first marriage away. Her connection with the Stirling family wouldn't hurt when she found someone else rich, of course. Lots of young women were raised to find a good husband. A rich husband preferably, or at least one who could keep them in style. She knew some of Melly's university friends had gone to university to find prospective husbands. That made perfect sense to Marigold. Let Melly marry her dull, old Oliver. Marigold hated academics. They didn't include her in their conversations.

"I need to speak to you after dinner, Jimmy," Marigold said, unsmiling. She considered she needed to enforce her position, as her sense of entitlement grew.

"Feel free to speak to me now," James responded, a ripple passing over his face. "We all know you're here to discuss divorce."

Marigold didn't beat about the bush. "You're right," she said. "We can't possibly live together after this."

"Maybe you should speak privately, Jimmy," Royce suggested. Marigold appeared to be blaming James entirely for the breakdown of the marriage, let alone the sad fact she had miscarried their child.

James shook his head, his sun-bleached hair falling onto his forehead. It made him look very young, very vulnerable to Amelia's eyes. She had a bad feeling about all this, or more precisely about Marigold and her methods. Amelia felt she was allowing herself to be compromised. She could imagine how her being party to any form of deception would appear in the family's eyes. Especially Royce's. Her need for him to believe in her grew daily. She couldn't hide from her own heart. She was in love with him. Surely he had to be a little in love with her? Not just a man who desired a certain woman? She knew it was her move next. Marigold had to be made accountable for her actions. The truth could not be buried. The truth could help Jimmy. She could see how deeply disturbed he was. She suspected Royce did too.

"I want to be open about this," Jimmy was saying. "What is it you want, Marigold? Hang on, let me rephrase that. How *much* do you want?"

"The kind of money I'm entitled to," Marigold retorted, as if his even asking was a disgrace.

There was a moment of stunned silence around the table.

Sally surprised them all by speaking up. "Is that why you married my son, for the money?" she asked, knowing it could well be true.

"Not really," Marigold shrugged. "I fell madly in love with Jimmy. Lots of girls did. Even Melly was attracted to him."

Amelia sat back in her chair, knowing Royce's brilliant, dark eyes were on her. "I think we've heard enough of that, Marigold."

Marigold smirked like a cat finishing off a bowl of cream. "I know. It's utterly confidential. You're promised to your enormously *boring* Oliver, even if he is loaded down with academic achievements."

"You're like a broken record, Marigold," James groaned. "There was nothing in the world I wanted more than for Amelia to be attracted to me. We both know she wasn't. Not in any romantic sense, which is what you're determined to put about."

"That's okay. Jimmy. I forgive you." Marigold spoke as though she was the one to show maturity, not James. "What man could fail to be attracted to Amelia?" she asked, coyly.

"Let it go, Jimmy." Amelia met Jimmy's anguished blue eyes. "Please, Jimmy. Once started on something, Marigold persists. Best to let it go."

"Why are you here with her, Amelia?" Jimmy implored her. "You must know she hates you."

"How dare you!" Marigold lashed out in a big hurry. "Melly is my sister. We grew up together. I *love* her."

"Like hell you do!" James said. "You don't fool me anymore."

Royce intervened. "I think that's enough!" he said in a hard, emphatic voice.

James turned his head to appeal to his brother even though Royce was wearing his most formidable expression. "I'm sorry, Royce, but I have to say it. There's no love in Marigold's heart for Amelia. If someone told me Marigold had murdered her, I'd believe it. Marigold is a warped soul."

"If that were true, Amelia should know it," Royce said, bluntly.

Anthea gently touched Amelia's hand. "Why *have* you come, Amelia, dear?"

Why have I allowed Marigold to do these things to me, Amelia agonized. She was less free of Marigold and her schemes than she had ever been.

"I think a reply might be in order, Amelia," Royce pointed out in a dark-toned, challenging voice.

"Allow *me!*" Marigold cut in loudly. "Melly is my *sister*. Need I repeat myself? I think it very unkind of anyone who might doubt our closeness. Jimmy is plain raving mad. Melly is here to support me."

"With what?" Royce asked, sounding more questioning than kind. "Is she here as your lawyer? Divorce isn't Amelia's field."

"God knows she sees a lot of broken marriages, Royce," Marigold said. "We have that in common along with everything else."

Amelia sat, her beautiful face as still as a marble statue. "Believe it or not, I'm here for Jimmy's sake."

"And I need you." James flushed with gratitude, not afraid to admit it. The intensity of his adoration of Amelia was clear to all of them.

"See, what did I tell you!" Marigold threw up her hands as though neither Amelia nor Jimmy could deny her allegations. She gave Amelia a look so stark she might have been demanding an instant apology. "I'll need more wine if I have to listen to any more of this."

Royce ignored her. *It wouldn't take Marigold long before she would be able to down enough alcohol to keep a football team happy,* he thought.

It was Sally who spoke, her forehead creased in consternation. "I don't understand any of this. Amelia is here to support Jimmy?"

"Jimmy's a wimp," Marigold said, as though that explained everything.

"You're the only one here who thinks so," Royce told her coldly, trying to hold his anger in check. "Enough has been said tonight. None of us can overlook the fact you recently suffered a miscarriage, Marigold. It's a surprise to find you looking so *well*."

To James's mind, there was something unspoken in his brother's last remark. "Hey, what's going on?" He looked from his brother to Amelia, whose creamy skin had gone very pale. "Have I missed something here, Amelia?" He appealed to her. "I'm not that dense I can't see you have some anxiety of your own."

She knew she was showing outward signs of her inner distress. "You and Marigold should talk, Jimmy," she urged, accepting blame for putting herself in Marigold's trap. "I can't be a part of that discussion."

"But you allowed yourself to be dragged into it." Royce had been staring at Amelia with great intensity.

Again, Anthea clasped Amelia's trembling hand. "It's wrong to blame Amelia for any of this, Royce," she admonished her nephew.

"Is it?" Royce returned, a sombre expression on his face. "I think we all saw there was no love between James and Marigold at the wedding. When Marigold told him she was pregnant, he made the decision to marry her. The real challenge for us all is, do we believe Marigold was pregnant at the time of the wedding and subsequently miscarried?"

Amelia felt her entire body go cold. The fabric of their lives was about to be torn apart, left in a pile of tatters. How foolish it was to lie! One was always caught out.

Hot colour sprang into Marigold's cheeks. She gave a gasp of pure outrage. "Jesus!" she blasphemed. She put her hand to her throat as if Royce had attempted to strangle her. "Tell them, Melly," she snapped. Sainted Melly would be believed. "Tell them about my miscarriage. This is a bloody insult. I can't believe it of you, Royce."

"Believe it," he said.

Amelia remained silent. All the support she had given her adoptive sister over the years now seemed for nothing. Clearly, Marigold believed she would back her to the death. The moment had presented itself. She needed to be herself and suffer the consequences. She released a breath of total weariness. She was more disgusted with herself than Marigold, who truly lacked the sensibility to know better.

"This is *your* business, Marigold," she said, almost pitying her adoptive sister. "It would be a cruelty for Jimmy not to know the truth."

"Truth?" James cried, fully conscious now there was something very wrong. "What the hell is going on here?"

Amelia bowed her golden-blond head, revealing her vulnerable nape.

"Bitch! You bitch!" Marigold jumped up from the table, sending her chair flying. She was practically spitting venom. Marigold hadn't allowed for betrayal. It shouldn't be happening.

Amelia felt the terror of Royce Stirling's piercing black gaze. This was a nightmare. What would her parents think of her, of Marigold? Of the whole rotten business? Her whole body seemed to be losing strength, limb after limb. There was a mist before her eyes. Even then, she couldn't fail to see the naked hatred on Marigold's face.

Her heart stumbled. She couldn't get up. Instead, Amelia, for the first time in her life, fainted dead away.

When she came to, she was lying on a sofa in the living room. Anthea was gently stroking her face. "It's all right, Amelia, dear. Lie still for a moment, dear. Everything will be fine shortly."

"I've *never* fainted before," she murmured, embarrassed. "Not *ever!*"

"We could all see how distressed you were."

Amelia attempted to sit up. "Where's Marigold?"

Anthea's lips tightened as she eased Amelia back. "Apparently, she's locked herself in her room. I have a set of keys to every room in the house, but naturally we have no wish to invade Marigold's privacy. Both of you appeared desperate in your own way."

Amelia felt as though she was drowning in sadness. "All our lives, I've supported Marigold. I was the elder, the steady one. Marigold has always had problems that she hasn't yet resolved."

"Ah, yes," Anthea said, compassion on her thin, fine features. "I have no wish to offend, Amelia. I hold you in high regard, but I think with the very best intentions, you've helped Marigold get on with her tendency to destroy things. Destructiveness can turn into a habit. I've seen it first-hand."

Amelia swallowed down Anthea's analysis. She went to say something more, only she caught sight of Royce's tall figure. He moved across the room to the sofa where she lay, her hand in Anthea's, looming over them. "I'll get Amelia upstairs." He bent to speak quietly to his aunt. "I've moved her down to the west wing. I think it best. Marigold may well take it into her head to take her condemnations further."

"What a sorry, sorry, business!" Anthea said, shaking her fine head of silver-grey hair that had once been the Stirling golden brown. "How Marigold manoeuvred herself into our lives!"

"She did have help from Jimmy," Royce pointed out. "He too has gone off to bed. I'm going to suggest he go back to university next year. Finish his architectural degree. Jimmy has a lot of ability in that direction. Time he learned to use it."

"Amen!" Anthea spoke fervently. She moved off the sofa so Royce could scoop Amelia up.

"I can walk. Truly," Amelia protested. Lightning sensations were sweeping through her. She had to lean back against him, one arm around his neck. A pulse beat in her throat. She had lost the comb she had used to pin up her hair. It tumbled all over the place, golden strands clinging to his shirt. She felt so emotional she had to fight off the weakness that might cause her to burst into tears. "*Please*, Royce," she said.

He ignored her, the line of his clean-cut jaw tense.

She might have weighed little more than a child for all the effort it took him to carry her up the stairs. She supposed he was used to lifting far heavier burdens than her. She prayed the anger she could feel in him would ease up, that he wouldn't blame her too severely when the truth came out.

If it ever did.

Marigold was quite capable of sticking to her story even in the face of overwhelming evidence to the contrary. It was a dubious accomplishment. Her job had been to defend the indefensible. She hadn't been able to do it. The Stirlings would pull together as a family. The Boyd family would never be the same again. She remembered with a great sinking of spirits Marigold's expression as she had looked at her. It had contained as much hatred as anyone could muster. She thought the sheer awfulness of it would remain with her forever.

Chapter 6

Amelia slept deeply for five or six hours before she woke with a muffled cry. Where was she? She sat bolt upright in a strange bed. In the space of a couple of heartbeats, she oriented herself. Her hand moved to the right to turn on a bedside lamp. She could plainly see it. She hadn't awakened in pitch black, which had a calming effect. The radiant silver light from a full moon streamed across the room through the open French doors. It was a huge room like all the other rooms in the house. The first Stirling who had built the homestead evidently intended it to be his castle.

She looked around her. Dark walls, either dark blue or navy. White ceiling with a lot of white trim to relieve the colour of the walls. The decor spoke volumes. This was a man's bedroom, though it wasn't the sort of place a man could tramp around in. Certainly not with muddy boots. Or even lounge in. No time for lounging. There were huge blown-up photographs of thoroughbred horses on the walls. A striking portrait of a handsome elderly gentleman who looked very important was given pride of place. A large desk and chair filled one corner, with a tall bookcase alongside. Books everywhere. In a way, it was like travelling back in time. She wondered who the bedroom had belonged to. She knew it wasn't Royce or Jimmy.

She felt thirsty, in need of a drink of water. Anthea had left her a jug and a glass. She stood up in one fluid motion of long legs and long arms. She felt steady enough on her feet, but she couldn't ignore the fact she had fainted hours before.

Picking up the jug, she poured herself some of the contents, taking a large, refreshing swallow. The water was still cold. Even the breeze that moved the heavy white curtains was decidedly cool. She knew the desert and the desert fringe could get very cold after the burning heat went out of the sands.

Despite the size of the room, she was starting to feel claustrophobic. The drama of the evening was coming back to haunt her: Marigold had made a holy show of them. She most remembered the look of burning hatred on Marigold's face. There was something implacable about it. *It had to be some sort of chemical imbalance.* Marigold's behaviour had not improved with age as the family had hoped.

She remembered how her mother had once taken Marigold to a clinical psychiatrist after some incident had worried her. Marigold had been around eight at the time. Amelia would have been ten. It had been some behavioural problem that had given their mother concern.

Marigold's attachment to Amelia had always been strong, if not affectionate, she thought as she sat down on the side of the bed. Although she had tried hard to interest Marigold in any number of pleasurable pursuits, Marigold's range of interests had been and remained limited. She had not been a happy, smiling child, but then she had never been a child to join in even when her parents had been alive. The conclusion was reached Marigold might need professional help.

Marigold had undergone tests. The conclusion: She wasn't handicapped in any way. Marigold was herself. Marigold had lost both her parents at a young age. The loss would have affected her deeply. There were behavioural problems, certainly, ones she would probably outgrow.

Marigold was prone to blame the world for her problems. To a family who knew her well, to Jimmy, Marigold had "issues." That was as far as it went. The worrying thing was, the older Marigold got, the more exploitive she became. Marigold had exploited Jimmy. She had exploited Amelia, prevailing on her to return to Kooralya. If the concerning traits veered towards sociopathic, people Amelia had watched pass through the Family Court had exhibited similar traits. What was normal, anyway? She thought a "normal" person displayed kindness and understanding, a self-discipline one could see exhibited in even well-adjusted six-year-olds.

The large room suddenly seemed too confining. It was a familiar feeling. Both she and her mother were mildly claustrophobic. She remembered how she and her father had to escort her mother off the crowded plane they were supposed to be travelling to London on. Long flights still remained a challenge for both her and her mother, though flying to New Zealand three hours away was a breeze. She wondered if Marigold were fast asleep. She would have to confront Marigold in the morning. It had been a long, long road they had travelled together. They both needed to free themselves.

For now, she needed air more than anything else. She had often felt that way when staying in hotels: the pressing need for air.

Her satin robe lay gleaming across a chair. She picked it up, sliding her arms into the long sleeves. The gold cord was attached. She tightened it firmly around her. She would go downstairs. She could even step out into the garden. There wouldn't be a soul about. Work on a cattle station started at dawn and finished at dusk.

She wished she were at home, back in her apartment.

She went quietly down the staircase, compelled to hold on to the banister. The great house was never in total darkness in case some member of the household might want to get something from the kitchen or one of the other rooms. A few strategic wall sconces were burning. She didn't think she should try the front door. One of the French doors in the drawing room seemed the better option.

Moonlight was streaming through the tall stained-glass window that rose from the first landing. Even so, she wished she had a torch. The last thing she wanted to do was trip over the hem of her robe.

When she reached the bottom of the stairs, she realized a breeze was ruffling her hair. How odd! Where was it coming from? Should she call out and ask if anyone was downstairs? Who would be roaming around at just after two? An intruder never crossed her mind. No one came to the big house unless they had business there. Had she done the right thing, leaving her bedroom? As she moved across the central entrance hall, darkness was surrounding her. She was certain she wasn't alone.

"Is anyone there?" she whispered, though her voice was like distant thunder in her ears. She could feel the thump-thump of her heart. She had to calm herself. This was ridiculous. She was perfectly safe even if she believed the colonial mansion harboured a few ghosts. She wasn't a weak woman. She wasn't a nervous woman, but she was a highly imaginative one.

She listened for an answer, her ears strained. The night was the time for listening.

"Why wouldn't a witch be wandering around at night?" a male voice asked, before he came into view.

Her breath caught short in her throat.

"Royce?"

Life did have a way of presenting you with your hopes and dreams. Or *was* she dreaming? Even sleep walking. She moved on slippered feet towards the tall, wide-shouldered figure. He hadn't gone to bed. He was still wearing the same clothes he had worn at dinner, minus the light jacket.

"You startled me," she said. The breeze she had noticed was coming through an open French door in the drawing room. Part of her wanted to rush back up the stairs, only he exerted so much control, she stayed in place, staring up into his face. She didn't realize she had been holding her breath. "I wanted air," she said by way of explanation. "I couldn't sleep."

"Why would you?" he asked, sardonically.

"What do you mean? I don't understand."

"*I* do."

> *Tis the witching hour of night,*
> *Orbed is the moon and bright,*
> *And the stars they glisten, glisten,*
> *Seeming with bright eyes to listen*
> *For what listen they?*

"Keats," she said instantly. He spoke the lines beautifully, in his deep, vibrant voice. "Only it's well past midnight."

"Opinions differ over the witching hour," he said smoothly. "Witches can be active anytime between midnight and three. Extraordinary time for mere mortals to walk around."

"Is three the time *you're* hanging around for?" she asked. It seemed strange she should meet with him at this time of night. Morning, really.

"Ah, you're referring to the 'devil's hour'?"

"As I've said before, Royce, you do have a devil in you."

"Then we're well matched. Only witches can claim some *extra* power. It has something to do with the way they move," he said, as though he had given the subject long consideration. "Your walk has an element of *floating*."

"Years of ballet lessons," she explained. Both she and Marigold had attended ballet lessons for years. "Do you really think witches exist?"

The breeze through the open French door whipped a long strand of her hair around her throat.

Royce reached out a hand to tuck it behind her ear. "If there is such a thing as a witch, it's *you*." His voice had roughened slightly. "You have a power. I know it. You know it. You fascinate me."

She turned away from him, with a ragged sigh. "Ah, Royce!"

He caught her back to him.

"You're angry with me?" she asked, a tremble in her legs.

He put out an imperative arm, steering her towards the drawing room. "You wanted air. Let's go for a stroll in the garden, shall we?"

She was walking through a dream. "Aren't you supposed to start work at dawn?" she asked.

"Here's your chance to talk to me."

She took a deep breath. "What is it you want to know?"

He glanced down at her. "We might leave it for the time being. You did faint last night."

"A first." she said. This was unreal, the two of them walking in the gardens under a big silver moon.

"But not surprising after Marigold's tirade," Royce said.

"It was a very angst-filled night."

"Angst-filled? Is that a word?" There was humour in his voice.

"It is now."

"Let's walk on to the lake," Royce said, keeping her lightly clad body close to his side. He could smell her special fragrance above the myriad scents of all the shrubs and flowers.

"Why? Would you like to drown me?" She stared up at him. The moonlight was so bright she could see his expression clearly.

"No, Amelia. I'd like to make love to you."

"I'd say you're determined to."

"Would you stop me?" he asked.

"Would it be any use?"

"I'm certain I would have your consent."

"Is *droit du seigneur* your *modus operandi*, or is it your natural arrogance talking?"

"It's not as if you hate me," he said in a maddeningly reasonable voice.

"You're worth hating."

He laughed. "You don't mean that, Amelia. You're afraid of real involvement. Isn't that true?"

"As I've said before, that makes two of us."

"Perhaps. But the heart, the mind, and the body still want what they want, don't they?"

"I'm afraid so." She knew she wasn't safe with this man.

They had reached the lake with its stands of iris and arum lilies. The pure white lilies had a lovely incandescence. The full moon glittered on the water, for the most part covered in water lilies. The moon, like Narcissus, had found its own perfect silver reflection.

"Oh, look at that! Isn't that marvellous?" Enchanted, Amelia moved out of Royce's light grasp. "You've seen this before?" She turned her head to ask.

"Quite a spectacle, isn't it?"

"Magic! The illumination is quite unique. I think Anthea might consider getting Vernon to make a curve of the water lilies," She made a sweeping S-shaped curve with her hand. "As it is, the water lilies are growing right across the surface, clustered at the borders."

"You can speak to Vernon yourself, flower child!" he said with a faint laugh. "He's always open to fresh ideas. How are you feeling now? You said you needed air."

"I wasn't expecting anything like this!" She was transfixed by the beauty of nature.

He moved down to where she was standing. She was illuminated herself. "So I'm not the arrogant, insensitive man you claim I am?"

"No, but that doesn't mean I'm about to fly into your arms."

"However desperately you want to?" There was mockery in his voice.

"I think we should go back to the house." Before her legs gave way and she sank down onto the grass. This man had too much power over her. She was losing her direction, her sense of autonomy. She had played into his hands far too quickly.

"You fear our *enfant terrible* could be watching? She's a very odd young woman, your adopted sister. But then you know that?"

"I do." Things had gone too far to deny it. Marigold wasn't odd. She was dangerous.

"High time then you took a stand," he suggested crisply.

"No lecture, please, Royce."

"Of course, you're right. Who would want to spoil the magic? But you know how much she's hurt James. I don't want to see her hurt you." His tone had hardened. "I will do everything in my power to keep you from harm."

They were back inside the house, walking up the staircase together. Guarded with most men, Amelia had no defence against Royce Stirling. Her ability to think analytically about all male admirers was no more than an illusion with him. She was trying very hard to will away images of them in bed together. She felt the intense physical attraction between them. It hadn't gone through phases. She had been powerfully attracted to him on sight. Now her emotions bore a resemblance to a volcano about to erupt. She was engulfed by sexual heat.

Then there was the sense of inevitability. She *knew* what was going to happen. She foresaw the passionate intensity of it. Electricity was thrumming through her veins. It was a wonder she didn't burst into flame. The pedestal clock in the hallway had pealed three as they walked in. Three o'clock, the true witching hour.

Outside her door, they stopped. Royce wasn't moving away. She stood with her back to the door. "Good night." She had to rise above this great swell of desire. She *had* to.

"Good morning, don't you mean?" he said.

Neither of them moved. How long were they going to stand there? He might have already stripped her of her robe and nightgown, she felt so without the protection of clothes. And something else she had never felt. *Voluptuous.* She felt like a woman who was truly *wanted*.

Royce pulled her slowly to him. She had plenty of time to get away. She didn't even try. She was utterly magnetized.

He slid his elegantly shaped hands inside her robe. There were little callouses on the tips of his fingers that increased the erotic build-up. The shock and the excitement of it took her breath away. Anything could happen. She was allowing it.

"Do you want to go to bed with me?" she whispered, compulsion sweeping over her. She was no longer a woman in control of herself, able to retreat.

"Why, Amelia, I have," he answered in a low voice. "In my *dreams*." He brought up his hands to cup her breasts with exquisite gentleness. His thumbs worked her highly sensitive nipples through the veil of her satin gown. He caught her deep sigh. Her slender body fell against his as though it were impossible for her to stand alone. With one hand, he reached back to open the door behind her. It came open. He drew them both inside.

"This is what you want?" He took her shoulders, looking down into her face.

The question was both challenging and heart-stoppingly tender.

Amelia could only stare up at him. "It is." There was no blaze of victory in his eyes, only a burning desire to merge that matched hers.

What was the use of denying it, even if she could have cause to regret it? This man could seriously hurt her. Not physically, but emotionally. She knew she was jumping head-first into a fathomless chasm. Yet it didn't seem to matter. She was quivering all over as she waited for the longed-for touch of his hands on her exposed breasts.

His hands did envelop her breasts as though they cherished her womanliness, allaying in part her desperation.

She allowed him to pick her up and tumble her softly onto the bed.

"Whose room is this?" she whispered.

"It used to be mine," he said. "That's why I put you here. I wanted you in my bed."

"Do you love me at all? Otherwise, what is this storm all about?"

He bent over her, kissed her until she was clutching at the pillows.

"I thought you said I didn't know what love was?" he gently mocked.

"*Do* you?" She stared up into his brilliant, dark eyes that seemed to hold enormous delight at the sight of her lying in his bed.

He straightened, giving a slight shrug. "I wish I knew, Amelia."

She found herself understanding his answer. "I don't know, either. Is this some form of bondage, do you suppose?"

He laughed as he began to strip the clothes from his lean, darkly tanned body. He was tanned all over, she saw, unable to look away from the splendid male physique so unselfconsciously on display. "I do know you're perfect to me," he said, his broad chest expanding with his every movement.

"You mean physically?"

"No room for doubt. As for the rest! I won't let you leave until we clear a few things up." He moved over to the bed. "That's a beautiful nightgown." Her robe had slipped off unattended. His fingers trailed down her long neck. Her bones were so finely formed. Her skin was satin. Her beauty mesmerized him. "We'll leave it on for a moment or two."

To Amelia's surprise, instead of moving onto the bed beside her, he slipped to his knees. From there, he began to stroke her all over while her body rose and dipped under his exploring hands. She couldn't control the excitement that was quickly becoming too much to bear. She was drowning in sensation. There was such an ache in her lower body. For a strong man with strong hands, he had an exquisitely delicate touch.

"What about . . . Oliver?" he asked very softly while watching her face.

Her answer came on a whisper. "He's a good man." She had moved her body so close to the very edge of the bed, she could easily fall off.

"I'm sure he is." He bent to kiss the upper contours of her breasts.

"There will only be *one* man for me." She had to close her eyes before the tears that threatened started to flow.

"I know that, Amelia." He rose to his feet, folding her arms above her head. She lay quietly as he lifted her nightgown from her. "God, you're beautiful!" he said, brushing her hair, as satiny as her gown, off her face. "Beautiful women leave a man powerless." He said it with a kind of infinite sadness. "Why were you sent to me, Amelia?"

She was aware of the seriousness of his question. She held his eyes, her own full of light. "For *this!*"

The motion of her long, slender arms was unmistakable. She drew him down onto the bed with her. She felt his weight, the strength of his strong muscles as she ran her hands down his back. She felt his arousal, powerful with need. There were no misunderstandings when their naked bodies came together, only the overwhelming desire to mate.

How was it possible to fall in love at first sight? Amelia thought in a delirium of pleasure.

Giving her heart to Royce Stirling would leave her defenceless.

"What's the matter?" Momentarily he drew back as though he registered her every thought. "Well?" He held her head in his two hands, searching her eyes.

"Why is it you mean so much to me?" She made it sound as if her question was too big to contemplate alone.

"You think I'll hurt you?"

She was losing her breath. "You can."

"We're not having an affair, Amelia," he said, as decisive as ever. "It's far more than that."

She sucked in her breath sharply as he touched the tender, petal-soft flesh between her thighs, exploring with his fingertips before sliding them gently into her. "How can I deny it? Yet we hardly know one another."

"Trust me," he said.

She could do nothing less. If he did turn out to be her enemy, he surely wasn't now. The feeling of intimacy was a cause for wonder. The nakedness. The madly erotic tingle of skin on skin. Royce fell back into kissing her. Deeper and deeper until every single thought was wiped out by the wildest euphoria. She half-lay on him. He lay on her. She was letting him into her in all sorts of ways. He was moving urgently deeper and deeper inside her. Filling her as she had never been filled before. She had to shut her eyes tight against the explosion of excitement that had her thrashing beneath him. Incredible as it seemed to her, Royce Stirling was her lover.

Was it just a dream he could become her life? Fate *had* propelled them together.

"Royce. . . . *please,*" she begged after a while, her womb contracting near painfully, at the mercy of this relentless ecstasy.

Head over heels mad for her, Royce gave a near-tortured sigh. He gloried in the possession of this miraculous woman. He was on fire. He lifted his upper body off her, dipping his head, as he surrendered his seed deep inside her.

Eventually, both lay back, their bodies still shaking from the aftershocks. After tonight, neither of them would be the same again. Neither of them would be able to draw back.

Normally, she fell asleep within moments of her head hitting the pillow. Only the events of the evening, Melly's betrayal, played endlessly on her mind like a disc she couldn't turn off. It was betrayal really. She didn't deserve it. Melly had to be punished for her disloyalty. She didn't know exactly *how* in these moments, but she would find a way. One way did present itself. The Boyds, her family that wasn't, were very private people. In the old days, she could have cited Melly as the woman responsible for the breakup of her marriage. These days, unfortunately for her, divorce was no longer fault-based.

She had to apply for a divorce certificate. She knew that. She had to be separated from Jimmy for at least twelve months. No problem there. Jimmy wouldn't want to fight the divorce. The family would already be getting ready to fight *her*. She needed a blue-chip divorce lawyer. One wouldn't be hard to find. The Stirlings were loaded. Everyone knew that.

Her love affair with Jimmy mightn't have started in heaven, but it was going to end in hell if she didn't get what she wanted. Life had been cruel to her. Life had pushed her into the Boyd family as an adopted daughter. But the Boyds had already had a daughter. The perfect child.

Melly.

It kept on amazing her how easily people fell under Melly's spell. She had really wrecked poor, old Jimmy. Even that arrogant bastard Royce had been drawn to her whether he liked it or not. Settling Melly in a bedroom far away from her had been the last straw. She had opened her own bedroom door a crack, in time to see Royce Stirling's tall, commanding figure carrying Melly away down the corridor of the west wing with his stuck-up aunt closely following him up like she was Melly's new best friend.

She quickly gathered from the few words that were spoken that Melly had fainted. Serve her right! She knew for a fact Melly had never fainted in her life. How sweet it felt knowing fit-as-a-fiddle Melly had passed out.

She closed the door and went back to her bed, but she was still awake at dawn, her whole body awash with anger and resentments. At least she had dozed off some of the time. Threadbare sleep. She had to get to Melly before the household woke up. She staggered out of bed, grabbed a robe. Maybe Melly had locked herself in? She unlocked her own bedroom door, opening it slightly so she could peer out. That silly bitch Pippa could well be about. Pippa! Another one of Melly's conquests. Melly made friends endlessly. All *she* seemed to get was conflict. She had thought as long as Melly was near, she had the most loyal of supporters. Melly had taken to the "sister" thing like some sacred vow. There was great satisfaction in knowing clever Melly had been clay in her hands. There were all kinds of cleverness.

There was no one about. That would have put paid to her efforts. Still, she felt a touch nervous. She padded down the hallway on her small, high-arched feet, pausing for a moment to look over the gallery into the entrance hall below. Who did these people think they were? This wasn't a house. It was a bloody museum. She knew work on the station began at dawn. She knew pitiful old Jimmy was actually trying to do his bit.

The coast should be clear. Her head was throbbing. She looked sick. She felt sick. All Melly's fault. All Melly had to say was that she had arrived not long after she had miscarried her and Jimmy's child. Instead Melly, her rock, had betrayed her with her silence. She had even said she was there for Jimmy. If that wasn't an admission, what was?

Marigold had caught the expression in Royce Stirling's darker-than-dark eyes. Melly didn't know who she was dealing with? The master of all he surveyed no more trusted Melly than her.

She didn't dare call out in case heads started popping. Very quietly, she tried the brass knob on the bedroom door.

Eureka! Yes!

As silent as a thief, Marigold moved into the bedroom that just had to have belonged to a man. It couldn't have been more different to the feminine bedrooms she and Melly had been allotted. She looked towards the bed. It was *huge* by normal standards. She felt she would get lost in the bedsheets, it was so big. Melly was lying on her side, her body turned away, facing the open French door.

"Melly!" she hissed. Melly didn't stir. She felt like screaming. She tried again. *"Melly?"*

Amelia sat up with a visible start. "What the—"

Marigold was astounded. "I don't believe this!" she cried. "You're *naked!"* Modest old Melly didn't appear to have so much as a stitch on.

"For God's sake, Marigold!" Amelia felt a prickling of anger. She reached for the sheet, pulling it up around her. "What are you doing here?"

"What are you doing *naked?"* Marigold shot back, genuinely shocked. She had never seen Melly naked in her entire life. Even getting out of her swimmers, there had always been a towel to hand.

"I was hot," Amelia said languidly, still lost in euphoria.

"Hot? The bloody place is like a refrigerator at night." Marigold sounded almost hysterical.

"Would you mind passing me my robe?" Amelia wanted the subject dropped.

"What's it doing on the floor?" Marigold demanded to know, still sounding outraged and not moving an inch. "Have you got messy all of a sudden?"

"I could never be as messy as you." Seeing Marigold wasn't going to help out, Amelia slid out of the bed, making short work of shouldering into her robe. Marigold was staring at her as if she had either grown two heads or three breasts.

She had come briefly awake to feel Royce's swift kiss before he had left, and then she had fallen back to sleep again. Thank God he hadn't been lying beside her when Marigold had taken it upon herself to barge in.

Marigold now appeared murderously angry. "I hear you fainted?"

"Why do you make that sound like I near-impaled myself? Have you come to check it out? Ask after my health?" Amelia moved to pick up her hairbrush, running it quickly through her long hair that crackled with electricity.

Marigold's blue eyes continued to rake over her. "That was a rotten thing you did to me last night. You just switched off all loyalty."

Amelia tightened the cord around her robe before she turned about. "Talk to Jimmy, Marigold. Don't keep on lying and lying. I said I would back you if you told him you truly believed you were pregnant and begged for his understanding."

"What, and sacrifice a huge hunk out of my settlement?" Marigold cried as if Amelia were out of her mind. "I'll never forget your treachery."

"While pretending you haven't done a darn thing wrong? It's a great pity you can't recognize your own treachery, Marigold. Jimmy would never have married you had he known the truth. We both know he was desperately unhappy over what he thought happened to his baby. What you *told* him happened to his baby in your super-sensitive way."

"Impossible to tell him," Marigold dismissed that suggestion.

"You acted very badly last night," Amelia reminded her.

"Okay, I freaked out. No need to go on about it."

"You drink too much, Marigold. It has to stop. It's not hard to turn into an alcoholic."

Marigold laughed. "I'd expect that coming from a wowser." She moved right up to confront the taller Amelia, speaking through clenched teeth. "You weren't on your own last night, were you?" She grabbed Amelia's arm, a familiar storm gathering on her small face.

Before Amelia could formulate any sort of an answer, the door opened. Royce's voice rang out with authority. "Take your hand off Amelia, Marigold." It was a compelling order.

Only Marigold was burning with barely suppressed violence. She turned to face Royce's formidable figure. He was fully dressed in his working uniform, the cattleman's elastic-sided riding boots, jeans, blue denim short-sleeved shirt he somehow made look like a million dollars. "She's had Jimmy in here. I'm sure of it. Aren't you shocked?"

Royce's reply was sardonic. "What shocks me most is the way you're always attacking Amelia. Aren't you supposed to love her? I know she's overprotective of you, which I suppose goes with the territory. You were raised as sisters. To answer your question, I know for a fact James wasn't here with Amelia."

"How *can* you know?" Marigold's voice soared as she reproached him. "I told you Jimmy was her lover. Don't you feel the least bit disgusted?"

"I might if I had reason to be," Royce said. "I suggest you go back to your own bedroom, Marigold. I expect you'll want to return home as soon as possible."

"You bet!" Marigold confirmed. "But first, we need to have an important discussion." Marigold was clearly seeing herself as a woman with new found power. "Melly has been apologizing to me for the way she acted last night. She wants to tell you all about it."

Amelia didn't think she could take much more. Marigold had turned lying into an art form. "Just go, Marigold," she urged quietly.

Marigold stood there as though she wasn't about to do any such thing.

"What say we meet in my study around ten-thirty?" Royce suggested, a movement of his tightly muscled arm encouraging Marigold to move.

"I'll be there." Marigold jutted her small chin. "So will Melly. I might as well tell you, we'll be going home together. Melly's being here for me is a psychological thing."

"You haven't considered *you* might need some counselling?" Royce asked.

"I *am* under massive pressure," said Marigold, truly believing that to be the case.

"Breakfast might help," said Royce. "Come along now. Amelia needs to dress." His outstretched arm shepherded Marigold to the door.

"I'm going, damn it!" she burst out, crossly. "I'm going." She hadn't read His Lordship as a guy easily impressed, yet here he was acting as if Melly was his great favourite.

"Bravo!" said Royce.

It wasn't a compliment.

Chapter 7

Marigold made an excuse not to go down to breakfast. She requested a tray in her room. Bacon and eggs and all the extras, including chips. Marigold had developed quite a hearty appetite. Fearing she might pile on weight given her small stature, Amelia had once suggested Marigold start the day with fruit.

"Fruit?" Marigold had snorted. "All right for you. You're a bean pole. I need to keep up my strength." Marigold always acted as if a big ordeal lay ahead of her.

"I gather there's a meeting at ten-thirty?" Anthea asked, accepting another cup of tea from Pippa. "Thank you, dear."

"Another coffee for you, Amelia?" Pippa asked.

"That would be lovely, Pippa." Amelia smiled up at the housekeeper.

"A bit of a chat, is it?" Pippa had no hesitation asking as she refilled Amelia's cup.

"I'd say Marigold is about to pull rank," Anthea sighed. "She wants you leaving with her, Amelia?"

"We've been together nearly twenty years, Anthea."

"I know, dear. That's a very long time." Anthea's sympathetic touch on Amelia's wrist was as delicate as a butterfly's.

Amelia lowered her golden head. "I've always been there for her. Maybe not right now."

Pippa plonked rather than sat herself down with a cup of tea. A kindly-looking woman with a round face, Pippa always wore her sandy hair held back by different-coloured headbands. Pippa was the sort of woman who could inspire agoraphobics to take to the streets. "Mightn't it be the right time to let go, love?" she asked, gently.

Pippa had seen enough of Amelia's younger sister to consider her unstable. Pippa had to wonder what Marigold had been like as a child. A closet holy terror? *Both young women, however, were hiding a secret,* Pippa thought shrewdly. It had to do with Marigold's miscarriage. A terrible blow for Jimmy, causing him so much grief. On the other hand, Marigold was showing no sign whatsoever of inner devastation. Had Marigold truly lost the baby? If so, she had recovered extremely fast. Or had Marigold only been playing at being pregnant? Pippa had spent many an hour speculating. After all, there was no hard proof.

Anthea broke into Pippa's speculations. "I'm truly sorry to say this, Amelia, but I can't feel Marigold is a safe person to be around."

Who would after last night? Amelia thought. She had been suffering her own concerns. "I've made my decision," she said quietly, looking from Anthea to Pippa. "I'd love to stay on a little while if you'll have me."

Pippa drained her tea cup and then stood up as though reenergized. Time to clear the dishes. There was a big smile of relief on her motherly face.

"That's great news!" Anthea said, a light in her eyes. She and Pippa had been down on their knees nightly, praying for just such an outcome.

At ten-thirty a.m., Pippa wheeled a delicious morning tea into the study. The menfolk, Royce and Jimmy, had returned to the house. They needed sustenance. That was a priority, feeding the men.

The atmosphere was a bit like a trial with everyone waiting on a verdict, Amelia thought.

"Were you happy for even five minutes of our marriage?" Jimmy abruptly asked his wife.

"Jimmy, I *loved* you," Marigold turned on him a distressed face. She was dressed very simply that morning. Yellow cotton pants, oval-necked white cotton top. No make-up. She didn't need it. A light touch of peach lipstick. She looked more her age than she did in her newly acquired sophisticated gear.

"God help me, I'd never have known," said James.

"Let's all keep calm, shall we?" Royce advised. "You know,

Marigold, you and James have to live apart for at least twelve months before you can file for divorce?"

Marigold gave him a sorrowful smile. "That it should end like this!" she mourned.

"You could, of course, seek counselling," Royce suggested, nodding faintly at his brother. Probably to shut him up, Amelia thought.

That look of sadness and deep disappointment remained in Marigold's blue eyes. Amelia had to hand it to her. The world stage had lost a truly great actress.

"I'm going to say this once more," Marigold told them, a prophetess forced into repeating her prophecies. "I will never say it again."

"Can we count on that?" James swivelled to face his wife. He was fully aware of what was coming. The indictment.

It came.

"There were three in our marriage," Marigold said with the quiet acceptance of a martyr.

"Sounds familiar," James drawled. "Princess Diana?"

"She knew the *pain* of it!" Marigold was swift to respond.

"Only there *were* three in her marriage, Marigold," said Anthea, who continued to hold a very soft spot in her heart for the late princess.

Marigold turned to face her. "You don't know Melly as well as you think you do, Miss Stirling," she said respectfully. Although Anthea had asked Marigold a number of times to call her Anthea, Marigold continued to act as though that were tantamount to calling the Queen of England "Liz."

"Oh, bin it, Marigold," Jimmy implored, rubbing a hand across his face. "No one believes your story."

Marigold looked around, searching those faces. "I endured it as long as I could," she said, her eyes suddenly glittering with tears.

James jumped to his feet as though goaded beyond endurance. "I'm outta here!" he cried. "I can't listen to any more of this self-serving bullshit!"

"Sit down, Jimmy." Royce's voice held a good dollop of parental sternness.

James sat down again.

"Have you a settlement figure in mind, Marigold?" Royce asked, maintaining his air of civility.

Marigold spread her little hands, the nails painted post-box red.

"What the hell! Go for it." Jimmy shouted, indignation and despair written all over him.

Royce looked about to rebuke his brother, but let it slide. "You must have a figure in mind, Marigold."

"Jonty Martin got ten million dollars," Marigold said, naming a young woman recently divorced from her prominent wealthy husband some twenty years older. "The whole business was lurid, don't you remember? Really juicy stuff! It gave me something to go on. George Martin wouldn't have as much as you Stirlings. I sort of thought, twenty million?"

"Good grief!" Anthea sat back, as though in the presence of the most outrageous of blackmailers.

"You're joking! That's peanuts to you lot." Marigold gave her girlish laugh.

"That's it . . . sure?" Royce asked with no expression on his dynamic face. "Twenty million dollars?"

"Marigold!" Amelia groaned. She had run out of all patience with Marigold, who was acting like a stupid, greedy, petulant child. Was that what she actually was?

Marigold swung her head, breathing hard. "Do shut up, Melly. You know they've got it. You're the one who pushed me into this."

"Come on," Amelia shook her head "You have to stop this," she said, with what she hoped was the voice of reason. Marigold had to listen in her own interests. Not turn nasty.

"Twenty million dollars should keep you in dresses," Royce spoke in a considering manner. "Houses, cars, jewellery, handbags, shoes. It could even extend to a small yacht."

Marigold's pretty face broke into a smile. "I don't need a yacht. I get seasick. Just sick to my stomach. I'm not Melly the mermaid. Good at everything is Melly."

"And you find that hard to deal with," said Royce. "Only what we all want to know is . . . *did* you get pregnant?"

Marigold yelped. There was no other word for it. "Dammit, dammit, dammit!" She threw out a hand, an over-the-top gesture that knocked over her coffee cup. "You're calling me a liar now?"

"Leave it, Amelia," Royce said, as Amelia rose to pick the pieces of fine bone china off the Persian rug.

Amelia did.

"Why are you doing this to me?" Marigold persisted, a persecuted note in her voice.

"As I've explained to you before, Marigold, questions will be asked. Proof will be needed." Royce gave her a cool look.

"*Excuse me!* It isn't Elizabethan times, is it?" Marigold retorted, colouring up. "Proof of virginity. Proof of pregnancy? Ask Melly. She was there."

"You can't hide behind Amelia anymore," Jimmy said with a grimace of disgust.

"Melly is the true culprit in all this," vowed Marigold. "She knows the truth, but I see now she's trying to ingratiate herself with the family."

Royce broke in with great patience. "We're prepared to make you an offer of five million dollars, Marigold," he said. "I'd advise you to take it. That's around a million for every week of your marriage. I'd call that a good deal."

Marigold wriggled her bottom around in her chair this way and that. This way and that, as if it was impossible to get comfortable. Her breath came in a gasp of bitter disappointment. "How *mean* of you, Royce!" she said, huskily, genuinely fighting tears.

He looked less than contrite. "It's a considerable sum, Marigold. Had you and James had a child, it would have been a great deal more."

"We would have!" Marigold cried, over her tearfulness. "I'm going to consult a top lawyer. I'm warning you. I'm warning the lot of you."

"Ooh, look out, guys!" James cried. "This is the real Marigold bitching about everything in the most unethical way."

"Well, I for one, Marigold, have been on guard since I met you," said Royce, ignoring his brother's outburst.

"You should have been concentrating on Melly," Marigold blurted, belligerent to the end. "You can't rule her out of all that went on."

Amelia stood up purposefully. She'd had enough. She went to Marigold, placing a firm hand on Marigold's narrow shoulder, not for the first time in their lives. "Stop now, Marigold. *If you can.*"

"And you're gonna stop me?" Marigold challenged in an excellent parody of a gangster's moll.

"You need to give this offer very serious consideration," Amelia said, undeterred. She was debating dragging Marigold out of her chair, only Marigold had wrapped her arms around it, guessing correctly Amelia was about to yank her out.

"Some offer!" Marigold burst out, surprised and aggrieved. "I want to go home."

"I can arrange for you to fly out tomorrow morning," Royce assured her in an expressionless voice. "You can contact me when you're ready regarding our offer. You can have the money in stages, if you like, starting with your acceptance of our offer. This is on the understanding, of course, that the divorce proceeds as quietly as possible."

"I'm not agreeing to anything yet," Marigold retorted, as if the offer reeked of intimidation. "You all hate me, don't you?"

"Hate?" James scrunched up his face. "I don't hate you, Marigold. You're not worth hating."

Marigold jutted out her chin, her most marked mannerism when things weren't going her way. "What's wrong with this world?" she implored.

No one in the study appeared to have the answer when Marigold had wanted a free-for-all. They were all too damned polite.

"You're coming with me, Melly?" she asked, rising to her diminutive five-two.

Some expression in her blue eyes—the vision of a despairing eight-year-old, lying on her bedroom floor madly kicking her legs—tore the heart out of Amelia. "I'll see you safely home," she said. Her eyes went to Anthea, seeking to convey she would be returning to Kooralya.

"Thank you, Melly." Marigold whispered her gratitude, while Jimmy rolled his eyes.

"Keep hanging around with your little sister and you're just asking for trouble, Amelia," he said. "I couldn't even count on one hand the nice things she's said about you."

"Why?" Marigold stared at him with angry blue eyes. "Because I didn't have to. Melly's *perfect*. She's the only one who has ever worried about me."

"Not true, Marigold," Amelia said. "We all worried about you, your *family*."

* * *

Moments later, Royce signalled to his brother. "Ken Pearson will be arriving pretty soon. Bill can't handle everything. We'd better get back to the yards."

"If I had to stick around here with Marigold, I'd go totally insane," said James. "It's like being on a roller coaster."

"God only knows what you saw in her," said Royce. "Go on, Jimmy. Get back to work." Royce watched as Amelia shepherded Marigold out the door. He turned to his aunt. "Keep an eye on things here, will you?" he asked. "I need to speak to the vet, then I'm coming back to the house. Jimmy can hold the fort for a while."

"Count on me, dear," said Anthea. "Amelia can't free herself of the past overnight, Royce. She's protected Marigold all their lives. We have to accept that. But I believe Amelia when she says she will be loosening that bond very soon."

"What if it's unbreakable?" Royce glanced down sombrely at his aunt.

"You said that as if you really care about Amelia," Anthea asked.

"She *is* running away!"

There was such a dark, brooding expression in her nephew's handsome face, Anthea gave his arm a comforting pat. "No, my dear, she isn't. Amelia isn't a heartless, shallow creature like her adopted sister. Despite that Marigold is—and the best spin I can put on it is a *handful*—Amelia feels pity for her. It's not a case of unending devotion. It's Amelia's kind heart. That's why Amelia is accompanying Marigold home. I too am reluctant to let her go, but I trust Amelia. I know she will return."

"Then you're saying I *should* let her go?" Royce asked.

"On the condition she comes back? Yes, of course, dear." Anthea gave him a little hug. "Don't let me keep you. I want Amelia to meet Vernon. I'm certain they'll hit it off splendidly. Marigold won't want to join us. She's free to wander around as she pleases."

"Jimmy made a huge mistake when he married Marigold," Royce said, a bleakness in his dark eyes. "Now we all have to pay for it. That includes Amelia."

Back in Marigold's assigned bedroom, Marigold gave vent to her frustrations. "Five million and you agree with them?" She turned on Amelia, protective arms wrapped around herself.

"It's more than you deserve," Amelia said. "I think the family have come around to believing you weren't pregnant at all."

"So what? They can't prove it."

"I'm not a medical person, so I don't actually know. But you can be certain it will be checked out. Take the money, Marigold."

"How good of you to say so," Marigold scoffed.

Amelia turned to leave the room. "If you can't behave in a courteous way for the remainder of the time we're here, I won't go back with you."

It was obvious to Marigold that Melly actually meant what she said.

"Wait, Melly," she cried, the picture of contrition. "I'm sorry. Sorry. It will take me ages to get over this. I'm not strong like you. I'm still the messed-up little girl. I truly am suffering."

"You need help, Marigold," Amelia said. "We can find someone very good in that field." She still saw herself as having obligations. Marigold hadn't asked to be born bipolar or whatever she was. The right medication could well work miracles.

"I'm afraid I'll never be able to function properly on my own." Marigold flashed Amelia a sad smile.

It was a familiar lament.

"Have you ever really tried?" Amelia asked. "You can function when you're shopping. You can function when you're spending money."

"Well, I am smarter than most. I'm just wired wrong. I love you, Melly," she said, her tone sweetly girlish. "You're my soulmate."

"No, I'm not, Marigold." Amelia said. "We're two entirely different people, but I do care about you. I have worried so much about you. But you're a grown woman. The Stirlings are offering you a great deal of money. Life certainly won't be arduous. Take it. I'm going to join Anthea in the garden now. I'm so looking forward to meeting their master landscaper. You don't care to join us?"

"Bloody hell, no!" Marigold reverted to her alter ego.

"Then what *are* you going to do?" Amelia asked, with an unwanted softening for the troubled young woman she had always thought of as her little sister.

"Well, I'm going to call down for some ice cubes to put on my aching head, then I've got to pack," Marigold said, ticking off her fingers. "Afterwards, I'll wander around the place. I might come and find you after a bit. We could take a dip in that creek. It's running a bumper, I believe. Who could live in this godforsaken place?" she complained, although a lovely breeze fanned in through the open French doors. "The heat is unbearable. By Christmas, it will turn into hell."

Amelia spent a most enjoyable and calming hour wandering around the garden with Anthea and her brilliant mentor, Vernon, who had not lost his English accent for all the years he had spent in Australia. Amelia felt so comfortable with him she broached the subject of forming a long *S* curve in the glittering, still green pond instead of the massed flowering across the pond's surface. Despite the bright metallic sun, the glorious water lilies, blue, pink, and white, were blooming profusely.

Anthea spoke with delight, as she visualized the concept. "I think it could work, Vernon." She turned to him.

Vernon held up a hand. Dressed in a long, loose, khaki shirt and cargo pants, Vernon was a tall, upright, well-kept man in his eighties with a clipped moustache and copious frazzled white hair that stood up in a quiff that reminded Amelia of a cockatoo's. "Just let me think, ladies," he said, putting a hand to his deeply creased forehead. "Simple enough to do, of course, but rather more difficult to maintain. As you can see, the water lilies are thriving here. We can certainly form the long sweeping curve, Amelia, and it would look wonderful, but plants like to fight back. Still, it could be tried. We would then have to sit back and wait for the regrowth. It's bound to be within a few days."

"It was just an idea, Vernon," Amelia said, seeing the sense of what Vernon had said.

"A *good* idea, m'dear!" He smiled benevolently, something he didn't often do. "We can call it an experiment."

"Amelia flew to London to see this year's Chelsea Show," Anthea turned to her mentor and friend. It was very clear they were the greatest of friends as well as collaborators in Kooralya's gardens.

"Did you now?" Vernon showed his interest. "Not another flower show to match it," he said proudly.

The talk fell to the world-famous Chelsea Flower Show. Vernon, in another lifetime, had actually met the young Queen Elizabeth, an honour he had never forgotten. The three of them took a slow, rambling walk around the unconventional gardens. Amelia could see they had been planted by an expert with a superb design vision allied to the knowledge of which plants would survive the hot Outback conditions. Vernon and Anthea together had come up with the idea of the fascinating abstract metal sculptures that were strategically placed around the large area. *It wasn't the garden for classical statues anyway,* Amelia thought.

All the while they were touring, Amelia could hear the bright, rippling cries from the creek. The creek was omnipresent in the compound. Water had a magnetic power, its voice and the sound of the shifting currents. It would be lovely to take a dip. She had a vivid recollection of Royce's dark all-over tan. He had confirmed he had been skinny dipping in the creek since boyhood.

Marigold actually came out to join them as their tour was coming to an end. She wore an orange halter and white shorts. Amelia knew beneath the shorts was the other half of the bikini. Marigold obviously intended to go for a swim. She was swinging a beach bag, a towel draped over one arm that made that conclusion easy to arrive at.

"Hi, there!" she called in the friendliest fashion.

"It's my sister, Marigold," Amelia told Vernon.

"Of course. Jimmy's young wife. She looks like she's going for a swim," said Vernon, shading his eyes. "She doesn't look a bit like you, Amelia. And she's *tiny!*" Vernon had heard about Marigold, but he had never laid eyes on her.

"Marigold is Amelia's adopted sister," Anthea explained.

"Aah!" Vernon ran his fingers under his luxuriant moustache. "That explains it."

Marigold joined them, giving Vernon a fetching smile. "So you're the famous gardener?"

"Landscape designer, m'dear," Vernon corrected.

"I would have joined you, only I so feel the heat," Marigold said, puffing a little. There *were* circular spots of colour in her cheeks. She put an arm around Amelia and hugged her. "You'll join me for a swim, won't you, Melly? It's always better with you around."

"I don't have a swimsuit with me," Amelia said, none too happy about letting Marigold go off by herself. Unlike her, Marigold wasn't a strong swimmer.

"All taken care of!" Marigold beamed happily. "I have one in my bag for you. Do come, Melly. I'm *dying* in this heat." She hugged Amelia harder in case Melly tried to break away.

Marigold was doing an excellent job of playing her engaging young sister, Amelia thought, as Marigold continued to chat away.

"Perfect day for a swim in the creek," Vernon agreed. "Lord knows how many times I've cooled off there. So off you go!"

"I'll come with you," Anthea said. "I can sit on the bank."

"Goodness, who would ask you to?" Marigold exclaimed. "We'll be fine on our own, Miss Stirling."

Vernon looked much taken aback. "Aren't you being a bit too polite, Marigold? You're family now."

"I have so much respect for Miss Stirling," said Marigold, straight-faced and sweet-voiced. "It's the way I was brought up."

Amelia bit her tongue.

It was a beautiful spot. Pristine. The creek, refreshed and replenished by torrents of life-giving rain, had turned into a river that ran swift and deep. The sun flashed diamond patterns all over the surface. The water appeared sparklingly clean to Amelia's delighted eyes, with no odour other than freshness. Tall river gums grew on either side of its banks. Their forest-green lent the water its glittering, deep-green colour.

"Come on," Marigold urged, much as she did as a child. "It looks great!"

"Since when have you been so keen on a swim?" Amelia asked.

"Since I arrived in this bloody back of nowhere. Here, catch!" She withdrew a Moroccan-style print bikini from her beach bag and pitched it towards Amelia. It was one of Amelia's that had gone missing. For years on end, Marigold had liked to purloin objects that belonged to her sister. Lipstick, scarf, earrings, bangles. Nothing of any real value. Amelia had dismissed it as one of Marigold's odd little quirks.

Amelia immediately looked about her. No spreading shrub to duck behind. Where to change?

"Don't pretend to be so bloody modest," Marigold jeered. "You were stark naked this morning."

"Anyone would think it was a sin. Turn around."

Marigold laughed, but she did what she was told.

Amelia made short work of changing out of her clothes and into the bikini. She took time to fold her clothes neatly. Under her feet grew hundreds and hundreds of tiny purple wildflowers with silvery-grey leaves. They formed the prettiest ground cover. Crushed, the little flowers gave off an attractive light scent.

Marigold stood at the edge of the grassy bank like a young woman transfixed. She was staring down into the rippling, flowing water like someone contemplating drowning herself.

"Don't jump in, Marigold," Amelia advised. "There could be fallen branches, hidden stones, and some small rocks. Lower yourself into the water."

Marigold turned her fluffy blond head. "Your middle name should be 'Caution.'"

"I'd be happy with that. One of us needs to be cautious."

"I'm sick and tired of all this!" Marigold suddenly cried. She totally ignored Amelia's warning. She launched herself into the creek, arms raised, head-first as she used to dive into their home swimming pool.

Had she truly thought Marigold would take any notice of her? Her own entry into the creek was much less spectacular. Amelia had to sink to the bottom to find the sand, her toes curling into its thickness. The creek was deep, six feet at its borders, deeper towards the middle, but the water was so clear she could see no weed-strewn rocks, no fallen branches, no submerged logs. Warmed by the sun or not, the water on entry hit her as *really* cold. She surfaced, treading water as she looked up at the trees where birds, parrots from the flashes of brilliant colour, were dancing about in the branches, squawking at the invasion of their territory.

Pulling the pins from her long hair, Amelia let it coil wetly down her back. The chill was fast wearing off. She felt invigorated.

"I can swim rings around you," Marigold yelled at her, a silly taunt from their childhood. She was swimming about in a peculiar fashion that was almost manic.

Amelia didn't answer. What was the point? She was enjoying herself. So was Marigold, really, she thought. Marigold swam up to her. "You could get Jimmy if you wanted him," she said, blinking water out of her eyes. "He's always been mad for you."

"Do shut up. I'm enjoying myself."

"Only you don't want Jimmy, do you? You want Royce. He's the man for you."

Amelia didn't answer. All her pleasure in being in the water, in pristine bush surroundings, was about to be ruined. "Why do you do this, Marigold?" she groaned.

Marigold was now floating a few feet away. "Can't help it! I wish I could stop. I do!" She swam closer, splashing water at Amelia's face.

"*Why* can't you stop?" Amelia asked. She was slow to anger, yet now she felt a simmering burn. She retaliated, splashing back *hard.* She was raising twice the volume of creek water, chopping up the glistening surface.

Angered, Marigold made a dolphin leap, grabbing onto Amelia's long, wet hair.

"Stop that. *Let go!*" Amelia tried to prise Marigold's fingers off. It was surprisingly difficult.

"What if I don't want to let go?" Marigold was spluttering for air, yet she strengthened her hold on Amelia's wet hair, giving it a painful tug. "You're such a bitch!" She flailed out at Amelia's face, making contact.

Amelia was stunned. "Are you *mad?*" They had never struck one another in their lives.

"Could be." Marigold put a shushing finger to her lips.

"I don't think you know *what* you're doing." Amelia said, dazed by Marigold's action. She needed to put distance between them to scotch any further attempts. She was by far the stronger swimmer. She would swim a good distance down the creek, and then pull herself up onto the bank.

Striking out freestyle, she powered through the water like in her old days at school and university when she had been part of the winning swim teams. Things seemed to be going to hell with Marigold. It had to be dealt with.

Even at a good distance away, she could hear Marigold piteous cries. "Melly, Melly! Don't leave me. There's something in the water. Some bloody thing. It's got me by the ankle. Melly, help me!" Marigold's mouth opened as she gave a frightened scream.

What now? It couldn't be the Loch Ness monster. The creek had been safe to swim in for years and years. Marigold craved drama, even as a kid. Nevertheless, she did appear to be floundering. Immediately, Amelia changed course. There was little else she could do but go to Marigold's rescue. She was such a little thing. Such a tormented little thing. She had probably come into the world that way, spewing affront at doctors, nurses, even her mother.

All hands were needed for the job of rounding up the cattle, the cleanskins who were unused to any form of discipline, and herding them into the yards. It was a dusty, sometimes frantic operation, lassoing the bellowing calves, branding them, castrating the males, and then nicking ears for future identification. Bill Wiseman, Kooralya's long-time foreman, was busy superintending the operation, with the help of a half-dozen young aboriginal stockmen who knew the country, the animals, the plants, the trees, the seasons better than anyone.

Bill and his wife had a comfortable bungalow much like Vernon's, not far from the compound. Bill's wife, Maeve, ran the station store where the staff could buy just about anything they wanted; clothes, boots, towels, sheets, blankets, camp gear, magazines, books, and so on.

"You can give Bill a hand." Although Royce was a magnificent rider and James had his own natural style, Royce had elected to take the Jeep. "I'm going back to the house."

"But we've only just arrived." Worriedly, James searched his brother's face. "Is something wrong?"

Royce took off his Akubra, running a hand through his thick, dark hair. "I have a bad feeling about leaving the women," he said. "Amelia in particular. I've asked Anthea to keep an eye on things, but it could be asking too much of her. If I have any kind of a sixth sense, it seems to be working now."

"God!" James groaned, like a man carrying a great weight. "Want me to come back with you?"

Royce shook his head. He planted his Akubra back on his head and gave it a good twist. "Bill needs you. I shouldn't be long. I'll just check everything is okay."

James sighed deeply. "It's all my fault, isn't it?"

Royce laid a comforting hand on his brother's shoulder. "You couldn't possibly know what you had to know about Marigold. Amelia doesn't either. She's been making excuses for Marigold for the past twenty years."

"Marigold is four inches high. She's no match for Amelia."

Royce gave him a tense look. "Then you've got it wrong."

* * *

Royce parked the Jeep at the very foot of the short flight of stone steps leading onto the broad veranda and then into the entrance hall, something he rarely did. He had barely entered the house when Anthea came rushing into the hallway as though she feared something was amiss.

"Is Amelia with you?" he asked, his urgent tone matching the expression on his face.

"She was," Anthea answered, starting to feel real panic. "Marigold persuaded her to go for a swim. They've just left. I wanted to go with them. I said I'd sit on the bank, only Marigold clearly didn't want me there. Did I do wrong?" Anthea was wringing her hands.

It wasn't like Royce to panic about anything, but some big concern was eating away at him.

"It's okay," he said, his tone softening. He was aware of his aunt's sudden distress. "Don't worry. I'll find them." He turned rapidly on his heel.

Anthea ran after him. "Marigold would be no match for Amelia under any circumstances, my dear," she called.

Royce didn't turn back. "Jimmy said the same."

They were both wrong. Marigold had mental issues.

Amelia was swimming fast towards her sister. She couldn't just switch off caring about Marigold, no matter how badly Marigold behaved. It would take time, but she was determined to make the break. She would have to speak to their parents about getting help for Marigold. She needed therapy.

"I'm here. What's wrong?" she called as she stroked through the clear water.

"Something under the water," Marigold gasped in fright. Rivulets of water were running down her small, anxious face.

"I can't think what. A fish, maybe." Having said that, Amelia plunged deep below Marigold to investigate.

Nothing. Nothing that she could see.

Next thing she knew, Marigold was coming down on top of her, throwing her body at her, kicking out with both feet. It was as bad as having a rock thrown at her head. Amelia threw herself sideways, trying to rise up for air. Marigold caught hold of her foot, dragging her down again. Amelia's body shot out signals of alarm. It took ninety seconds to drown. What was going on here? Was Marigold trying to drown her? It wasn't possible. It had to be some manic game she couldn't understand. She drew on all her strength to kick free and rise to the surface. Her head completely out of the water, she drew in a shuddering breath. Her whole body was signalling physical and mental distress. It was a mad joke that had gone too far.

"Amelia!"

Royce was on the bank. He yelled her name, his voice ringing around the whole area, scattering the birds. She watched him yank off his boots and then he dived right in. He reached her in record time, putting a strong arm around her as if he intended to hold her tight forever.

It was Marigold's voice laughing a little wildly behind them. "Feel like a dip too, Royce?"

"Get out of the water, Marigold," Royce thundered at her. *"Out. Now."*

"Heck, we were only playing," Marigold yelled back. "What's your problem?"

"Get out or I'll drag you out," Royce said.

Neither Marigold nor Amelia doubted he meant it.

All three of them were on the bank. Amelia lay back motionless, trying to swallow her laboured breath. She needed to settle her nerves. Marigold, seemingly exhausted, was sitting on the sand, a slumped little figure like the wrath of God was about to come down on her. Royce stood over her. A man. A powerful man who clearly didn't like or trust her.

Amelia found herself flinching from what had just happened. Marigold hadn't been playing any game. Some part of Marigold had cracked. Amelia had accepted a lifetime of making excuses for her sister. As a family, they had all made innumerable allowances for Marigold, the sad, little five-year-old who had lost both her parents. Who wouldn't? Marigold hadn't been trying to give her a good fright. Yet how could Marigold have such a terrible desire to hurt her? What madness had got the better of her? Lacking a jealous streak, Amelia didn't fully appreciate how destructive jealousy could be, yet she saw it in the courts, day after day.

"What did you think you were playing at, Marigold?" she asked on a panting breath. Marigold's small face was red and moist with tears. She knew she had gone too far. Amelia put out a hand to Royce.

He passed her a towel. He was soaking wet, his shirt and jeans clinging to him, but he didn't appear to notice it.

"You started it," Marigold burst out. "You splashed so much water at me I thought I was going to drown."

"Don't talk rubbish," Royce told her curtly.

Marigold stared up at him. "It was a *game*, Royce. We always played games in the pool at home. I would never harm a hair of Melly's head. She knows that. How could you think I would?"

She scrabbled up. Royce helped her. She seemed to him like a child who had no real conception of right and wrong, only she was twenty-four. She was not a child younger than five or even seven, when a child was deemed to have reached the age of reason and could differentiate between right and wrong. As a woman of twenty-four, that made Marigold dangerous to others.

"I'll take you both back to the house," he said as though he didn't want to hear a word out of either of them. "I have to insist you stay in your room, Marigold. Anything you want can be sent up to you. Don't attempt to speak to Amelia. I've heard your version of what was going on here. I'll hear Amelia's. I'll tell you right now, I'll believe her story over yours."

"Well, you would, wouldn't you?" Marigold didn't conceal the effects of long years of resentment. "Why does everyone love Melly? Is it because love and Melly go together? She's so utterly selfless?"

"And you feel a powerful jealousy," said Royce.

Marigold didn't look ready to consider that one. "I wasn't plotting to hurt Melly, Royce," she said. "I love her."

"That's what you were demonstrating, was it?" Royce said, picking up his discarded riding boots. "Love?" His hair was already starting to dry in deep, thick waves that curled up at the nape. He raked his fingers through it, clearly troubled.

"Sorry, sorry, sorry, Melly," Marigold spoke like a severely reprimanded little girl. She put out her hand to take Amelia's.

For the first time in their lives, Amelia turned away.

Chapter 8

There was no quiet family dinner that night. All mention of the afternoon's upsetting incident was held back until after Pippa had served coffee. Amelia was feeling a tremendous unease. Jimmy was looking very unhappy.

Royce, on the other hand, looked formidable, a man on a mission. He was clearly determined to get to the bottom of exactly what had happened at the creek. He hadn't attempted to get Amelia's version of events. That would happen soon.

Back at the house, Marigold had claimed she was ill, yelling at Pippa, who had been sent upstairs to check on her. "Goddammit, I want to see Melly," Marigold had shouted. "What is this? Am I a prisoner?"

"Not at all, dear. We're anxious for you to rest."

"It's Melly's fault. I need you all to know that. I'm coming downstairs."

Pippa had stood firm, although she was a little wary of what Marigold might do, like throw anything to hand. The Royal Worcester Water Bearer figurine was far too close. As unobtrusively as she could, Pippa shifted it. "I'd advise you not to, dear. Mr. Royce won't take kindly to that. You're to rest. Lie back now."

They were gathered in the drawing room in a council of war. "I always knew Marigold might attempt to hurt you," James said, feeling great responsibility for his past misdeeds. "Hers aren't petty jealousies. There's something wrong with her. I did warn you. You didn't listen, Amelia."

"I did listen, Jimmy." Amelia turned towards him. "Marigold has always had her little problems—"

"Little?" James raised his eyes to the ceiling. "You know she tried to kill you."

"It took *you* time to see Marigold clearly, Jimmy," Amelia reminded him. "None of us are happy about Marigold's behaviour, but she's never been as bad as this."

"Are you saying Marigold has had some kind of a breakdown?" Royce asked sardonically.

"I think she needs therapy," Amelia said, feeling the full force of his eyes, brilliantly dark and alive. "For her own protection."

"And what about yours? At this point, you should acknowledge she was trying to drown you," Royce said.

"Dear God!" Anthea murmured. She was looking thoroughly appalled.

"I think she was trying to punish me for something, Royce," Amelia hit back. He was judging her and finding her wanting despite the intimacy they had shared, hungrily kissing and caressing each other for hours. This was something entirely different. Royce was a different man. She was another woman.

"She *was*," James agreed. "It makes me want to bawl my eyes out."

"Why does it have to be so hard to admit it, Amelia?" Royce asked her, as though her head wasn't on straight.

"I've never learned to hate anyone, Royce. But I could hate you!" she retaliated, her green eyes flashing in her pale face.

"For insisting you see the truth? Not only see it, but admit it before it's too late. Marigold's behaviour isn't slowing down, or improving as she matures," he said.

"I said she needs therapy," Amelia insisted doggedly.

"You are a very generous woman," Royce replied, his eyes on the pulse in the hollow of her throat. How many times had he kissed her there? Kissed the soft, warm velvety skin.

"What did you expect? Marigold is a very vulnerable person."

"A danger to herself and others. You in particular," Royce argued.

"That being the case, how can I let her return home unaccompanied?" Amelia challenged him.

"*I'm* still Marigold's husband," James broke in. The tension between Amelia and his brother was so palpable James felt like he could reach out and touch it. Following that trail, he realized Royce and Amelia were madly in love. *If Amelia should be one man's woman, who better than Royce's?* he thought. "I'll take her back to Melbourne," he said. "Marigold is my responsibility, not yours, Amelia. I agree, she shouldn't head off on her own."

"It's out of the question, Amelia, that you be left alone with her," Royce ruled.

"What could she do?" Amelia turned on him. "Bring down a plane?"

He gave a laugh that held not a trace of humour. "God knows! But I'm not prepared to take the risk." His black brows knitted. "I suppose there's never a good time to be away from the station, but I've come to a decision. I'll fly you home myself. That's you, me, Jimmy, and dear little Marigold, who is showing every sign of not being normal. I'll leave it at that."

"When would you leave, dear?" Anthea asked, looking at him with anxious eyes.

"First thing in the morning would be a good time. I'm quite sure Marigold will be desperate to shove off. She's even deluded enough to think Amelia will be going alone with her."

"I will need to speak to my parents," Amelia said. "No use persisting with *our* parents. For all the love and attention that was lavished on Marigold, I'm beginning to believe she was born with little or no capacity for loving."

"There was no baby, was there, Amelia?" James asked, very quietly.

She drew in her breath, her expression deeply sad. "No, Jimmy. It may or may not have been the worst kind of lie, but Marigold swore to me she truly believed herself pregnant."

"You don't *really* believe that, Amelia?" Royce challenged.

"You want me to give in, don't you?"

He held her eyes. "I want you to admit the truth, Amelia."

"Of course I believed her. I didn't think she could be so dishonourable." Her hands fluttered up helplessly. "Okay, Royce. She *lied.*"

"Because she knew I would marry her," James said. "It's as simple as that!"

"We leave in the morning," Royce said. "Pippa can let Marigold—child-woman, lying-woman, unstable-woman—know. I understand she requested steak and chips, chocolate mousse, and a bottle of the best pinot noir for dinner. She got the first two. A pity, but the best pinot noir was denied her. She was granted a glass of chardonnay. I believe Pippa cited health and safety reasons," he added suavely.

After a long meeting with Amelia's parents, who had tried hard to absorb her news, Marigold was admitted to a highly regarded private psychiatric hospital, ostensibly for observation. Jeremy Boyd had met them at the airport, for the first time establishing contact with his adopted daughter's husband and his very impressive brother, Royce Stirling. Both men had courteously declined to come home with him. They took themselves off to a hotel. Royce Stirling had told him he had to return to Kooralya as soon as possible. That would be first thing the following morning. He would collect Amelia on the way. She had promised his aunt Anthea she would be returning.

Amelia hadn't contradicted him. She *had* promised Anthea, after all.

At first, Marigold had flown into a rage, saying she wasn't going to any hospital. There was absolutely nothing wrong with her. Melly had provoked her into a temporary madness.

Clearly, there was a lot wrong. Marigold needed help. It was the Boyds' responsibility to see she got it.

"I'm afraid for her," said Amelia's mother. "I seem to remember now Grace had a strange aunt or a cousin somewhere in the background. It's all so sad."

Both parents had thought it unbelievable Marigold and James Stirling had been married only a few weeks before they had acrimoniously split up. Knowing Marigold as they did, they did not believe her story. Marigold had always wanted to find not her prince, her soulmate, but a rich husband. The script had been written countless times over.

James didn't fly back with them. He stayed on in the city to consult a divorce lawyer. Jimmy had at long last seen the error of his ways. He had been incredibly stupid and careless allowing Marigold into his life. He had always known she didn't love him, or even like him for that matter. He had long been a target for young women looking for a well-heeled husband. He felt better now. Lighter. He hadn't lost his first child as he had believed.

His first child had never existed.

He wasn't happy inside, but his heart was lighter. Royce had suggested to him he pick up his architectural degree. He had another two years to go. He had done well at university until he had let *la dolce vita* take him over. For him, more like the road to ruin.

He had found deliverance. It was a good feeling. There was something else he planned to do. Something he should have done years ago. Charlene had meant a good deal to him in the past. Why not the future?

When they were finally back on Kooralya hours later, they were greeted by Anthea and Pippa with beaming smiles no one could fake. Pippa actually leaned her sandy head on Amelia's shoulder. "I'm just so happy to have you back."

"You're going to have a bite to eat, Royce?" Anthea asked, staring up at her tall nephew. Unlike the rest of them, he wasn't smiling. He looked preoccupied. "It can wait, Anthea. There are things I have to attend to. I can't leave it all to Bill."

"Not for ten minutes?" Anthea persisted, aware of the constraint between Royce and Amelia.

"I have to go. The keys in the Jeep?"

"Yes, dear."

Royce turned away. He didn't say anything to Amelia. She didn't say anything to him. Amelia understood he wasn't happy with her. That was the way things were.

The three women stayed together all afternoon. There was much Amelia had to tell them, much they deserved to know. Anthea and Pippa didn't make her feel guilty about anything. They understood her whole story and Marigold's darkening mind. All three prayed that with the right treatment and the right medication, Marigold would learn how to quell her angers and resentments and master her self-absorption. There was a good chance it could happen. Many deeply troubled people had reshaped their lives once they sought help.

There were no romantic walks in the garden that night. Royce had to make up for lost time. He had correspondence to attend to. He took himself off to his study. He had been invited by the government to be part of a trade delegation to Japan, Australia's biggest trading partner. He had represented the national Cattlemen's Union on former occasions. Japan trusted the high quality of Australian beef. That would be a talking point on the agenda: The Japanese population had taken more and more to beef. Supply had to keep abreast of demand. Kooralya beef was very highly rated. The station had hosted Japanese businessmen in the past.

Amelia didn't see Royce again until mid-morning of the following day, when he returned to the house to come in search of her. At the time, she was in the kitchen with Pippa. When she heard Amelia often didn't have time to make herself a proper evening meal, Pippa had elected to show her how to put a few healthy, tasty dishes together in less than twenty minutes.

Royce interrupted their session as Pippa launched into how to prepare pan-fried pork wrapped in prosciutto with sage and capers to be served on English spinach.

"Course, you could use veal, dear, but I reckon pork is tastier."

Both looked up in surprise as Royce walked into the huge farmhouse-style kitchen that had every possible amenity. On occasions, with the help of staff, Pippa had had to cater for large numbers of people, guests, or visitors. Pippa wasn't a home cook: She had learned to become a chef.

"Sorry to interrupt the cooking lesson, ladies," Royce said, smooth as dark molasses. "I thought I'd show Amelia more of the station. That is, of course, if she's willing to come with me?"

"Would she say no?" Pippa looked shocked by the very idea. Royce Stirling was king in his own kingdom.

"I would consider it an honour, Royce." Amelia gave a mock curtsy.

"So you do!" Pippa exclaimed. "Aren't you two friends anymore?" she asked, looking sharply from one to the other.

"We haven't known one another long enough, Pippa."

"Then let us try to change that," Royce returned smoothly.

"You're funning, you two, aren't you?" Pippa looked from one to the other.

"Whatever gave you that idea?" Royce gave Pippa his infrequent but very beautiful smile. "Come on, Amelia. I don't suppose you ride?"

"As in horses?"

"Of course, you wouldn't need to." He made it sound as if she were all the poorer for not being able to ride a horse.

Amelia shot him a sparkling glance. "I'm confident I can stay on."

"Course she can!" Pippa patted Amelia encouragingly on the back. She thought Amelia was having Royce on. "Well, on your way. I have things to do."

They walked in near-silence to the stables where Eddie, the head stable boy, was in attendance.

"Mornin', miss." Eddie smiled, admiring the beautiful young lady's golden-blond hair that shone like a halo in the sunlight. Aboriginal people, particularly in the Centre, had blond hair, straight or curly, which gradually darkened with age.

"Good morning, Eddie, isn't it?" Amelia returned the wide friendly smile. Eddie was obviously happy with his lot in life.

"Eddie Emu, miss." He looked up at Royce. "Goin' ridin', Boss?"

"Marika, Eddie." Royce named his favourite. "We need a nice, safe horse for Miss Boyd here."

"Then you'd really like Toby, Miss," Eddie said, eager to please. "He's an old codger, but he's still a sound ride. Won't try to throw yah off or anythin' like that. Come this way and I'll introduce you."

"After you, Amelia," Royce said with a wave of his hand.

"You are the very worst of men," she said, hanging back and keeping her voice to a murmur.

"I should say we're evenly balanced."

It sounded familiar.

They followed Eddie into the stables down the line of neat and tidy well-kept stalls. Eddie walked with such a bounce in his step that she wanted to bounce along with him. Amelia knew aboriginals were wonderful natural dancers.

The horses were immediately alerted. Horses were very sociable animals. Even when they had plenty of space to roam around in, they usually stuck together for companionship, a good gallop, and games. Now all of them, some seven in all, were showing their curiosity by poking their heads out so they could see what was going on.

Toby, a bay gelding with a white star between his gentle eyes, greeted them with a soft whinny. Amelia could see at this stage of his life, Toby would be a fine mount for a beginner who couldn't handle a spirited horse. She petted him for a while, and then began to move on, stopping in front of a very elegant young horse that had to have Arab blood. There was the dished face, the large eyes, and wide nostrils to go on. It was a small animal compared to Toby, who had to stand at least 17 hands high. All thoroughbreds in the world had some Arab blood in them, but this horse hadn't been bred for the track. It was domiciled on Kooralya.

"Not that one, Missy," Eddie said, a mix of laughter and surprise in his voice. "That's Tamara. Tell her, Boss."

"Isn't there a Royal Arabian stud called Tamara?" Amelia asked.

"You're very well informed, Amelia," Royce said. "Morocco. I've been there. Tamara is a Moroccan Arab."

"She's gorgeous!" Amelia said warmly. "I love horses, the most beautiful, the most elegant of animals. I've even been a racegoer in my time, though only a token gambler. Oddly enough, I won more than I lost. I took time out to study the conformation of the horses."

"A lawyer and you'd know about that?"

"Don't be such a snob. City folk know about horses, the things to look for when evaluating a horse. Race horses are natural athletes. Everything hangs on the conformation. I don't have to tell you that."

"You're a bit of a dark horse yourself," Royce commented with a humorous twist to his handsome mouth.

"I had a great-aunt who was quite a famous show jumper. As a matter of fact, she won major competitions in Europe in her day." As she spoke she was petting Tamara, who had no objections to her, her smell, or her touch.

"Name, please?" Royce asked.

She turned to him, with sparkling green eyes. "Ann Hardy."

Royce frowned. "Ann Hardy is your great-aunt?" Anyone in the horse world had heard of Ann Hardy, the Olympic contender on a number of occasions.

"*Was*," Amelia said. "She took a bad fall when she was holidaying with friends in England. A freak accident. Her horse balked at a fence."

"That happens," Royce said, grimly. He knew all too well.

"She never fully recovered," Amelia told him, a sad look in her eyes. "She never rode for the last ten years of her life."

"I'm sorry to hear that." Royce's voice held all the feeling of a born-in-the-saddle horseman. He looked Amelia right in the eye. "I expect you're hiding the fact you're a competent rider. Miss Boyd?"

He was deliberately trying to stir her. "Well," she shrugged in a mock self-deprecating manner. "Not as good as you, of course."

"Of course," he agreed. "I'm still not going to allow you to ride Tamara."

"You mean you're going to try to stop me?" Colour washed into her creamy skin.

He arched an eyebrow. "Not *try.*"

Eddie the stable boy was agog at this exchange. Who argued with the boss?

"Get Eddie to saddle up Tamara," Amelia said, a touch of hostility in her voice. "Let me walk her around the courtyard. If you're not satisfied I can ride her to your exacting requirements, I promise to dismount immediately."

Eddie stared up at Royce. "Boss?" There was a whole world of respect in the word. Eddie would not disobey the boss under any circumstances.

"*Do* it, Eddie," Amelia said, before she could stop herself. She couldn't tolerate controlling men. She couldn't tolerate men who threw a long shadow.

Eddie didn't move until Royce nodded.

Amelia already knew Kooralya was as big as some European countries. It would take ages to see over it. Necessarily by Jeep. Having passed her riding test with flying colours, warmly congratulated by Eddie but not by the boss, who just briskly nodded his satisfaction, they headed towards the hill country, an area Amelia particularly wanted to see. Anthea had told her all about the aboriginal rock paintings on some of the cave walls. Many people had heard about Kooralya's rock paintings, but none had been allowed to photograph on site. It was aboriginal hallowed ground. The family and the aboriginal people who lived on the station or roamed it didn't want the ancestral rock paintings exposed. They had to be protected at all costs. Amelia fully appreciated she was being granted a great honour by being allowed to see into the caves. Apparently, she had displayed the right reverence.

The horses cut a great swathe through the fields of wildflowers, which were already starting to wither under the hot sun. Judging from the gradual build-up of clouds in the silken opal-blue sky, Amelia thought there could be an afternoon storm.

"Endless storms pass over without a single drop of rain materializing," Royce told her. Though his dark eyes revealed little, he admired her prowess in the saddle. She had confided that her mother, a

good weekend rider, had initially taught her to ride before she had
joined a very good pony club.

"At one time, I was horse mad!"

No wonder the problematic Marigold had said there was nothing
Melly couldn't do.

"It must be immensely frustrating," she said, referring to the cloud
build-ups that yielded not a drop of the all-important rain.

Royce shrugged. "It's the way it is."

"How Irish is that?" she said with a laugh. She tipped back her
blond head, protected by the wide-brimmed cream felt hat Anthea
had found for her.

It had never looked remotely as good on anyone else, Royce
thought. "I don't know what you mean."

"The Irish coined that phrase," she said.

He nodded. "I believe the Irish also have a saying, 'God does take
an interest in your prayers, but most times, He can't be bothered.'"

"It must seem that way to too many people," Amelia said. "Even
God must be flat-out tired of coping with our manmade ills and disasters."

"Governments of the world are taking too long to get their act together," Royce said.

They rode on.

For the time being, in perfect harmony.

The late spring rains had performed their miracles all over the station. Amelia had found the wildflower display phenomenal. Kooralya
was in fine condition. Great flights of tiny wild birds native to Australia, the budgerigars, green and gold, streaked ahead of them in
near-perfect squadron formation. Their speed was fantastic, a blinding sheet of emerald.

"I'm fascinated by the birdlife on Kooralya," she called to Royce,
riding a short distance away. She had marvelled at the huge flocks of
pink and grey galahs, the cockatoos, the millions of red-beaked
finches, not to mention the predators: the hawks, the falcons, and the
wedge-tailed eagles with their nests in the hill country.

She was enjoying this shared experience immensely. There had
been no bucking, no rearing, no prancing, or signs of ill humour from
Tamara. The filly too was thoroughly enjoying her outing with her
female, sensitive-handed rider.

"The desert and the desert fringe are among the hottest, driest places on earth," Royce said, "but it's alive with birdsong and these extraordinary flyovers we're looking at now."

Amelia stared up. "The leader or leaders have to make an amazing decision where to land."

"That's right." Royce was impressed. Miss Amelia Boyd, lawyer, might as well have been born on the land. "They descend as one. Thousands and thousands of nomadic birds arrived here with the rains. God knows where they all come from, but they always turn up to breed in our lignum swamps. I have to tell you, the lignum swamps are barely accessible."

"Where the pelican builds his nest?" Amelia turned her head to smile at him.

Once more, he surprised her.

> *The horses were ready, the rails were down,*
> *But the riders lingered still—*
> *One had a parting word to say*
> *And one had his pipe to fill*
> *Then they mounted, one with a granted prayer*
> *And one with a grief unguessed*
> *"We are going," they said, as they rode away—*
> *"Where the pelican builds her nest."*

Amelia's heart gave a little excited leap. She decided to contribute some remembered lines of her own.

> *No drought they dreaded, no flood they feared,*
> *Where the pelican builds her nest.*

"We all learned that poem in primary school," she said.

Royce looked away into the distance. "My mother used to read it to me," he revealed, most unexpectedly. "I couldn't have been more than three or four. She had a wonderful way with children. Visiting kids, relatives, loved her. She was a fine, natural rider like you. Maybe a shade reckless, which I suspect you are. She could lift everyone's spirits with a smile. My father was a *hard* man, immensely abrupt. No one stood against him. There were no bedtime stories for a small son. No poetry readings around him. No pat on the head. God forbid a kiss goodnight. No kisses, yet he was *passionate* about my mother. It was primitive. So wildly pronounced. He thought he owned her."

Tears shimmered in Amelia's eyes. She blinked them back. "When you are blessed with children, Royce, will you find the time to read to them?" she asked.

He flicked her a wry glance. "I have to find a wife first."

"Answer the question."

"It would have been good to have my mother around."

"Maybe she didn't desert you at all, Royce." she said gently. "You never have bothered to find out the real story."

"Maybe I can recruit you to do it," he returned, in a hard, mocking voice. "Let's move on, Amelia."

"Yes, Boss."

Amelia remained quiet as requested. To this day, talk of his mother disturbed him. *He and Jimmy must have had a brutal time of it with their dreadful father,* she thought. Her own father was the loveliest father in the world. She adored her parents. She was one of the lucky ones. Both Charles Stirling's sons had responded to their father's harshness differently. It had toughened up Royce. It had almost broken Jimmy.

The hills were close. "Opal matrix was found up there from the early days," Royce told her. "My father gave my mother a magnificent opal necklace and earrings as a present. The opals came from Kooralya. I suppose if we ever had the time, we could go prospecting again. I'm certain the opals are still there, ready to be mined. My father was always plying my mother with jewellery. He insisted she wear the jewellery he gave her to dinner, even when they were on their own, and certainly whenever we had guests, like the family friend she ran off with."

"And never married. He could simply have been helping her escape."

"No, he was in love with her. They all were."

End of story.

Only there was a story begging to be told.

Amelia found this ancient land breathtakingly beautiful in a wild, mysterious way. Apart from the extreme remoteness, the great width and openness of the desert that gave the spirit a great sense of liberation, the stark contrasting colours played a big part. There was the dense furnace-red of the soil, the gold of the dry but luxuriant grasses, the lacy leafed trees and the pure white boles of the ghost gums under the intense blue of the sky.

Even the passing storm clouds pierced by shafts of gold had such a depth of colour, silver-grey, ink black shot through with plum-purple, acid green and streaks of a pinkish-red. A pair of emus, which thrived in the Outback, had joined them. Probably mates, male and female. The taller bird stood some two metres in height, the other noticeably shorter. In size, emus were second only to ostriches in the bird kingdom. They were pacing along on their ungainly long legs, yet Amelia knew emus were incredibly fast. They could reach speeds up to sixty miles an hour in short bursts. They looked amazing in their natural habitat.

Gradually, the flightless birds got bored and moved off. The bigger bird, the male, was making loud drumming sounds. A prelude to mating?

"'Emu' isn't an aboriginal word," Royce turned his head to her, having noted her interest in the birds.

"I always thought it was."

"It comes from the Portuguese *ema*. It means large bird. Even aboriginals stuck to it. Our aboriginal people have lived in peace in this land for upwards of fifty thousand years. My family took up this vast holding a little over one hundred and fifty years ago. Just think of it! In the main, we treated our original landowners well."

"I'm glad to hear it. A treaty with the aboriginal people, the first landowners, is long overdue."

"Agreed. Still, may I point out, Miss Boyd, it was the white man who pioneered this land and built up the nation's great stations both for sheep and cattle? Aboriginal people may respect the white man. I hope, know, they respect me, but I can never become a blood brother. That's out of the question."

"Yet this is your kingdom?" She glanced over at him, so straight-backed in the saddle. No slouching. Not for one minute. He looked so splendid he took her breath away.

"A king without a queen," he said, dryly.

"What about Charlene? I would have thought she was eminently suitable."

"She is. Charlene is my friend. I wouldn't like to lose her friendship. I wouldn't have made love to you if I were committed to Charlene, Miss Boyd. I'm not. At one time, she and Jimmy hit it off very well. They were, as they say, an item. Charlene has the qualities Jimmy needs to keep him on track."

Amelia shot him a surprised glance. "I could have sworn she was madly in love with you. It looked that way at the wedding."

"Sorry to be so ungallant, but that's wishful thinking. I suspect Charlene's mother, Stella, had something to do with it. Why go for the younger brother when the older brother is the bigger catch? I know the thinking."

"So what happened? This is very surprising news. Jimmy never mentioned a Charlene, though I did see him dancing with her at the reception."

"Jimmy had it drummed into him he couldn't compete with me. I told you. Dad was a cruel man. Never physically cruel. No beatings. Maybe the occasional biff I managed to duck. He couldn't have taken me on from about age sixteen. I was already over six feet. It was more prolonged mental cruelty. Instead of staying here and maybe getting engaged to Charlene, Jimmy took off. I find it very hard to be angry with him."

"Then you should understand how I found it very hard to be angry with Marigold."

"Except James has a conscience," Royce pointed out shortly. "It gives me no pleasure to say it, but I believe Marigold was born without a conscience. Not so extraordinary, when you think about it. Thousands and thousands of people—men, women, children—have been born without a conscience. They're indifferent to the feelings of others. You must know that's true."

Amelia swallowed. Essentially, she did. "We're hoping Marigold will benefit greatly from therapy and medication."

"There's always hope." Then after a minute's reflection, he said, "Some people have great inner strength. Take Pippa. She won't have told you this. None of us can bear to talk about it, for that matter, but Pippa's husband, Cliff, was gored to death by a bull."

Amelia was aghast. Pippa was always so cheerful. "Here on the station?"

"Where else? Station work is dangerous work. We've had broken legs, broken arms, serious kicks in the head, all over the body, fatal riding accidents, but nothing as bad as losing Cliff. He was a great bloke."

"When was this? I'm so sorry."

"Eight years ago. Pippa is a stoic. We took her into the house. Anthea looked after her until she got back on her feet. I wouldn't mention it to Pippa. If she wants to talk about it, she will."

"Of course. I wouldn't dream of bringing up such a painful subject. Nothing is ever what it seems, is it?"

"No. Many, many people experience tragedy. Just as many don't talk about it. Stirling men, the ones who went off to war and managed to come back, never spoke about their experiences."

"Too horrific."

"Our young men, all the young men particularly of the New World were innocents. Some thought they were going off to a great adventure."

"And perished. War is such wanton destruction. Men blindly obeyed lunatics like Hitler and Stalin and their modern counterparts. Human life was treated as meaningless. Yet instead of hating it, men live to keep wars going. Men, not women. Out here, thank God, war seems so very far away."

"We're blessed," said Royce, "but if our country and our allies are threatened, we fight."

"Let's pray it doesn't come to that. Some men must hate life if they're so ready to die. I would hate to think peace was just a fantasy."

"Men also fight wars for justice," Royce said.

The long line of hills to the west and northwest was so lit up it was as if gigantic coal fires were burning inside the caves. When they arrived at the base, they took the saddles off their horses and then left the animals loosely tethered to one of the ubiquitous mulga trees. The broad, deep, overhanging rocks acted as a shelter from the hot sun. A little grass and vegetational cover, a sprinkling of wildflowers, were growing in the shade for them to munch. It was clear these two stable-mates were happy together.

"Take my hand and don't let go." Royce ordered.

"What do you think I'm going to do, race you to the summit?" She gave him a scornful look.

"I wouldn't put it past you." He put out his hand.

She held on, her fingers laced through his. It came to her like a revelation: She would go anywhere with him. To the ends of the earth.

"Watch where you put your feet," Royce called back to her, his tone imperative. "Hug the wall. Don't look down. It seems we're going to get a shower after all."

"Told you."

A sea of shadow was descending on them. As yet, no drops of rain had fallen, but Amelia could smell it. She was happy. So happy. Madly in love. Was it wise to be?

They barely made it into the chosen cave before the rain fell down. There was no violence to it, no strong whistling wind, but if one were standing out in it, one could get very wet. There was plenty of light inside the cave, which was great. Amelia had expected deep gloom. Brilliant spears of lightning were shooting down from the heavens to fork into the receptive earth, increasing the amount of light.

"Will the horses be okay?" she asked, concerned they would be frightened by the bluster.

"They're used to it," Royce said. He watched on while Amelia stared all around her, From her expression, she was caught in a spell of wonder. It gave him immense pleasure that she felt such kinship with this ancient land and all it had to offer. Not everyone felt that way.

Amelia tread carefully over the bone-dry pale yellow sand. It was thick and crunchy underfoot, deep and clean. No lizards ran hither and thither, for which she was thankful. The interior was the land of the lizards: the great perenties, the giant goannas. The roof of the cave soared to about ten feet at the highest point. She looked up. The ceiling and the sandstone walls were covered in all manner of drawings.

"Oh my gosh!" she murmured, as prayerfully as if she were in a cathedral.

"Quite something, aren't they?" Royce said. "These are the best and the clearest of the drawings. They may not be the oldest, but they are plenty old enough."

"They're fantastic!" Her eyes swept around her. Normally, she would have felt a bit claustrophobic, but not here. Not in this place. Not here with Royce.

The grace with which she moved and acted, as always, had a powerful effect on him. In the strangely eerie light, her beautiful skin had a lambent quality, like the lustre of a pearl. These caves were sacred places. Ancient meeting places. He had known about the caves all his life. He would never have been allowed to see them by his father, only his mother. He had ridden out into the great landscape one afternoon when his father was overseas on business. Those were the times when they all had freedom from his endless brutal remarks and piercing scrutiny.

He would have been seven or eight. His mother had been his touchstone. It was Amelia who had turned the key on the lock on all these memories of his mother. Amelia didn't speak to him as others spoke to him. She was her own woman. They were on an equal footing. After his traumatic childhood, he firmly believed men and women should be partners; equals. For all that, his closest women friends continued to act as if he were somehow their superior, the alpha male. He had grown impatient of that.

Inexorably, he had to question his own behaviour. For all he appeared to show little in the way of emotion on the surface, his emotions ran very deep. His mother, the woman who had given birth to him, who had appeared to have loved him as much as he loved her, had run away and abandoned him, was *still* his mother. Some families were safe sanctuaries, where members could turn to each other for love, for support, for comfort.

Other families were battlegrounds. He had to acknowledge his family had been the latter, only it had been his father's behaviour that had accounted for most of the unhappiness and discontent within the Stirlings. They were many accounts of happy times under his grandfather, his father, and the father before him. Happy photographs, letters, snapshots. There was plenty of evidence his ancestor Captain Richard Stirling had been a fine man who had bound the family, his workers, and the aboriginal people on the station into a cohesive whole.

"This is the giant Rainbow Snake, isn't it, Royce?" Amelia called. Royce was standing still near the mouth of the cave. He hadn't joined her. "These undulating coils? There are stick figures caught inside the coils."

He could hear the excitement in her voice. He closed the gap between them. He had been deliberately keeping some distance in an effort to tamp down the strength of his feelings. He wanted to take hold of her and pull her into his arms. He wanted to lie down with her on the sand, watched over by the ancient erotic drawings on the cave ceiling.

"The great Rainbow Snake," he confirmed, stuffing his hands in the pockets of his jeans. "*Wanambi* to the desert people. The Rainbow Snake is a terrifying and powerful snake hundreds of feet long. Whenever Wanambi was angered, which was often, he used to rear up into the sky. There he was even more powerful. Wanambi could wreak punishment wherever he pleased. He could stop the rains. He could cause the drought. The desert people believed he lived on earth at Uluru, Ayers Rock. Yet they didn't fear Uluru. They love it. It's their most sacred place."

"I've never been there," she confessed, suddenly feeling a sense of shame she hadn't made the pilgrimage to the Centre. So many did, and reported on its wonders.

"Yet you've been all over Europe?" Royce said.

"I'll get there," she promised, on the defensive.

"You will. I'll take you."

She dared not look at him, such was the effect of his closeness to her. "These images are magic."

"They are."

"A bit spooky too. The Rainbow Snake looks like it's moving. Surely that's not a crocodile there?" She pointed to a creature executed in ochres with a broad primeval snout and a long, upturned tail.

"Don't they call Australia 'the land where time began'?" Royce asked of her. "That *is* a crocodile. Ancient aboriginals might have seen them here. When our continent broke away from Gondwanaland over 100 million years ago, the Centre was covered by a vast inland sea. An American team in the 1930s from Harvard discovered a fossilized head over six feet long of *Kronosaurus queenslandicus*, a fearsome predator. They shipped the great hunk of dynamited rock containing the skull back home. It took them twenty years to get it out."

"Good grief! So the early explorers set out in search of the great inland sea and found nothing but sand. Imagine how they felt!"

"They should have asked the aboriginal people," said Royce dryly. "Even if they had to use sign language. The aboriginals had a 50,000-year start. Captain Sturt set out from Adelaide, Oxley from Sydney, Leichhardt's from Brisbane. Leichhardt's expedition disappeared into the interior, never to be seen again."

"I know. We learned the tragic stories of our early explorers at school."

"Sadly, most of them came to a very sticky end. Man can't live without water. They had hoped to find it."

Amelia began to move about in an effort to break a mounting tension. Whatever he said, however much he appeared to condone her actions over Marigold, she knew he didn't really trust her. Desire her? Yes. But there could be no real bond without trust. It was easy to pick out the warrior's spears in hand, the kangaroos, the emus, and a goanna as big as a crocodile. She lifted her blond head to stare up at the ceiling. It was covered with stick people, clearly delineated as male and female. Many appeared to be on the verge of having sex. Most were actually conjoined. The ancient drawings were so graphic, her whole body flushed. The male buttocks were as full and rounded as any ancient Greek statue, the women's breasts upthrust, pointed.

"Men and women have been making love since time immemorial," he said, with a hint of mockery in his voice.

She didn't answer.

A strong wind full of raindrops suddenly blew into the mouth of the cave, startling her. "Perhaps we should go." It was the oddest thing, but even to her own ears, she sounded out of breath.

"It's still raining," Royce pointed out.

"I'm more afraid of you than the rain."

There, it was out!

"Works both ways, Amelia," he said almost gently. "It appears we don't trust one another enough."

"It's because you have such a suspicious nature," she accused.

"It's difficult not to be suspicious with some people," he said mildly.

She met his dark, mesmerizing eyes. "I've told you almost from the moment I met you that I played no part in the breakup of Marigold's and Jimmy's marriage. Jimmy only fancied he was in love with me."

"He didn't fancy it, Amelia. He was. He is."

"He'll get over it. He will."

"Not if he comes back here," he said crisply. "Well, not for some time. Because *I'm* not letting you go."

Her heart fluttered so strongly she had to put her hand to it. Even her hand couldn't still the flutter. "Do you really think I'm going to fall into your arms?"

He gave a brief laugh. "A dangerous question. I'd say it was inevitable. Some things just *are.*"

"What? A blessing or a curse?"

"Neither seems to exist for me," he said, almost to himself. "What I feel for you is something quite apart."

"A quirk of fate? Karma?"

He put out his hands to cup her upturned face. "Tell me this, Amelia. When you first saw me, did you feel a sense of recognition?"

She wasn't about to lie to him. "I felt overwhelmed." Hadn't her heart taken off like a rocket? "Yet you looked back at me with barely concealed hostility."

"It went beyond you, Amelia," he said. "In a strange way, you reminded me of my mother. Bewitching women, a man like me would say. Women who capture a man's heart, his soul, his imagination, and never let go. Do you think I don't understand Jimmy's fascination?"

"That's all over with." She shook her head, in the process freeing it from its long, smooth coils.

"Yes and no," he replied in an ironic voice. "Beneath the surface, feelings always flow. Jimmy will move on. He may even connect with Charlene again. That would be a good thing. Charlene is not a predatory woman like your adopted sister."

"Wouldn't you prefer to believe I am too?" There was a kind of despair in her voice.

"No. You're beautiful," he said, grasping a fistful of her glorious hair. He was burning for her, burning to take her in his arms.

"So it all comes back to Frances, your mother?"

"I wonder if she *ever* loved my father? I can't imagine how."

"Your father was a very handsome man. He was heir to a great station. Your mother may well have fallen in love with one man and then found he wasn't the man she thought she'd fallen in love with at all. Why don't you ask her? Or have you decided you never will?"

"I know what I've decided," he said. "I want *you*" It was true. If he only admitted it, he cried out for her. Really and truly cried out for her. His enchantment was absolute. The weakness he had despised in some men, including his father, now extended to him.

"You want to make love?" she asked, huskily, her heart swelling with desire.

"God, more than anything else." The days and the nights were starting to feel endless without her. He wouldn't tell her that. Not yet.

"Desire and love can be polarized, Royce. Men have their . . . needs . . . but . . ."

He kissed her midsentence, cutting off her voice.

It was a kiss so deeply passionate, so ravenous Amelia was left breathless unable to swiftly recuperate. He hadn't appeared to move at all, yet he had full control of her swaying body.

Holding the whole luscious length of her against him was not nearly enough for Royce. The ache, the longing had to be appeased.

She felt his hand move to unbutton her shirt.

"You can stop me," he murmured in a hypnotic voice.

Not when his hands were radiating such heat.

The first button, the second, the third, the last, and her cotton shirt was hanging open, exposing her undergarment, a flimsy cotton and lace bra. There was a kind of tantalising terror in sexual excitement. It was agonizing and blindingly blissful at one and the same time.

"Say the word," he invited, in one smooth movement reaching back to unclasp her bra.

"So I can topple into your arms?"

"You *are* in my arms." Now he was easing first her shirt then her bra off her.

"Could I make you pregnant, Amelia? You must tell me."

He looked and sounded utterly serious, as he should. "Would you want our child?" she asked, knowing how terribly upsetting the whole topic of pregnancy had been.

"You know the answer to that." He had to express what he felt. He bent to kiss her beautiful, generous mouth. He wanted all the time in the world with her,

"As I know how to protect myself," Amelia told him, gently

drawing back her head. "No, you can't make me pregnant, Royce Stirling. Not today. Not tomorrow. Not until *I* say. Do you suppose the ancient spirits will be happy about our making love here?"

"I don't see why not." He began to unbuckle her soft leather belt. "We are ourselves, Amelia and Royce. We are them. We are everyone. I think I've been waiting for you since the day I was born."

There is a corner of heaven on earth.

It's reserved for lovers.

Chapter 9

A melia called her parents when she got back to the city. She had total respect for them, love, admiration. When they were all together, it was like being under a protective shining light. Her mother invited her to dinner that evening, as Amelia knew she would. There were so many life-changing decisions to be made. She needed her parents' approval.

How Marigold was faring would be one topic of discussion. Amelia had tried to put out of her mind what she believed Marigold had attempted to do. Had she been successful, Amelia would be dead and Marigold would be locked up in some psychiatric unit of a jail. None of them—not her, not her parents—had rushed to blame. There were people like Marigold in the world. She had grown up under their roof. All three genuinely cared for her. All three continued to pray Marigold would respond to proper treatment.

"I've been assured Marigold is responding well," Ava Boyd, said. "She doesn't want to see any of us at the moment, but apparently she's behaving like a model patient."

"Let's hope it lasts!" Jeremy remarked in a dry voice. He knew enough to know how the worst criminals could behave like model citizens if they could turn it to their benefit.

"So what is *your* big news? I know you have it." Ava turned to her daughter. They had almost finished a delicious dinner. "You're in love, I take it?"

"Mum!" Amelia's voice wavered. "How do you know?"

"Mothers are very intuitive people. Apart from the fact you're looking positively glowing, you spent your vacation on Kooralya station. Obviously you enjoyed it there."

"It was wonderful. The Big Sky Country. Channel Country is a revelation. The wildflowers were out after all the rain. A glorious, unforgettable sight! I have photographs."

"And I've seen Royston Stirling," Ava said, with a mischievous gleam in her eyes. "Very impressive. I simply put two and two together. It is Royston, isn't it?"

"You certainly didn't let *me* know, Ava." Jeremy spoke as if she had somehow betrayed him.

Ava reached out to pat her husband's hand. "There was a reason, darling. Marigold caused such pain in the brief time she was with James Stirling, it could have rubbed off on Amelia."

"It did," Amelia confessed, nervously twirling her wine glass. Her father wasn't on side like her mother, leaving her with a sudden frisson. "Marigold actually told Royce I was Jimmy's 'golden enchantress.' It was a term he apparently used. He even used it when he told his family he and Marigold would be getting married."

"And the minute Royce laid eyes on you, he *knew* you were the golden enchantress, not the bride-to-be?" Ava guessed correctly.

Amelia nodded. "That's exactly what happened. Jimmy's behaviour didn't help. On the very eve of the wedding, he begged to kiss me."

"You didn't let him?" her father asked, looking quite scandalized. "What sort of man does that?"

"Dad, what is it?"

"You're such a level-headed young woman, Amelia. A lawyer!"

"Even a lawyer can make mistakes, Dad." Amelia turned imploring green eyes on her father. "It happened because he looked so sad."

"Sad? Good God, Amelia!" her father exploded. "Why wouldn't he be sad, marrying the wrong woman?"

"Well, he wasn't going to marry *me*. I had no romantic interest in Jimmy. He was my friend. He knew that."

"James took advantage," Jeremy Boyd said. "I know all about your mother's and your tender hearts, but really! James Stirling went through with the wedding because he believed Marigold pregnant?"

"Jimmy loves children. He will make a good father."

"He has a lot of maturing to do before that," Jeremy responded severely. "At least there's some honour in telling Marigold he would marry her."

"You'll like him, Dad, when you get to know him better."

"Will I indeed!" Jeremy grumbled, shaking his handsome head.

"They'll never get the truth out of Marigold," Ava broke in. "The last time I saw her, she was still maintaining she had lost the baby."

"There *was* no baby," Amelia said. "Or I'm 99.9 percent sure."

"There *had* to be a baby for James Stirling to marry her," Jeremy said. "Is he a complete fool? Didn't he check it out? I've made it my business to find out all about him. He's one of those 'Another champagne, Charlie!' types."

"Oh, Dad! Jimmy has reformed. He's getting back on track. There will be a divorce."

"Have you ever!" Jeremy spread his hands. "How long were they married? Five minutes, ten?"

"Let's forget about Marigold and James Stirling for the time being," Ava said. "We want to hear about *you*, Amelia. What are your plans? I'm assuming you have plans?" Ava raised her finely arched eyebrows.

"It's as you suspected, Mum. I love Royce. He loves me. For both of us, that means total commitment."

Jeremy, for once in his life with his womenfolk, looked about to hit the roof. "You love Royce. This man you hardly know. The man we don't know. He loves you. I can understand that. What about your career, Amelia?" Jeremy asked. "You have a very bright future. Are you going to throw that away to go live in the back of beyond? Just about as far from your mother and me as you can get? I mean, *is this it*?" Jeremy Boyd was clearly upset. It must have seemed to him like the old life was gone forever. Vanished.

"Calm down, darling," Ava said, in her soothing voice, knowing her husband doted on Amelia and couldn't face the thought of her moving so far away. "Let's go into the living room."

"This is *my daughter!*" Jeremy cried, not about to be soothed. "Isn't that true? My daughter. Your daughter. Our precious daughter. Our only child together. She's so clever!"

"You're going to have to remember, Jeremy, you passed on your cleverness to her. I'm absolutely certain Amelia can turn her cleverness to account. Now I've been doing a spot of detective work."

"*W-h-a-t!*" Jeremy, the brilliant barrister, managed to croak the single word.

"I know for a fact the Stirling fortune is spread over many enterprises. They've long been diversified. The grandfather, Sir Clive

Stirling, was a top-notch business man. Apparently so is Royce. The Stirlings have a finger in many pies. They have a team of accountants, solicitors. You might remember, my darling," again Ava patted her husband's hand, "Amelia studied accountancy as part of her degree."

"So?" Jeremy Boyd couldn't have looked testier. He had been seized by upset.

"Our daughter could prove very useful to the family businesses. Amelia will find a way. We haven't raised a young woman who is prepared to sit back like a Jane Austen character."

"More like being told to get out there and help muster the cattle," Jeremy huffed.

"I daresay she can fit a bit of mustering in. She's a splendid rider, thanks to me."

"What you're saying doesn't solve the many problems for me, Ava," Jeremy told his wife sternly. "I don't know this young man. We barely said hello, though I grant you he has presence. And he's very courteous. But I can't help feeling Amelia is *rushing* into things." He put great emphasis on the word.

"*We* did," Ava gently reminded him. Her father hadn't approved of a young man who could end up prosecuting criminals.

"We were madly in love. I still am."

"So is our daughter with her Royce."

Jeremy wasn't mollified. "When it comes to who is marrying our daughter, I have to tell you *both*, I'm very, very old school. It's been an unfortunate start with Marigold acting so badly. There's another worry. You were complicit to a certain extent, Amelia. You should have contacted us. We would have come home."

"It is as I said, Dad. It wouldn't have changed a thing. Marigold had arranged it that way. She only told me she was pregnant on the eve of the wedding. I believed her. Jimmy believed her."

"Let's face it. She's a pathological liar," Ava gave a heavy sigh.

"This is something entirely different, Amelia." Jeremy maintained. "I know you want your mother and me to support you. We always will. You know that. But first I need to have a long meeting with this Royce. I'll know whether he qualifies as a suitable husband for our beloved daughter. I can assure you of that."

Amelia leapt up from her chair, going to her father and flinging her arms around his neck. "He will, Dad. He *will!* I promise."

Jeremy accepted his daughter's hug and a kiss on the cheek. "We'll see about that. I have to tell you, I didn't see this coming."

"Me either," Amelia confessed." It was love at first sight, Dad."

"Your father knows all about love at first sight," Ava smiled. "Don't you, darling?"

"We didn't get to be married, Ava, until I had satisfied your father I would be able to support you in the manner to which you were accustomed. He gave me quite a grilling. Were he here now, he would agree with me."

"Dads generally do," said Ava. "Let's have dessert in the living room. I whipped up some chocolate truffles. We can have them with coffee."

"I'll help you, Mum," Amelia said, keeping an anxious eye on her father.

If she married Royce Stirling, it would be the break-up of their old lives. That she would be living so far away was a major part of it. At the moment, her father was acting as if he had forever lost her. That would *never* happen. Royce was a stranger to her parents. Her mother apparently had seen enough of him to understand how the bond between her and Royce had been so swiftly forged. Her father was yet to be convinced . . .

Amelia already knew where Frances Stirling lived. The deep rift between Royce and his mother seemed to her like an open wound. Wounds could be healed if mother and son were able to breach the huge gap.

Amelia had seen sadness in the beautiful portrait of the young Frances, soon to marry a most unsuitable man. Had her parents pressed her into it? It happened all the time, parental pressure. Charles Stirling would have been considered a great catch with a most prestigious, landed name. Royce had lost his paternal grandparents, but his mother's parents had never spoken to their daughter again after the divorce. Incredibly, they had taken their son-in-law's part at the time, or actually, they had taken their son-in-law's version of what had happened. Their daughter had cruelly abandoned both her husband and their child when they adored her and she had everything a woman could want. Not long after the very public acrimonious divorce, they had gone to live in Spain. The whole family was fractured. The fractures had never healed.

Amelia continued to go into work. She had cases that had to be settled. She scheduled an appointment with her father. Even *she* had to make an appointment. Her father's time was precious.

He looked up the minute she entered his spacious office. "Is everything okay, Amelia?" he asked, searching her face. "Please, darling, come and sit down."

"Thanks, Dad." Amelia took the chair opposite. "I won't disturb you for long. I just wanted to tell you I'd like to fly to Adelaide to see Royce's mother, if that's okay with you."

Jeremy frowned. "They're estranged, aren't they? Have been since he was a boy. Your mother has been busy filling me in. It must have been very hard for a child, losing his mother like that. Your mother's far-flung sources have told her Charles Stirling was a very hard, unlikeable man. A very possessive man. No one dared look sideways at his beautiful wife."

"I think she was frightened of him, Dad. I think that's why she ran away."

"Your mother would never have run anywhere without you," Jeremy pointed out.

"I need to hear her story, Dad," Amelia persisted. She was used to persisting and ferreting out the truth.

"Surely it's Royce who needs to hear her story?" Jeremy said.

"The way things are, I believe he needs a go-between."

"And he asked you?" From his expression, her father definitely did not approve.

"No, he did not."

"Then he may not welcome your intervention, Amelia. I gather this is a very sensitive matter?"

"I'm prepared to take that risk."

"There would be *no* risk if he truly loves you," Jeremy pointed out.

"No risk." Amelia was able to smile. "Maybe a few cross words. If I'm going to marry Royce, I can't allow this situation to go on. I could never be parted from you and Mum, but then you've been the most loving supportive parents. Royce had a totally different upbringing, with a very harsh father who burdened him from boyhood with massive propaganda."

Jeremy gave it a moment of quiet consideration. "I see that. He had to get his son on side. By the way, we received an email. Your

Royce will be flying in next weekend. He wants to visit. He wants to speak to me. I hope it's to ask your hand in marriage."

"He's a fine man, Dad. Everyone on Kooralya looks up to him. He has earned everyone's respect. He is not his father. He even looks like his mother. It's Jimmy who most resembles the Stirlings physically. Their aunt Anthea is a wonderful woman. We've become great friends."

"You love the place, don't you? Not everyone does. The heat, the isolation, the droughts, the floods."

"The Outback has tremendous mystique, Dad. When you're free, you and Mum have to come for a long visit. You know what they say: 'If you never, never go, you'll never, never know.' Kooralya isn't as far away as you think."

"Well I can't afford a Beech Baron like your Royce." Jeremy actually smiled. "I have spoken about this to your mother. My workload has been getting heavier and heavier these past years. You know that. We're both in our late fifties, although your mother looks nothing like it."

"Neither do you, Dad. Are you going to tell me you're thinking of retiring?"

"Well . . . yes," Jeremy admitted. "I'm not spending half as much time as I would like with your mother. We have a wonderful time when we're on vacation. Your mother is all for my retiring. She even has plans we drive around Australia. We've seen more of Europe and the U.S. than our own country."

"I think that's a great idea!" Amelia said, watching her father's expression soften.

"Enjoy life while you're both so wonderfully fit and healthy. We both know you've almost driven yourself to burnout."

"That's the price of being too successful, dear girl. Okay, then, Amelia. Take the time off to visit your future mother-in-law. If anyone can bring two people together, it's you. I've seen it happen with your clients. You're a born peacemaker."

"What more could I ask?" said Amelia.

Amelia thought long and hard about ringing Frances Stirling beforehand to request a visit.

Finally, she decided on taking a taxi to Frances's address. Frances didn't live in an apartment. She maintained a residence in one of Adelaide's prettiest suburbs. With any luck at all, Amelia might find her at home. If not, she would just have to try again, or ask a neighbour if Mrs. Stirling was at home or perhaps away.

The house sat comfortably with its neighbours, reflecting the prosperity of the Cathedral City. Amelia walked up the pathway to the house, butterflies flitting about in her stomach. Royce knew nothing about her plans, but she had difficulty letting go of her belief that, given goodwill on both sides, mother and son could be reunited. As a young woman, Frances had found herself in an impossible situation. She couldn't have taken her son with her. He was at boarding school at the time. But she could easily have visited him there, requesting the headmaster to release her son into her care.

So what had happened?

She was about to find out.

She walked up to the door of the house, and knocked. Soon she heard footsteps headed her way. The door opened.

It was startling to see the woman Amelia had so admired in her early portrait. Frances Stirling was still a very beautiful woman, as Amelia's own mother was. Both had the kind of bone structure that defied age, excellent unlined skin, good thick hair. Both had retained their elegant, slim figures.

"Can I help you, my dear?" the woman asked politely as Amelia stood momentarily speechless.

"Forgive me." Amelia found her smile. "My name is Amelia Boyd, Mrs. Stirling. I live and work in Melbourne. I've flown here to see you. I felt I should. I'm marrying your son, Royce."

The woman sucked in her breath. Her velvety dark eyes widened. "And you've sought me out?"

"Yes," Amelia answered gently. "I do hope you don't mind?"

"Does Royce know you're here?" There was a measure of alarm in Frances's voice.

"No, he doesn't," Amelia confessed. "But don't worry. I've never fully understood your story, Mrs. Stirling. It grieves me you and Royce are estranged. I've come to see if we can talk about it."

"Then you'd better come in, my dear."

* * *

Frances Stirling did indeed have a tale of woe to tell. They sat companionably in the lovely airy living room over coffee, which Frances had insisted on making.

"With my own parents so supportive of Charles, I felt unable to turn to them for help, Amelia. You have loving, supportive parents?"

"I do."

"You're very fortunate. I had to turn to a close family friend, never a lover. Royce's father, Charles, may have been obsessed with me, but there was so much unkindness, so much intimidation, I found married life increasingly unbearable. I stuck it out for my son's sake, but when he was sent away to boarding school, the loneliness was unbearable. And there was the extreme isolation. It was like being a prisoner. Back then, I had decided I would take Royce out of school. I had *some* money. I could sell some pieces of jewellery. God knows I had enough, but when I finally arrived at Royce's school, I was told by the headmaster he had been contacted by Mr. Stirling. Under no circumstances was he to allow me to take my son out of school. He was to call the police if need be."

"So you were thoroughly warned off."

"Indeed I was. The headmaster clearly believed I had come to kidnap Royce. I would have done it too. That's the thing. The headmaster would have been told I had run away from the family home with my lover. I remember he looked at me as if he despised me. It was Charles who took Royce out of school. He brought him back to Kooralya.

"Charles was a terrible man when thwarted. He would have filled Royce's head with endless lies. I could never go near Royce's school again. I got the message. Don't forget, the Stirling family had long been associated with the school. They were big financial supporters. Charles had real clout. I had none."

"You were never able to seek Sir Clive Stirling's help?" Amelia asked. "I understand he was a very fine man."

"Oh, he was," Frances agreed. "But Royce was the *heir*. In a small way, it was like Princess Diana running off with her boys. It wouldn't have been allowed to happen. If Royce came to me, I might flee the country. If I didn't manage to get away, I would certainly show my son a different way of life." Tears sprang into the great dark eyes. "There was a time I feared for my life. Harry, my friend, escaped overseas. Charles was a violent man. It was a great mercy he had to run the station. He couldn't be long away. It would have been Sir Clive who steered Royce into adulthood. Then Anthea came to stay. A good woman, but she could never have gone against her brother. No one did. The poor woman Charles married after must have had a ghastly time."

"She did. So did her son, James."

"She still lives on the station?" Frances asked, trying to collect herself.

"Yes. She's a quiet little woman. James, we call him Jimmy, married my adopted sister, Marigold. A disaster that should never have happened. They will be getting a divorce. I was Marigold's bridesmaid. They were married on Kooralya."

"Where you fell in love with my son?"

"At first sight," Amelia admitted with considerable feeling. "Though it wasn't smooth sailing. Still isn't, until we sort a few things out. Why didn't you contact Royce at university, Mrs. Stirling?"

"Frances, please. Royce didn't answer any of my letters. I was told he *hated* me. Really hated me. He never wanted me back after his father died. I gave up."

"Who told you he hated you, Frances? That sounds so cruel."

"The wife of one of Kooralya's neighbours," Frances said quietly, with a bent head.

"She doesn't have a daughter, Charlene, does she?" Amelia didn't know, but she thought it worth a stab in the dark.

"That's right." Frances momentarily closed her eyes in thought. "Little Charlene. Such a pretty little thing. She and Royce were hardly more than babies when Stella began to make plans to marry them off together. Stella was that kind of woman."

"She still is, apparently," Amelia said. Royce's mother was just as she had pictured her. She had taken to her at once. Frances was her late husband's victim. "Royce loves you, Frances," she said softly. "He's still very conflicted, but he does love you. I *know*. That's why I'm here. I would say he didn't receive any of the letters you sent to his university. Someone could have been paid to collect them. I'm sure he would have told me had he received your letters. He didn't. What it boils down to is he truly believes you wrote him off. I mean, can you imagine how his father would have raved and ranted? Royce had to cope with all that from a young age. It all went very horribly wrong. Jimmy suffered. Royce suffered in his own way, but he's a far stronger man than Jimmy. The thing is, you've been mourning your son. Royce has been mourning you. Let me try to bring you together."

Frances drew a sad, resigned breath. "It won't work, Amelia. Others have tried."

"Extended family. Yes, I know. I do have a tremendous advantage, Frances. Royce loves me."

Frances went to speak, but there were so many tears gathered in her throat, her voice had shut down.

Impelled by a rush of sympathy, Amelia rose from her armchair to join Frances on the sofa. She took the older woman's hand. "I can do this, Frances. Will you trust me?"

Frances' little sob turned into a laugh. "I do. Yes, Amelia, I do. I've prayed for someone like you."

"Well I'm here now," said Amelia the crusader.

Royce emerged from Jeremy Boyd's study after a good thirty minutes of close conversation. Amelia could only hope it hadn't turned into an interrogation. If so, Royce would probably shut it down.

"Relax, sweetheart," Ava said. "I imagine your Royce is a match for anyone. Even your father. I should tell you now, your father expects you to be married from home. You will have to have a second celebration on Kooralya."

"If we get married at all," Amelia only half-joked.

Eventually, both men emerged, both smiling.

Amelia could breathe again.

They could have had dinner in one of the city's many fine restaurants. Instead, they elected to go back to Amelia's apartment. The eyes told it all. After a couple of weeks of separation, they needed to be together. Alone.

"So it went well?" Amelia asked as she drove out onto the street. Her parents had waved them off. That was a great sign. She knew she would marry Royce no matter the strength of any opposition, but the last thing she wanted was to marry without her parents' blessing. "Come on, I have to know."

"Well, I had to agree to our wedding being held here in Melbourne," Royce said. "No problem. You wish to be married from home?"

"Ideally, yes."

"So, yes it is. The time passed quickly. We actually got onto world affairs."

"What, you weren't asked how much you love me?"

"Your father didn't need to ask, Amelia," Royce said dryly. "I would have liked to get married sooner, only I had to agree to a three-month wait."

"But it will take all of that time to arrange the wedding," Amelia said. "I'm only going to be a bride once."

"I should hope so."

"I want you to remember me as I'll look on that day for the rest of our lives."

"Count on it," he touched a finger to her cheek, his touch as electric as a kiss. "Now can we get home please. I'm absolutely mad to make love to you. For hours and hours."

"That can be arranged."

Royce sliced fillet steaks while Amelia put together a salad. She had bought a really good bottle of shiraz from Hunter Valley to compliment the meal. She intended to wait until after they had coffee before she told him about her visit to Frances.

"What are you keeping from me? Royce pinned her shimmering green eyes. "Tell me."

"Who said I'm keeping anything from you?" She was suddenly very nervous.

"What is it?" he repeated his glance leaping over her face.

"Let's sit on the sofa."

He followed her. "You've been up to something." He sat in a corner of the sofa, drawing her back against him.

Amelia put her arms and her hands over his. "I went to see your mother."

Royce sat up straight, forcing her to do the same. "You're joking, aren't you?"

"I'm dead serious." She looked at him.

"Amelia!" he groaned. "I didn't want you going anywhere near my mother."

"Well, I have. What are you going to do about it?"

"This is too much!" he said, standing up like a man on the point of leaving.

"She's just as I imagined her, Royce," Amelia said. "She's a lovely woman."

"Is she?" he asked bitterly.

"Face it, Royce. You can't stand there and tell me who I should and should not meet. We're getting married, aren't we?"

He didn't answer.

"I'll sue you for breach of promise if you call it off."

He dismissed that out of hand. "There's no such thing anymore."

"Maybe not, but it was a good idea at the time. Men being what they are. All you've heard about your mother was totally warped. She was a *victim*, Royce. Why can't you see that? Please sit down again. You've really got to hear this. I love you. I wouldn't hurt you for the world, but I'm not going to allow you to bury your head in the sand."

"Really? In the sand?" he questioned, his handsome face saturnine. "You think *you* can call the shots?"

"Sit down. *Please.* Just hear me out."

"God, Amelia!" He lowered his tall frame back onto the sofa.

She took his hand. Lifted it. Kissed it. "Did you know your mother went to your school to get you out? The headmaster warned her off. Your father had already been in contact with him. He was told your mother would attempt to kidnap you. He was to call the police."

Something flickered on Royce's face. "I don't believe this. The headmaster had met my mother many times."

"It was your father who had the clout. She was turned away."

He hardened in an instant. "She could have been lying to you, Amelia," he said his tone brittle.

"No. I'm a very perceptive woman. I fell in love with you, didn't I? You would believe your mother if you met her. She sent many letters to you when you were at university."

"Now that *is* a lie," he said bluntly. "I never got a one."

"Couldn't someone have been paid to intercept them?" Amelia searched his darkly tanned face.

"Like who?" he challenged.

"The purser?" she suggested. It was worth a shot. "Pursers collect all the mail for distribution—"

"Pursers don't pry into student's affairs," he said with cool deliberation.

"They certainly do. Another thing you should know. Your friend Charlene's mother, Stella Warrender?"

"What about her?" Royce fired back.

"She met up with your mother somewhere, a function maybe, and told her you *hated* her. You never wanted to see her again. She would never be welcome on Kooralya. "

"Amelia, darling," he groaned. "Why would Stella Warrender do that?"

"Jealousy, maybe? Or she didn't want your mother back. Don't forget she sees herself as a marriage-maker. Your mother loves you, Royce. She has never stopped loving you. I guess as the years passed, she felt defeated. You didn't answer any of her letters."

"Which I didn't get," he said, but an element of doubt had crept into his voice.

"The rift became as wide as the universe. It would have stayed like that—"

"Only *you* came along."

"You could at least smile when you say that." She willed him to relax.

"I don't feel like smiling."

"Okay, you're a bit fragile at the moment."

"Me, *fragile?* " His dark eyes blazed.

"If you love me, you'll meet your mother," she said.

"That's an ultimatum, is it?" He pulled her back into his arms, imprisoning her.

"It's a *request*. Underneath the formidable façade, you have a loving heart, Royce. You still love your mother, no matter the lies that were fed you. I'll go to any lengths to make you happy. I love you. Every day I feel it more deeply than ever." Tears sprang into her eyes.

"Don't you dare cry, darling. Please don't." His heart melting, Royce bent his head, finding almost blindly her moist, lovely mouth that tasted like some delicious fruit.

"I'll come with you," she whispered into his parted lips.

She defeated him every time. "You'll always come with me," he said. In his mind, they were inseparable. The kissing went on. Breathing as one, tumultuous thoughts as one, the same pressing hunger until he moved to lift her high into his arms. He was deeply moved she should go in search of his mother, even if it was without his permission.

Hadn't he known from the moment he laid eyes on her she would be a handful?

And at the heart of her?

Fulfillment.

Chapter 10

The Stirling-Boyd wedding held in Melbourne's flower-decked Anglican Cathedral was unanimously voted by guests and the media alike as the wedding of the year. Guests came from all points of the globe. The bride's gown was described in *Woman's Day*, the magazine that won the exclusive coverage for the big social event, as "quite exceptional. The wedding gown dreams are made of." The issue was expected to sell like hotcakes. It was later reported the happy couple had donated their share of the proceeds to one of the bride's favourite charities, an organization benefitting needy women.

The gorgeous wedding gown featured in the magazine was a strapless closely fitted column of white satin with a short train. The fabric had been richly embroidered with thousands of tiny beads, seed pearls, crystals, and silver thread. The style, difficult to wear for anyone who didn't have a great figure, suited the bride's tall, willowy figure to perfection. The bride had chosen not to wear a veil but instead wore white camellias fitted around her silky golden chignon. Around her throat and at her ears she wore magnificent opals set in diamonds, previously owned by the bridegroom's mother, Frances Stirling, and given to the bride as a fabulous wedding present. Frances Stirling dazzled, as did the bride's mother, Ava Boyd. Both women were recognized beauties. As mothers, they appeared overcome with joy that their two families were united.

Jeremy Boyd, the distinguished barrister, gave his beautiful daughter away. The bride was attended by two of her closest friends, in exquisite strapless chiffon gowns, with long floaty skirts: jacaranda blue for the brunette, deep complementary rose for the blonde. The bride carried a small bouquet of white rosebuds; the bridesmaids carried bouquets to match their gowns. Each had been presented by the bridegroom with a memento of the great day, which they wore: pendant earrings with precious stones set in gold to match their gowns.

The groom was attended by his half-brother, the well-known charmer James Stirling, and two of the groom's long-time friends from school and university. Formal dress was the order of the day. The guests had dressed accordingly. All four men looked stunning, but none more so than the tall, splendid groom.

The reception held at the city's finest hotel was lavish. No expense had been spared to make this wedding day as memorable as possible. It was clear to everyone that bride and groom were meant for each other.

"You had to be there to appreciate it," a well-known woman guest was heard to say. "Love, love, love. Is there anything like it?"

It was a day when love and happiness flowed in abundance. A unique experience for the bride and groom. A day they were destined to remember with great poignancy for the rest of their long, inspiring lives.

Epilogue

It had been briefly reported in the papers, Marigold Boyd, adopted daughter of one of the city's most distinguished lawyers, had married a visiting fabulously wealthy Chinese businessman and high-stakes gambler, Jonathon Wang. Ms. Boyd had met her future husband at the gaming table of the city's biggest casino. After a whirlwind romance, the couple flew to Macau, where Mr. Wang had many business interests, to be married. It was further understood none of the bride's family had been invited to the wedding. No doubt, they could look forward to catching up in the future.

USA Today bestselling author **Margaret Way** has written more than 130 books, many of them International Bestsellers. She has been published in 114 countries and 34 languages. Her novels are set in her beloved Australia, where she was born and lives to this day. Her stories always contain the beauty and rugged nature of the rural and Outback Australia, as well as the rainforests and coral reefs of Northern Queensland.

ife on the Australian Outback is a high-stakes game, even among
most privileged—and love must be strong to survive . . .

ng has all the strength, money, and power that his infamous father
he family cattle station deep in the dusty bush of Australia's Channel
rom the moment she sees him, Amelia Boyd knows Royce struggles
nan. His tense energy attracts her, fueling the spell of remote, manor
and its lush gardens of gardenia and roses—even as she recognizes
wedding bringing their families together is a terrible mistake.

s her sister has snared Royce's brother more out of greed than
he can't abandon her, no matter how conniving she seems. And
m besotted with Amelia even as he prepares to walk down the
sle, the ill-fated match stirs up nightmares of the past.

almost forgive Royce's suspicions. But the arrogance of a wounded
erful force, one Amelia knows too well. And as the desire brewing
e and Amelia grows irresistible, the distrust, heartache, and family
s seething beneath the surface are bound to burst forth . . .

ve never read Margaret Way before, you're in for a treat!"
—*New York Times* bestselling author Diana Palmer

Also by Margaret Way

Visit us at www.kensingtonbooks.com

ISBN-13: 978-1-5161-0160-3
ISBN-10: 1-5161-0160-X

ESS
N